He'll Never Let Me Go

ALSO BY SADIE RYAN

The Proposal
The Secretary
The Housekeeper
The Witness
He'll Never Let Me Go

HE'LL NEVER LET ME GO

SADIE RYAN

JOFFE BOOKS

Joffe Books, London
www.joffebooks.com

First published in Great Britain in 2025

Cover art by Nick Castle

ISBN: 978-1781899281

To Harry, Charlotte and Stephen

CHAPTER 1

Jill

The M40 morphs into a bleak ribbon stretching out of London as I merge from the slip road. Thumping heartbeats match the pounding in my ears. I indicate to manoeuvre into the fast lane. My leg on the accelerator trembles. I grip the steering wheel so hard my knuckles turn white. In front of me, a sea of red brake lights pulse dimly against the gloom, standing out like smouldering embers against the subdued winter daylight. With every jolt of adrenaline coursing through me, I try to push away thoughts of what I've left behind.

Two hours ago, I hoped to be further along this motorway. I expected an uneventful drive, but the city turned chaotic with London's gridlock, thick with protestors — surging bodies blocking my path unexpectedly. So I skip a planned stop, convinced it's too risky so soon. I can still hear the echoes of your routine — the hum of your car as it pulls into the driveway, the rhythmic bleep of the alarm, the jangling of keys. My stomach knots at the thought of you looking for me, annoyance creeping into your voice as you call my name, your footsteps moving impatiently through the house, seeking me in each empty room.

I force myself to concentrate on the road ahead, every second ticking down until you realise, I am gone. Time presses down on me like a vice, and I know I need to pull off soon. I seek the next services where I can vanish for a moment. A mile later I indicate, slipping around the back, tucked away from prying eyes where the lorries park. I swing out of the car, the world spinning as I rush towards a clump of trees, aware that the ANPR camera upon entry has clocked my registration. I double over, from the fear inducing waves of nausea that claim me, and throw up. Keeping my head down, my baseball cap pulled low, the unrecognisable clothes weigh down my identity — a massive sweatshirt and baggy trousers concealing the woman I once was. I nip quickly to use the facilities knowing I have to keep moving.

The timing of my departure is intentional; I can't leave a trail; I can't risk recognition. The police will indeed be hunting for me, but I've taken your money, and though it's ours, I made sure to withdraw only what I could without igniting suspicion. It's all been a rush in the end. A bit of a scramble to escape. I'm lucky I had things already in place.

I slip back into the driver's seat, stealing a quick glance at the time flashing on the dashboard. A mix of satisfaction and shame washes over me — I'm not exactly proud of how I came to possess this car. If there's one lesson I've learned, it's that young women should think twice before hanging their handbags on the backs of chairs. One never knows who might be lurking nearby, eyes keenly observing.

It took countless evenings of quiet observation, blending into the background, to truly understand how people behave when they're out socialising. There's a certain foolishness in most, a blissful ignorance of their surroundings and the potential threats.

When opportunity finally presented itself, lifting the driving licence of someone who had a passing likeness to me turned out to be surprisingly easy. Yes, my heart raced with the thrill of it, but the act itself was simpler than I'd anticipated. I took nothing else but that precious slip of plastic.

The ten-year-old Fiesta was a bargain, practically a steal. I bought it a couple of weeks ago through a private sale, disguising my identity with the false name and address I had stolen. It's been tucked away behind a row of shops near our house, where construction for new homes begins at the end of the month. To fund this little venture, I let go of bits of Mum's jewellery — pieces that you might not even remember existed. Each item carried a piece of her spirit, but desperation has a way of dulling sentimentality. I saved every shred from the small café job I had — cash in hand, under the radar that you know nothing about. It's not that much but it will have to do. My mother first showed signs that something was wrong when I was eleven, and it started with her obsession over climate change. That's when the hoarding began — 'Just in case, you know? There won't be enough food; we have to be prepared.' She would repeat it over and over. It became her mantra, and it drove me insane. I dreaded bringing friends home, only to be met with cardboard boxes stacked everywhere, filling the house with a sense of chaos I couldn't escape. So much canned food. She was diagnosed with OCD, obsessive compulsive disorder. She died three years ago from a sudden heart attack. I still bear the guilt that she'd been dead for a couple of days before I found her. I was supposed to call round, but things were busy and I wasn't feeling up to it, and I just never went.

I know that it won't be long before the DVLA starts making enquiries, especially once the supposed new owner gets the logbook in the post and decides to reach out. I can already feel the clock ticking against me.

The motorway hums with busy traffic as I rejoin, and visions of hitting Birmingham's rush hour set my nerves on fire. I tighten my grip on the wheel as a lorry swerves too close, and my instinct screams for a detour. I'll avoid the chaos, slipping off when I get further up north at Stoke-on-Trent, taking the A34 through Cheshire and into Manchester, then head further north. This will add confusion if the police are tracking the car with the ANPR cameras and give me more time.

You won't let me go. You can't. My heart pounds as my mind plays tricks and I think I see you in my rear-view mirror, your expression fierce and unrelenting, your determination driving you forward, closing the distance between us.

The image of you racing up behind me on a fiery, red Ducati, your eyes filled with anger, flickers across my mind, but I blink it away. Those days are behind me now. Memories pour in, hot and sticky like a blistering hot summer's day of how much I still love you. And that is why I must do this. I clench my jaw refusing to be claimed by the past.

Traffic slows, and anxiety swells inside me — I feel like I could leap from the vehicle and scream for help. I hold my composure, biting my lip to suppress a tumult of panic. I sip from my warm water bottle, and my stomach churns as I bite into an apple. I must keep my strength up, despite my fear. The radio blares cheerful tunes that feel entirely out of place in this moment. I stifle the urge to turn it off; silence will leave me alone with my thoughts, terrifying and suffocating.

We haven't moved in a frustrating ten minutes. I reach for the paper map — no electronic traces to connect you to me — and my mind races as I calculate the distance to Carlisle. The feeling of being boxed in sitting here among standing traffic on either side, with nowhere to go, sends fresh waves of dread washing over me. I remind myself that you'll think I'm close by, sheltered with friends, blissfully unaware of my escape route.

I remember that night — the knife catching the dim light, its blade glinting like a silent witness to everything unspoken.

The air felt heavy, charged with a tension that made it impossible to breathe. In that moment, the reflection on the blade seemed almost like a stranger staring back, a version of you — or maybe me — that neither of us wanted to acknowledge.

I remember your eyes — wild, almost electric, yet still holding a strange allure. The words hung in the air, sharp and venomous, cutting through the silence like a blade. It all felt surreal, like I was watching someone else's life unravel, yet the weight of it pressed down on me, unrelenting.

My heart raced — not in fear but awakening. *I will fucking kill you.* The words echo in my mind, reverberating like a claxon. They curled around my thoughts like ivy, suffocating the last shreds of dependence that rooted me to your side. I felt the wet warmth of blood trickling on the skin, a visceral reminder that I was still alive, still capable of choices — still capable of defiance.

As the memories flood back, I remember the quiet moments, the ones always brushed aside. The times I would stare at our reflection in shop windows, only to see a shadow of the girl I used to be. The whispers of friends who claimed to love me, watching from the sidelines, insisting how good our marriage seemed — how perfect we were together — echo in my mind, their words laced with a truth they couldn't possibly understand. They had no idea what really happened behind closed doors, yet their hushed reassurances felt like accusations, like screams masked in gentleness, tearing at the edges of my sanity.

Unstable, yes. That was often said, as if it were some undeniable truth, used like a weapon. But maybe, just maybe, no one truly understands — how the human spirit, no matter how shattered, can find its way back. The cracks weren't signs of weakness; they were openings, moments where something stronger was starting to emerge. Each accusation, each harsh word, only drove closer to the truth, revealing a strength no one could have expected.

In the aftermath of that night, the rebellious spark ignited into a flame fed by everything that had been overlooked, underestimated. I knew what you thought of me, the assumptions you made — and I was determined to slip through your grasp, like a shadow in the night, vanishing before you could hold on. You'll search every corner, every trace of our shared existence, every digital echo you think might lead you back to me. That's why I have to stay off the radar — no trains, no buses. All those places have CCTV, something the police will home in on. But you'll find nothing. I've become smarter than you anticipated.

The whispers of threats twisted, becoming something almost alive that stretched and shifted, taking on the shape of wings, dark and restless — beating against the edges of my mind. I learned the art of silence, the skill of disappearing among the noise. I began to build a plan of escape, woven carefully so it would never lead back to me. The image of freedom took form in my mind, intoxicating and bold — a life in vivid colours of autonomy.

I angle the mirror and catch my reflection; it's a stranger staring back, etched with fear and resolve. It's taken me far too long to realise that change was never part of our design. Or perhaps it was, just not the way we had imagined. My freedom had to be meticulous, every detail scrutinised to ensure you wouldn't suspect.

You will not find me. Not now, not ever.

CHAPTER 2

William

I stop by the quaint little off-licence before heading home, grabbing a bottle of wine that promises to brighten the evening ahead. Two nagging thoughts plague me as I stroll down the aisles: first, you haven't responded to any of my texts; second, you haven't even bothered to read them. With a sigh, I select a special bottle of red, our favourite, pay the cashier, and step out into the cool evening air.

As I pull into the driveway of our Holland Park home, nothing seems amiss. The autumn leaves lie like a patchwork blanket over the cobblestone path we had laid two years ago, and I can't help but frown at the lack of attention to the garden. The gardener was due today, but you clearly didn't think it important enough to have him tidy up the leaves. He's been getting very lazy recently. I think we'll have to find someone else. The house itself glows warmly from within, the soft light spilling out and inviting me into its embrace. You've always had a knack for creating a welcoming atmosphere.

I lock the Audi and rummage through my pockets for the house keys, taking the familiar steps up to our Georgian stucco home, which stands proudly opposite the autumnal looking garden square. As I open the front door, an unsettling silence envelops me. It's too quiet, especially given that I'm late tonight; if you'd read my texts, you'd understand why.

The kitchen greets me with chaos: the dishwasher door ajar, releasing a pungent odour from the neglected dishes inside. I toss in a detergent tablet from under the sink, close the door and switch the machine on. The twenty lights in the high ceiling blaze brightly, illuminating every corner. Yet the vibrant brightness does nothing to shake the growing sense of unease that curls around me. It's not like you to leave the kitchen in this state.

I unbutton my shirt, loosening my tie as I call out, 'Cat?' My voice echoes through the hallway as I step carefully over the expensive runner we bought during our trip to Turkey. I dart upstairs, hoping the wine will melt away some of the tension that has been simmering between us for the last eight months — ever since our attempts at starting a family hit a wall. But tonight, it seems, you have chosen to disappear without a word even though we'd made plans for *us*. 'Cat?' I call again, standing at the threshold of our bedroom. Everything appears in order, yet an intangible sense of discomfort hangs in the air. I strain to hear any sounds from the bathroom — silence. I rummage through the room for a note, something to explain your absence. But there's nothing. That unease begins to grow.

After checking each room in our sprawling house, I make my way back downstairs, glancing into the garage where your car sits, still and silent — offering no answers.

Things have changed over the past few months. You've become distant, sometimes flinching away from my touch. The IVF treatments have been a taxing journey, leaving you feeling as though my touches are burdens rather than gestures of love. I know that, even though you think I'm blind to your feelings. I refuse to accept defeat when it comes to our dreams of having a baby.

Last night, you seemed eager for a quiet evening, for us to reconnect, and we both decided tonight we'd really sit down and talk, but I sensed something was off with you. Perhaps it was the tension from me that made you tetchy — yet now, it feels as though the sands have shifted, and that I've been left behind. I know your job at the florist near the Ritz entails late deliveries, but you always communicate if you'll be delayed. I frown thinking how Rita often keeps you late for just one more delivery. I hated you taking that job. But now is not the time to get worked up about that. I check our shared calendar — nothing indicates you have plans tonight. Since we implemented it, I thought it would ease my worries about your late nights on that wretched bicycle laden with flowers, navigating the treacherous London streets dragging that ridiculous eco trolley behind you. You know how concerned I am about your safety. But it's a fight I don't want right now.

You hinted at something last night, and I brushed it off, too exhausted to dive into what felt like deeper waters. Especially when bloody Jason called you and I lost it with him for interrupting us. After I snatched the phone from you to tell him to sod off and leave you alone, he was abusive — I had to tell him to back off or he'd regret it. I know I snapped at him, but you did too. I was trying to protect you. Now, the weight of that conversation between us that we never got to have docks in my mind, cloaked in urgency. Maybe I should have been less irritable. I tried. I honestly did.

Frustrated at your phone going straight to voicemail time and again, I fill the sink with water and begin tidying the remaining bits cluttered about the kitchen. All I can think of is whether you've gone off sulking again because of how I was with you.

Nearly two hours pass, and I'm still left in an empty house with no sign of you. What's more important than us? If you've sought refuge in solitude after our latest setback with IVF, it would have been kind to share it with me. I know I probably didn't help, the way I was putting pressure on you. I shouldn't have had a go at you like I did. I know it's not your fault. We always talk — at least, I thought we did. Vanishing without a word? That's just cruel, Cat. But you know how desperate I am for it to work. I know I get cross, but I don't mean to take it out on you. *Where on earth are you?*

I can't shake the gnawing worry that I've driven you away. Have I unwittingly pushed you into this silence, as if to prove a point about our struggles? We've been a solid couple for eight wonderful years, but now it feels strained. It's my fault and I'm sorry I'm so pushy about it.

I'm transported back to the bubble of joy when you first moved in, filled with laughter and hope. You marvelled at the size of the house. 'It's huge, William! You must be kidding! Is this really all ours?' But ever since we embarked on this arduous journey towards parenthood, the smiles have faded, replaced by shadows of conflict and doubt. After this last failed IVF, you spoke of adoption, of returning to your old life as a lawyer, and I felt the weight of those words last night. I knew your return to work would mean the end of our chances to expand our family — you'd be pulled taut under that pressure. I was anxious too after this last failed attempt you'd stop wanting to try IVF and instead push for adoption. I was wrong to have been so selfish. I wouldn't rule out adoption. Not at all. Let's talk about it all as we planned.

At that moment, my phone vibrates, snapping me out of my spiral. I glance at the screen — your brother, Jason. What could he want now?

'Hey, Jason. How are you?' I brace myself for him to shake the balance once more. He always seems to take joy in our disputes, but I tolerate him for your sake.

'Cut the crap, William. Where's Cat?' His voice is sharp, laced with accusation, and my stomach twists at the implication that he may know something I don't.

I'm frustrated at his tone. 'I don't know,' I manage. 'She wasn't home when I got in, and she's not answering her phone.'

'Did you two have another fight?'

I wince. So, he is indeed privy to our private life after all. You confide in him, and I can't help but worry about what you've disclosed. 'No, we didn't fight. Didn't she tell *you* where she was going?' I try to maintain a calm facade. I'm certainly not telling him what went down last night. It's none of his business. You share too many secrets with Jason, and I'm anxious he knows more than I do about our marriage.

'I've been trying to reach her since six o'clock. Her phone goes straight to voicemail. I know you hit her, William. She told me everything. What have you done to her now?'

The weight of the accusation lingers, thick and unshakeable , pressing down on my chest like a vice. I open my mouth to defend myself, to deny the absurd claim, but the words catch in my throat. *What the hell did you tell him?*

CHAPTER 3

Jill

Carlisle is a small town in the north, quiet and unassuming, yet it takes on an air of mystery when night falls.

The rain begins, painting the streets with a slick sheen. The dim glow from the streetlights flicker like hesitant ghosts, casting long shadows that spiral and curl around the corners of the deserted streets. I drive slowly, obeying the speed limits, my wipers offering a squeaking protest against the relentless rain. They need replacing — definitely a task for someone else. Shadows dance as my headlights catch dark corners, casting an eerie glow across the quiet roads as I navigate cautiously, half-expecting you to spring forth from behind a tree or around a corner. Perhaps it's merely an old habit, that nagging sense of being watched.

I pull up under a lamp-post. An A–Z sprawls across my lap, the faint smell of worn paper rising from its pages. I squint at the cramped street names, feeling as if I am navigating a maze designed to keep me lost. A satnav would be so much easier; yet there's a comfort in the familiar rustle of paper, each page a promise of direction and no chance of you knowing where I am. I drive on looking for the street. At last, I spot the B&B and parallel park between two parked vehicles with a precision borne of practice and your insistence of doing it right. Gathering my rucksack and a crumpled food bag from the boot, I lock the car then brace myself against the downpour, heading towards the Victorian guest house that stands warmly ahead, its lights glowing through the heavy rain. I look around, taking in my surroundings, checking no one's watching. You made me be aware of everything so much that now I'm scared of my own shadow.

Inside a wave of warmth washes over me, a stark contrast to the chill outside. Soft, golden lighting envelops the reception area, and the comforting tick of a grandfather clock fills the silence. I drop my bags beside the desk, instinctively scanning for security cameras — finding none, I let out a sigh I didn't realise I had been holding. I'm tense and my neck and shoulders ache. I remove my baseball cap. My messy blonde hair falls free, mirroring the weariness etched on my face.

Out from a side door emerges a woman in her late fifties, and our eyes meet. A sharp note of awareness strikes me. I know she will remember me. I have stepped into her world — a new arrival, a single woman with a dishevelled aura who feels decidedly conspicuous. For now, I am Jill Hart, but I intend to reveal little more.

'Good evening! You must be Miss Hart, is that right?' she asks, settling herself on the edge of the chair behind the desk. Leaning forward, she taps her computer awake, her Geordie accent slicing through the stillness surprising me. Her ruby lips curve into a welcoming smile, revealing unexpectedly pristine white teeth, a feature at odds with her wrinkled top lip, suggesting years of indulgent smoking. Dressed neatly, dark hair frames her pale blue eyes that seem to absorb every detail of me and make me uncomfortable. As I step closer, I pick up the acrid tang of stale cigarettes threading its way through the air. I silently pray my room doesn't carry the same scent, having specifically requested a non-smoking B&B when I called up to make the booking.

13

Sadie Ryan

'Yes, that's correct,' I reply, pressing a smile that feebly masks my anxiety of my new identity. The moment feels too personal by the way she looks at me, clothed in a heavy veil of scrutiny of who I am and why I'm here at this late hour.

'Two nights. Is that correct, pet?' she probes, even though she knows my answer — it's staring at her on her computer — her tone friendly but curious.

'Yes, that's right,' I confirm, cautious to hold tightly on to my composure therefore making me rigid. I hope this woman doesn't see through my fragile facade even though she seems to be trying. The quiet makes me nervous. 'Are you from around here?' I enquire, realising how dumb my question is the moment the words come out. Her eyes dart between my rucksack and my expression, a gaze that feels like a soft interrogation. I stumble on, 'Sorry, God, that sounded so rude,' I stammer. 'I, eh, just wasn't expecting your accent that's all. Sorry. I mean, sorry, sorry, I'm tired and well . . . you know, just tired.' *Oh my God, I need to stop babbling.* I lift my arms in the air to emphasise my stupidity.

She regards me for a moment before responding, 'Well, I'm from Newcastle, pet. Been here thirty years for my sins after marrying a Carlisle lad.' Her laughter is warm, a fleeting comfort that tempts me to share more than I should. I'm not going to. She's not my friend.

'I, eh, didn't mean to pry, or be rude,' I say, the admission spilling forth unbidden. I ought to shut up now. 'I just . . . didn't expect it, that's all.' *Oh, God, I'm making it worse.*

'Don't fret, pet. Here's your key. Top of the stairs, second door on the right. Will you be wanting breakfast?'

'No, thank you. I have a lot to do, so I'll pass.' I mentally scold myself for not accepting. My stomach growls in protest, a sound undeniable amid the stillness. But the least I'm seen the better. I can grab something from the shops and eat it in my room.

'It's included in the price, you know?' she adds, her curiosity not yet sated as she spots the crumpled Tesco bag at my feet. 'I can rustle you up some sandwiches if you're hungry now?'

'That's very kind, but no thanks, I really won't need breakfast. I'll be out early — oh, I just wanted to confirm, you still accept cash?'

She raises an eyebrow, a flicker of something passing through her gaze. 'Well, we prefer not to as it keeps the books straight. But if cash is what you want, that's all right with me.' Instinctively, I touch the hidden money belt beneath my sweatshirt, her eyes narrowing imperceptibly, catching the movement.

'Here's your key,' she says, handing it to me with a finality that feels ominous. She's going to keep probing, I can tell. She's one of those kind people who want to help. I don't need help. I need to be invisible. 'We'd appreciate it if you didn't take it out with you — guests tend to lose them, you know how it is.'

I nod, pocketing the key as I make my way towards the stairs, the blue flowery carpet a path to temporary refuge. Just as I'm about to ascend, her voice calls out, 'Hey, pet, just a moment.'

A chill courses through me. Has someone been looking for me already? I shake off the irrational thought and turn back, meeting her gaze.

'I'm guessing you're here to get away from it all — *a bit of time to yourself*, is that right?' There's a wary subtlety lacing her words. 'If anyone comes asking for you, I won't say a word, pet.'

Shock blurs my senses, and I find myself fumbling for words. 'I doubt anyone will call for me,' I manage, bewildered by her presumption, wishing her mouth had remained closed and not said those words. Now I know she will remember me.

Her words linger, a foreboding blend of warning and understanding that quickens my pulse. Does she sense why I am here? I stare, horrified that she can read me so easily. Anger roils within; *I should be better at this.* I force a casual shrug, as though her insight

15

means nothing. 'I'm moving to the area for a new job. Just here looking for a temporary rental. I don't know anyone, so I'd be surprised if anyone does.' The lie is weak but necessary. I know I must prepare a more convincing story moving forward.

'Huh, is that right, pet?' she muses, eyeing my rucksack again. Clearly, I'm lying — who travels with no luggage? 'But you're not from around here, either, are you? Have you travelled a ways?' Her lingering gaze is irritating.

I wince at how easily I revealed too much with that comment about her accent. *Why didn't I keep quiet? You told me how stupid people are, feeling the need to fill the quiet therefore giving themselves away. I know this, dammit. I need to do better. This is what you'll be banking on.*

'Yes, exactly. Sometimes you just have to make a change. It's a great career move — great benefits.' I plaster on a smile that feels as forced as my story. 'It's all about the benefits these days, isn't it?' I refuse to tell her what she wants to hear.

'Well, I wouldn't know about such things, but I take your word for it, pet. If you need anything ironed—' she gestures towards my rucksack — 'I have a wonderful lady who does for me.' She approaches me, warmth radiating from her, causing a wave of urgency to swell in my chest that I've read her wrong and she is just a kind person. I long to escape to my room. *Like I would ever have smart clothes in a rucksack!*

She briefly rests a warm hand gently on my arm, just long enough for heat to surge into my cheeks — a touch that stings from its kindness. Turning away, I know she senses the truth buried within me — I'm running from something or someone.

* * *

Sinking onto the bed, the clean duvet and fragrant whiff of lavender offer a momentary reprieve, but my reflection in the bathroom

mirror reveals the tumult boiling inside. Her words echo menac-
ingly: *If anyone comes asking for you, I won't say a word.* Rethinking
my stay, two nights suddenly feels alarmingly long. I must leave
tomorrow, change my car, and ultimately vanish, putting as much
distance as possible between us.

Carefully, I remove my money belt — my lifeline. I can't afford
to lose this. After locking the door, I empty the contents of my rucksack onto the bed. It's a meagre collection: a driving licence, loose
coins, a few tissues, a pen, and two changes of clothes alongside a
crumpled food bag. This is all I own — along with a lone packet of
sandwiches. I ravenously tear it open, grateful the cold weather has
kept them fresh. A quick sip of coffee washes it down before I strip
off my clothes and shower, washing away the weariness of travel.

Exhaustion tugs at me as I collapse back onto the bed, damp
hair splayed across the pillow. My plan hangs by a thread of
sending you on a wild goose chase before I extinguish my trail
completely.

We first met at that awful meeting where I was working near
Tower Bridge. I was battling a cruel stomach bug, every second of
that meeting a contest against nausea. You noticed my struggle,
piercing through my haze as I calculated the torturous fifty steps
to the ladies' room. As my boss droned on, oblivious, I secretly
hoped the floor would swallow me whole.

You stood up, pouring water for those at the table, your gaze
landing on me. You offered me a glass, which I silently declined,
too terrified to risk a word slipping past my lips or anything else.

When your phone rang, you excused yourself, shaking hands
with my boss and, surprisingly, guiding me gently towards the
ladies. That simple, kind gesture ignited a wave of gratitude so
profound, I knew I'd never forget it.

You returned later, and I found myself captivated by your
presence. Handsome doesn't begin to capture you — rather,

you exuded an undemanding confidence that drew me in like a moth to a flame. Dark, thick hair framed your mocha eyes, complemented by strong features that ignited the space around you. When you smiled, my heart leapt, the weight of my world lightening for the briefest moment.

Now, as I lie in this clean, tired B&B, weariness pulling me beneath the waves of sleep, my memories drown me, tethered to thoughts of you. I don't want to think of you, but I can't help myself.

CHAPTER 4

William

I push myself off the bed, dishevelled and groggy in yesterday's clothes. A sense of grime clings to me, as if the weight of my choices has taken root in the fabric. The moment my foot hits the carpet, I stifle a yell. My toe collides with the broken whisky glass I must have knocked over last night, sending sharp pain shooting through me. Blood seeps from the cut, staining the fawn carpet — a silent witness to my muddled state.

Hobbling awkwardly, I stagger towards the bathroom, the sound of the shower roaring to life as I turn the tap. The scalding water cascades down my body, a temporary shield against the turmoil in my head. Eleven a.m., it reads on my phone. No calls from you. Just a barrage of missed notices from your insufferable brother. I've dialled your number too many times to count. Either I switched my phone to silent after his last onslaught, or I made it through the night without hearing the calls. My head recalls all too well the extent of my drunken stupor.

I know you hit her, William. She told me all about it. His words repeat in my head.

The water, relentlessly hot, wraps around me and I let it wash away his words, too absurd to acknowledge. I push aside my worry, my mind racing with scenarios. What could have happened to you while you were out delivering flowers?

As the water, mixing with my blood, runs pink, I can't shake the gnawing feeling that something terrible has happened to you. Perhaps you're buried in your own thoughts, making me suffer with uncertainty. I shake my head, trying to dispel the rising thoughts that cling like shadows in the corners of my mind.

Should I call the police before your brother does? Before they come banging on my door, demanding answers I can't provide? The tarnished state of our marriage weighs heavily on me as I step out of the shower and wrap myself in a towel. I reach for my phone to call your boss.

'Hi, Rita. It's William, Cat's husband. Just checking if she made it to work today?'

'No, haven't seen her. Left me in the lurch. Why? Has something happened?'

'She didn't come home last night.'

'Have you tried her brother?'

'Yes, no luck. He can't get hold of her either.' The words feel heavy against my tongue as I dry off, applying a plaster to my foot. I can't help but search for hope, grasping at straws. 'Maybe she's made a new friend? One of the clients? Is it possible?'

'Not that I know of. But with Cat, it's not impossible. I just wish she'd let me know if she wasn't coming in.' Her voice is tinged with worry and annoyance. 'I hope she's okay.'

'Maybe she fell off that bike,' I retort, bitterness creeping into my tone. I hated you using that damned thing around the busy London streets. And all because Rita's damned obsession with eco-friendly transport. I haven't heard of *her* using it.

'Unlikely, the bike's here,' she replies sharply. 'Have you checked the hospitals in case she was knocked down or something?'

Embarrassment crashes over me when I realise I haven't. I end the call, then phone the hospitals. There's no sign of you anywhere.

That's good but now my mind is thinking the worst — that you're lying somewhere, hurt. Switching on the TV, I search for some sign of a disaster I might have missed that you've been caught up in, but the screen flickers with mundane news. I finally get dressed.

'Damn it, Cat, where the hell are you?' I shout into the empty house. My finger hovers over your number, but it goes straight to voicemail — again. I call those of your friends I have contact details for. They all say the same — they haven't heard from you.

For reasons I can't understand, I drift over to your dressing table. Somehow, the disarray bothers me today, more than ever. This is you, a brilliant whirlwind of chaos. But today it feels like a riddle I can't solve, and then I see it — your phone, half-hidden beneath a discarded silk scarf.

My heart races. Why would you leave without it? My fingers tremble as I switch it on, and the screen floods with missed calls from me, Jason, Rita and your friends. A mounting wave of anxiety washes over me. I punch in the code and flick through your messages — nothing tells me where you are. *What the hell, Cat?* The familiar rush of anger rises that you've blocked me from your life once again. And vanished to hurt me, again.

I stride into the kitchen, ignoring calls from my office and sending them straight to voicemail. A quick glance at my work diary and I see I have no appointments today, Friday. I'm relieved I have the weekend to unravel all this before I have to speak to my boss. I pour whisky into a tumbler — yet another poor breakfast choice, but it's a coping mechanism at this point, I tell myself. Part of me believes this is some elaborate ploy to hurt me. My frustration builds: it's almost like you choose to disappear when you want to make a point. You've done this before. Your little secret you tell me, but you never tell me where you go. Yet deeper in my subconscious, worry gnaws at me. What if the worst has happened? And I've not done anything to find you? What if you're lying in a lay-by, hurt somewhere, and I'm too late contacting the police?

But pushing that thought away, I grapple with my instincts. I have to call the police before they take an interest in me if your brother gets there first. The burden weighs heavier with every passing minute — sixteen hours since I last saw you. What if something terrible has happened?

The doorbell rings, breaking into my thoughts, which I'm slowly losing control over as they head into dark places I don't want to go to. I freeze and glance at the clock. It's been a long and unproductive morning. I open the door, hoping to see you but it's the postman wanting a signature for something you ordered. I oblige, snatch it off him, close the door and dial Jason. Reluctantly.

'Morning, Jason. It's me, William.'

Instantly, I can hear the tension in his voice. 'I know it's you. My phone tells me who's ringing. Have you heard from her?' His question is sharp, like a knife.

'No, I haven't. I found her phone though. It was left behind. Switched off.'

A pause.

'Why?' His impatience flares, adding venom to each word. 'This doesn't add up. Why would she go out without her phone?'

'Are you trying to be aggravating on purpose?' I snap, my own frustration bubbling over. 'I don't know. I've called everyone I know. No one has seen her.'

'Aren't you worried? She's clearly missing. Or worse.'

'Calm down, Jason. I don't need your theatrics right now. Cat is a grown woman. She can take care of herself now.'

'Except when you're involved, right? What have you done to her?'

'Nothing! I can't believe you think that!'

'Cat has never disappeared. I'd know. Clearly something is wrong.'

'Would you though? She didn't tell you everything.' But even as I say it, doubt clings to my tongue like a bitter aftertaste. You agreed we ought to sit down and talk, get it all out in the open, the IVF, the adoption. What happened to make you change your mind and disappear?

'You need to take this seriously. I'm heading to the police.'

Panic overtakes me. I don't want him there before I can explain myself! 'Wait—'

But the connection severs before I can say another word. All I have left now is that growing ache in my chest. Why does it all feel like an accusation? A paralysing fear creeps in as I glance again at your neglected phone, the chaos of the unknown eddying around me. The stakes have been raised, and I'm caught in the middle — a husband desperate for answers against the very real possibility that you might never come home.

CHAPTER 5

Jill

In the morning, I consult my A–Z for the address where I'll buy my new car — only two miles away, I estimate. I call to confirm that the seller, Sam, will be there. He sounds okay, but what can you glean from a voice? My judgement hasn't been stellar lately, after all.

I park several streets away, ensuring I've left nothing in the car. I check the cash I've set aside and tuck it into my back pocket. I won't return to this car again. After wiping it down for finger-prints, I lock it up, heart pounding as I walk away.

Crossing a main road, I weave through stopped traffic, pulling my cap lower over my face as I spot a CCTV camera. A mother with a pushchair looks at me but a couple of teenagers glued to their phones are oblivious. The smell of fried food wafts from a nearby burger shop. At the bus stop, I note a few people — an old man, two women, a teenager. Did they notice me? I convince myself I blend in, just another face in the crowd.

As I turn down a side street, rows of Victorian two up, two downs loom around me on either side, the parked cars creating a claustrophobic atmosphere. Most are battered and ancient — no shiny new models here. I'm reminded that I'm not dressed in my usual smart casual attire; my joggers and sweat top help me fit in. The people at the bus stop didn't even look up when I walked by.

Ahead, a group of youths huddle together, and I feel a flicker of unease. I can't help but wonder if they can sense that I'm an outsider. My heart races and I want to turn back, but it's critical I secure this new car and move on. It had better be as advertised. Five hundred pounds isn't much for a reliable vehicle. I keep my head down as I walk past the youths, some turning to watch me. I slouch slightly and keep moving, their laughter stinging like a slap.

Every muscle in my legs urges me to run, to escape this moment. I think of you — wondering if you've already taken action. Have you started looking for me? I push the thoughts aside, focusing instead on the road ahead.

I finally arrive at number twenty-one, marked by its bright red garage door — the house Sam mentioned. My heart pounds as I knock, uncertain of what this man looks like. Just days ago, he was a stranger, but soon he'll be wrapped up in my deceptive scheme. Not that he'll get into trouble; how could he know I'm anything but legitimate?

A young boy, maybe sixteen, answers the door. 'Hi, I'm looking for Sam about the car,' I say, forcing a smile. My pulse races. Will he see through my facade?

'Dad!' he calls into the house. 'Someone's here for the car!'

I glance at the two vehicles parked out front. The Citroen I'm here for looks decent from a distance. I circle it, inspecting the tyres — my main concern. I couldn't care less about torn seats or the mileage. I know nothing about engines, so I have to hope that it's in good shape. All I need is a car to get me from here to St Andrews in Scotland, one hundred and sixty-one miles.

A man in his mid-twenties appears at the door. Surely, this can't be Sam, who sounded older on the phone.

'Hi, are you Sam?' I ask, my instincts on high alert that they might just rob me. That this is a con and there's no car for sale. I was adamant I would pay for it in cash. No bank transfer.

'He'll be out in a sec. He said you could look at the car, take a look inside if you want. Turn it on.' He tosses me the keys.

I catch them, keeping my head down to hide my face as much as possible. 'Great, I will, thanks.' I start the engine and go through the gears — they seem reasonably smooth. I don't hear any peculiar engine sounds; I'm not going to hang around long enough to give it a run around the block.

When Sam finally appears, he's unremarkable, just as I expected. He's squeezed into jeans that sag low on his hips, exposing skin at his midriff and the top of his buttocks as he bends to show me the tyres. 'They're relatively new — put them on two months ago. Solid. Good quality.' He gives one a kick for emphasis. 'MOT's good for another eight months. Enough petrol to get you to the next petrol station, about a mile out of town. You won't find better value for money.' He takes a puff from his vape, releasing smoke through his mouth that wafts into my ear.

'Right. So, had much interest?' I ask, forcing myself to act casual and normal, not take it and leave even though my mind is racing.

'Sure, sure. But you know how it is. People have their own ideas of what they want. Got someone coming in the next hour. So, you interested or what? I'll knock off twenty quid if you take it today.'

He's ready to haggle. I've always been one to negotiate, so I give it a shot. 'Knock off fifty, and I'll take it.'

'Fifty? You've got to be joking. Twenty-five.'

He'll budge closer to fifty, I can tell. 'Forty-five.'

'Come on, that's insulting. What d'you take me for? Thirty.'

I want to laugh; he doesn't realise I'm playing him. 'Nope, sorry, that's my final offer.' I start to hand him the keys back, feigning disinterest. 'Have a nice day, and thanks for your time.' I turn to leave, a rush of adrenaline coursing through me.

'Wait! Let's meet halfway. Forty?'

'Deal.' I can't help but smirk as we shake hands. Inside, we fill out the paperwork with my new ID. I feel a twinge of guilt for Jill Hart, who will soon receive the registration papers for yet another clapped-out car. I hand over the cash and drive away.

I avoid parking in places with CCTV, eventually finding a space on a quiet side street, away from shops. I can't be late for my next appointment, and Sam dragged this out longer than I expected.

The fast-food restaurant is hot and greasy, the air thick with the scent of fried food. I try not to recoil as I order a tea and a bag of fries, then head to the back where Simone told me to meet her.

Surprisingly, it's bustling for this time of day on a Saturday. A couple of mothers sit at a table, engrossed in conversation while feeding fries to their toddlers strapped into strollers. A rheumy-eyed old man nurses a cup of something warm, staring blankly into space. A group of teens huddle by the window, laughing and teasing each other over their meals. I brush crumbs off my table, pulling out my hand sanitiser and rubbing it into my palms.

I keep my head down but watch the window. Outside, some teenagers are shouting at others, laughter erupting in response. The walls are plastered with Friends of the Earth posters, hastily scrawled over in black marker.

I glance at my Nokia: my basic untraceable phone, a burner I think they're called. Simone is five minutes late. I didn't expect this. I thought I'd be the one running late. Staying in one place too long makes me twitchy. Have you found my phone yet? Have you searched through my things, wondering why I left without it? You've probably combed through my emails, but you'll find nothing there. I can't help but imagine your anger simmering, not knowing where I am.

I shift in my seat, acutely aware of the teenagers eyeing me, a lone woman nursing a cup of tea at the back of the room. I'm too anxious to look up or get another drink. I crunch on a fry, the tension in my fingers tapping on the Formica tabletop.

Suddenly, a motorbike pulls up outside, the roar of its engine grabbing all the attention of the teenagers. As I'm about to leave, a woman stands before me, holding a steaming cup. She's dressed in a white T-shirt, quilted black jacket and grey joggers — generic, forgettable, just like the rest of them in the café. We both wear baseball caps, making us look suspicious.

'You been waiting long?' she asks, sliding into the seat across from me.

'Long enough.' Irritation has crept into my voice. 'You must be Simone?' Which I know instantly isn't her real name. I glance out the window behind her, glad the motorbike has grabbed the attention of the teenagers.

'I had to make sure nobody was watching you.' Her strong East End accent surprises me. 'Wouldn't worry about him.' She nods at the crowd around the bike. 'He's deflecting nicely — couldn't have organised it better myself. What we don't want is people to notice us, if you know what I mean.'

I don't at first. It takes me a moment to catch on that she's talking about my husband. She looks like somebody you'd see in the park pushing her kid on the swings. Normal. But none of this is normal. It's interesting what you can find on the internet when you start to look and fall into one rabbit hole after another. Strangers out there ready to help if you know where to look. So many women in terrible situations who don't know where to turn. I followed the signs jumping from one site to another until I came to Simone, who helps women like me and who directed me to the National Domestic Abuse Helpline.

I didn't notice her come in, which is unsettling. Seeing as though I'm supposed to be vigilant about my surroundings.

'You okay for a drink? Want another?' I shake my head. She adds six packets of sugar and drinks half the cup of the steaming liquid before putting the BioCup down. I don't know whether it's tea or coffee until I see the same weak brownish liquid as my own and then I'm still not sure. I'm curious why we're meeting here and not a pub or the park or somewhere less — busy. 'You look nervous,' she observes after the third time I glance at the window. 'You worried someone is going to walk through that door? Don't be, I scouted the area when you walked in. Nobody is following you.'

I kick myself for again revealing too much of myself. But then she must have seen the signs a million times before of women on the run from abuse, to recognise them. She sits back waiting for me to speak, spinning the cup around and around on the Formica.

'You're a sales rep and move around the country a lot for your job, is that right? Sometimes even going to Ireland,' I say remembering our online conversation.

'That's right. I go where the work takes me. It's fluid, you know what I mean?' When I look confused, she explains further. 'What I mean is, I can move around without drawing attention to myself. This way, I can do what I need to do to help you and women like you. It's been very effective, and I've been doing it for years.'

Other women like me that I found online, she means, who recommended Simone. I didn't know they were all out there. This little band of *runners*. They had another name for her. She has lots of aliases. I suppose she has to keep herself safe too. She called herself Simone when she got in touch. There's help out there if you know where to look for it. Advice, on what to do. What not to do. How to hide in plain sight. When you're being chased, slow down, move slowly. Don't bring attention to yourself. What and where to avoid. Planning is everything.

I had a small tick list to fill, and she filled it. She's not married. No ties. I hadn't noticed her come in, and I guess, neither had anyone else. She moves like a ghost.

'How often do you travel?' I ask, remembering our brief online chats.

'Regularly. I drive, sometimes I take the train or the coach. Variety is the spice of life, right?' She takes a sip, studying me over the rim of her cup. 'Are you running from your husband or someone else?' she asks suddenly, and the question takes me off guard. I don't want to give her too much information. I know how smart you are; one slip up from her and you'll find me. I have to be careful who knows my business. I don't answer right away. All I told her in our chats was that I had to escape and not be found, but her eyes are sharp. 'Most men — by that I mean husbands, boyfriends, partners — don't bother looking for you after a while,' she adds, reading my silence. 'It's too much trouble.'

I nod. She has no idea how resourceful you are and how easily you can call on the people you need to find me.

I sip my cold tea. 'My situation is complicated,' I finally say, not wanting to divulge more.

'I see that look of fear in a lot of women's eyes,' she says, her voice softening.

I drop my eyes; she's completely unaware of how dangerous my situation is. I told the Domestic Abuse Helpline as little as possible, afraid it might get back to you.

'You'll have to blend in. You want to disappear, so you need to change everything about you. Leave no trace. Don't look the same in any new place you stay. What you need to understand is, continuity is the last thing you want. That's why you can't leave any trace behind. Understand? Because you need to do that if you want to hide in plain sight. It's too easy to get caught on cameras these days, especially if he calls in the police.'

I blink, feeling exposed — stupid, realising I've already let myself down by stopping on the motorway to use the facilities. 'The bank card has a thousand pounds on it, and the credit card is unlimited,' I say and pull them out of my pocket. 'I need you to spend wisely, but not all at once. Make it look like someone on the run. Small spends. Food, travel tickets that sort of thing. You'll have to look a little like me in case you're caught on camera.' I think of you spotting Simone on some camera and realising it's not me.

Her expression turns serious. 'You're green, love. Be careful out there. Trust no one. I mean it. I'll be okay, I know what I'm doing. But you really need to listen and do as I'm about to tell you.'

'Right.' I nod then slide the cards across the table.

She places her hand over mine, making it clear that this conversation is about survival. 'Keep your head down. You don't need to share your life story. Don't talk to anyone about the real you. Don't help anyone. Stay away from trouble, confrontation. Walk away from problems. I will scatter you around the country. Leave a trail that will drive him insane. But you need to lie low. Pay cash. Go to ground. D'you hear me?'

I nod, feeling a sense of urgency and panic. 'There's five thousand pounds in this envelope for you. Use the cards carefully and destroy them once you're done. No trace. Be careful. He's good and won't give up. He has the means to track the transactions — he knows people.' I know I keep repeating myself. I'm just scared. So scared.

She takes the envelope, studying me. 'You don't have to worry about me disappearing. Just focus on getting yourself to safety. You have a plan, right? A place to go?'

I nod. 'Why do you do this?' I ask, curiosity getting the better of me.

'Let's not get into that, love.' She dismisses the question with a wave. 'You've got what you need.' She taps her temple. 'Just keep yourself safe.' As she stands to leave, I feel a mix of gratitude and apprehension.

'Be careful,' I say again, not wanting her to draw attention as she exits.

She gives a nod, a knowing look in her eyes. 'Remember, don't underestimate yourself. You've come this far. If he's as smart as you say, he'll be expecting you *not* to do the opposite of what you'd normally do. Bear that in mind. So, be two steps ahead. Always think before you do anything.'

As she disappears into the crowd of teenagers outside, I let out a breath. I've set things in motion, but I know the hardest part is yet to come.

CHAPTER 6

Royce

I only stopped by the station briefly to check on something when the call came in. I'm not even supposed to be here — I was officially meant to start my leave today. But that's been cancelled I'm guessing, likely because Butterworth wants to see me. In a way, it works to my advantage, and having a work-related excuse will make it easier for my brother, Sid, to understand why I'm backing out of our plans.

'Super wants a word, boss,' my lovely DS and partner in crime, Camilla Santos, says. 'Jeez, what happened to you?' I touch the cut above my eye.

I had planned to drive to Cornwall to spend five quiet and relaxing days with my brother, Sid, and his wife, Mel, and my two nephews. However, things took a turn when my wife, Natalie, decided we weren't going.

Sid rang early this morning, full of energy. 'You're still coming, right? The kids are so excited to see you both. I wasn't going to tell them because, well, you almost always cancel on us.'

'Yep, all sorted here,' I said, wondering then what excuse I was going to give. Instead I said, 'All packed and should be leaving around midday.'

'You better. Christ, Royce, we haven't seen each other in ages because of your job.'

'I know, and I'm sorry, really. But you could always come here, you know. Show the kids the big lights of the capital?' I hated lying to him that way. And I am sorry, I love my nephews but sometimes seeing them is a little painful, to think we'll not have any ourselves.

'Yeah, no, we'll pass. Too much crap going on there. Have you watched the bloody news?' He had a point. If I had a choice of bringing my kids up in Cornwall or London, I know where I'd choose.

'Just bits and pieces,' I said, biting back a sigh. I *am* the bloody news. This is the same tired excuse every time I ask my dear brother to visit us for a change. It's not going to happen. We grew up in the East End, and now he acts like he's allergic to it. Claims he gets physically ill if he leaves the clean, calming air of Cornwall.

'Don't let us down, Royce. The kids will be devastated. They've planned to take you bodyboarding.'

* * *

'You wanted to see me, ma'am?' I ask, hesitating in the doorway of Superintendent Butterworth's office. I know the moment I step inside I'll be pulled into the gravitational force of yet another investigation.

'Ah, Royce, glad Camilla managed to catch you. You ready to head off?' Butterworth leans back in her chair, glasses perched at the tip of her nose as she peers at me over the rims. 'What happened to you?'

I step just inside the room, careful not to get too close. She's like a spider weaving her web, and I know better than to get tangled up willingly. I stay rooted to the spot, determined not to volunteer any information that might give her an opening. 'Long story, ma'am. Yes, my brother has been on at me, making sure I'm still coming.' I lie that I'm still going. The truth is I'd rather be working now it's off than be at home.

'Right,' she says, almost dismissively. 'Well, I just wanted to say goodbye. Make the most of your time off.'

I narrow my eyes, instantly suspicious. Butterworth isn't exactly the sentimental type and wishing me bon voyage feels entirely out of character.

'And,' she continues, casually slipping the real reason into the conversation, 'I was wondering if you wouldn't mind handling a quick missing person's call we've had. William Johnson-Smyth's wife has gone missing. I know you're officially off-duty now, but if you could just have a sniff around, get a feel for the situation, Camilla can pick it up from there and you'll still make it to Cornwall.' This feels like the perfect opportunity to cancel my leave and step back in, holding firm to my reasons for staying — without inviting any questions. Not that I'd feel obliged to answer them anyway.

Johnson-Smyth. The name rings no bells. From her tone, he sounds important, though. 'Is the husband someone I should know?' I ask, mentally sifting through my memory for any connection, but I come up blank.

'Well, he's high up in the upper echelons — you know, his father's a peer.' She waves her hand dismissively as if the rest of the explanation doesn't matter. 'The request came straight from the top, so I need you on it.'

And just like that, I'm roped in. Now I'm typing out a text to Sid, explaining why I won't be coming down today. I'm too much of a coward to call and face the disappointment in his voice, so I'll promise to reschedule as soon as the investigation wraps up.

I hate texting — it feels cold and impersonal — but sometimes it's the perfect escape route for dodging an uncomfortable conversation.

'Why this particular misper, ma'am? DS Camilla Santos is more than qualified to investigate. Are we looking at something unpleasant here? Having to keep things — quiet? Do you suspect the wife's been hurt?'

She sighs. 'The brother of the wife came in shouting that Smyth had done her in. We feel you ought to go check it out. It's not looking good for Smyth with the brother shouting the odds out there. We need to keep him quiet for the moment. See what has happened to the wife if anything or if she's just run off.'

'And if she has just run off?'

'Then they want to keep it out of the papers. Family don't want a scandal. Look, Royce, you know the drill here. No media on this for now until we know what we're dealing with. They aren't saying we must keep it under wraps, just find out what is going on first. It might be an argument, and she's left him.'

'I don't get why the brother is saying it's suspicious? Is there anything on the husband that we don't know about?'

Butterworth shrugs. 'The wife is a creature of habit. She works part-time at a florist. She's a kept woman. Easy life. We've had no reports on either of them in the past only that they seem a happy couple.'

I interrupt. 'Always a sign for concern then.'

She frowns. 'He works in stocks and shares — a venture capitalist. Has big clients. I mean *big* clients if you get my drift. The sort we don't want to rattle. Clients that have influence. Clients that don't want scandal. According to the brother, the husband didn't call it in immediately and he finds that suspicious—'

I interrupt again. 'But he has called it in?'

She narrows her eyes at my interruptions and continues. 'He phoned in, yes, but this morning. The brother says the husband hits her. We must be very careful here, Royce, that this does not get out if it's not true and, well, even if it is, it must be handled with kid gloves until we know the whole story. No scandal, do you hear me?'

Oh, I hear her all right. 'What you're not saying, ma'am, is that my leave is cancelled, and you'd like me to work this case. Is that correct?'

'You know I can't officially ask you that, Royce. You're entitled to your leave.'

Yeah, yeah, yeah, there's always a great big *but* though. 'But?'

'But they'd be very grateful upstairs if you could see your way to changing your leave. Do you think that might be a possibility, Royce?'

'I'm reading between the lines, here, ma'am, so correct me if I'm wrong — are you saying that there is a big possibility that this Smyth fella has hurt his wife?'

'I can't possibly comment on something like that. But what I can tell you is that there could be blood in the water, and we cannot let the sharks get a whiff.'

CHAPTER 7

William

Headlights cut through the dimness of my home, inching through the stained-glass window of the front door like spectres announcing their arrival. They're here. I called the police, knowing well enough that racing around the streets of London to find Cat was futile, especially with Jason lurking like a dark cloud above my head. The heavy thud of the door knocker reverberates in the pit of my stomach as a dark figure appears behind the stained glass. Anxiety claws at my insides. What if they think I know more than I do? What if they think, like Jason does, that I've harmed you? I take a quick breath, steeling myself.

'Mr Johnson-Smyth?' His voice draws me from my racing thoughts. 'I'm DCI Royce Benedick.' He holds up his warrant card, a shield against my mounting fears. 'May I come in?'

'Yes, yes of course.' I step aside, dread curling around my heart — a chief inspector no less. This can't be good. *What has he said to them?*

'You've reported your wife missing, Mr Johnson-Smyth. Her brother came to the station too, anxious about her whereabouts.' He enters, his gaze sweeping over the opulent hallway, lingering momentarily on the signs of wealth before focusing on the disarray in the kitchen. Guilt and regret tighten in my chest that I didn't call it in earlier, desperately wondering what Jason has spun into his tale.

I walk us through to the kitchen.

'Yes, Cat . . . Cat hasn't come home.' My voice sounds strained, each word wrested from my throat as I lead him further in. 'I — I should have gone looking for her last night.'

'And why didn't you?' he presses, his voice steady as granite. The air suddenly grows thick with tension. *I wasn't expecting that question — it's so accusatory.*

'I . . . I thought she'd come home. I . . . I just thought she'd gone to a friend's but the ones I called said they hadn't seen her, so I thought maybe it was a friend I didn't know of yet. It's not unusual for her to do that — she's friendly that way. She finds it easy to make friends.' I try to infuse my words with confidence, yet a creeping doubt eats away at my resolve that you might have been keeping something from me. I don't know why I feel that, but something is off here.

'Were you not worried that she'd not come home by the morning? You called us just before midday today.'

'Of course! Yes, I was worried!' My voice hitches, unravelling my calm. I don't like his implication. 'I just didn't think she'd gone missing as such. I thought . . . I thought, she'd come home later. I had no reason to think something had happened to her.' I stop. 'The thing is, she's done this before.'

'Not come home you mean?' DCI Benedick asks, intrigued.

I nod and mutter, 'Yes, that's why I wasn't deeply concerned. I don't mean I wasn't worried because I was. I am, I mean.' I feel helpless, the weight of it pushing into me, into my chest. I slump into the nearest chair, just managing to pull it out before I collapse.

'Does your wife have a habit of going off without telling you on a regular basis?' DCI Benedick is looking at the mess I've made after too much drink; a whisky bottle and bags of nuts are scattered over the worktop. I'm about to explain it away, but I just don't have the energy.

'She's done this before, yes. That's why I wasn't worried. She always comes back.'

'And the last time she did this, do you know where she went?'

'No.' I shake my head, staring into the middle distance. 'She wouldn't tell me.' It's always annoyed me that you wouldn't say. It's probably a friend I don't know and you think I won't approve of.

'So, she could have gone there this time. When was the last time?'

'I suppose. About four months ago. But as I don't know where that is, I can't check.' My gaze comes back, drops to the table. There's a stain I haven't noticed before and I start to rub at it with my thumb. 'That's why I didn't want to rush in — calling you. In case she came home. I mean there was no reason for me to think something has happened to her.' I sigh unable to budge it and look up at him. 'Not initially, anyway.' I deflate. *Why do I have this terrible feeling inside my gut you've been keeping something from me?*

'How many times has she done this?'

'A few.'

'And you lodged your call when you suspected some harm may have come to her. But if she's done this before and come home, why did you call it in this time?'

'I had a feeling. It felt different this time. But I had a feeling like this the last time, and she came home. I mean you always worry, don't you? You can't be certain something hasn't happened. I worried maybe she'd fallen off her bike.'

'Cat rides a bike?'

'A stupid bike for work, yes. Her boss is helping the environment by having nearby deliveries made by bike.' I punctuate *the environment* with air quotations. 'Cat has panniers on the bike and a cart she drags along.' I see his frown. 'It's a fancy cart with the shop's name on it, that sort of thing. I've never been happy about it. About her riding that thing. And she'd never wear a helmet, which annoyed me more. I mean the roads are so congested.' I snort. 'You don't see her boss ever using the bike, only the van.'

His eyes scrutinise me like a magnifying glass.

'So, you think she could have fallen off and been injured, is that it?'

'I did think that but then I thought the hospital would have called. And her boss said the bike was at the shop so that theory was out.'

'Have you rung them?'

'The hospital? Yes,' I say, dejected. My admission is like a punch in the gut. 'I should have done it sooner, I suppose. I just haven't been that worried as daft as it sounds, because she's done it before. Vanished, I mean. Like I said. It's Jason and his stupid accusations about us that's made me think differently this time.' I force a hollow smile.

'How so?' He scribbles in his notebook.

I throw up my hands, annoyed now. 'His lies of course. I mean it's all lies, the whole damn lot of what he's saying. I've never laid a finger on Cat. I wouldn't.'

'Tell me more about her brother, Jason.'

The shift in conversation pushes the knife deeper into my already raw nerves.

'They're close. Have been since the death of their parents about ten years ago. He's dependent on Cat, she not as much, but nevertheless they're incredibly close.' I fetch a glass of water for us and place his in front of him. I sit back down in the chair. And slouch. It almost feels too difficult to sit upright. I drink my glass dry, noticing the DCI doesn't sit down. 'I don't know what he's told you, but he hates me. He's always been jealous of what I have — what Cat and I have.' The words tumble from my lips, urgent and fervent. 'He accuses me of hitting her. A ludicrous notion. I'd never . . . I love her.'

'And yet, here we are, William. These are serious accusations.'

I sit up taller now, panic igniting me. 'I know that, Chief Inspector. Why would he make them up? It's extreme, I agree. I don't have an answer for you. But to go about saying things like that is unconscionable.'

'I agree, yes, but if he's overprotective of his sister, too protective, her disappearance could be quite unsettling for him.' His gaze pierces. 'Does he know about her other disappearances?'

'No. Well not from me. I don't tell him much, but Cat does, or so he thinks, but clearly, she hasn't mentioned them. At least, I don't think so, otherwise, I guess he'd have mentioned them to me and wouldn't be as worried as he is. Don't you agree?' I stand, agitated by the way this conversation is going; I need to defuse the tension building up inside me. I can almost feel his eyes probing, peeling back layers of my story.

Another knock reverberates through the hall, pulling Royce's attention away. Two colleagues enter — their presence only heightening the storm of chaos growing in my mind.

'William, these are my colleagues, Sergeant Santos and DC Glennon. They'll look around the place,' he says with a nod. They make their way upstairs. 'Do you have a photo of your wife we could have?'

'Of course.' I force another hollow smile, but the tension inside me remains like a taut string ready to snap. I leave the kitchen returning with a photo. I always liked you in this picture. You're wearing a summer dress of spring colours, floaty, off the shoulder. Your long chestnut hair is caught on the breeze; you are smiling up at me. I hand it to the sergeant.

'So, you've checked your home, I presume?' The chief inspector's voice cuts through my thoughts. There's an urgency behind his gaze that makes my skin prickle.

'Yes, everything looks as it should.' But a flicker of doubt lingers. 'Well, the kitchen was a bit of a mess, not a lot, but unlike Cat. She never leaves it like that.' Royce looks around. 'This mess? Is all mine. She left the dishwasher ready to go, unlike her, unwashed dishes in the sink, unlike her. She's a bit OCD about stuff like that.' I chuckle to myself, hating that I've ribbed you playfully about it before. Chief Inspector Benedick's eyes narrow.

'Any signs of a struggle?' His question is heavy and sits in the air.

'No. Nothing.'

'Anything out of the ordinary? Any missing items?' he probes. 'Things she may have taken with her? An overnight bag or a case?'

'No, not that I've noticed, but . . .' I swallow hard. 'You know what did bug me and it's why I think I feel weird about this whole thing, the dishwasher door . . . it was left half open, as if she'd meant to start it but didn't get to finish it. It's so unlike her.'

He scribbles everything down. 'Anything else?'

'Everything was the same as always.'

He pulls out a chair next to the one I've returned to, as if he's settling in for a long interrogation.

I tremble internally that I've missed something important here or in something you've said to me that would make all this make sense. I take in a deep breath, piecing together my memories. 'Her phone! I found her phone upstairs.'

DCI Benedick examines me closer. 'Phone?' he snaps, refocusing on me sharply. 'Where?'

'In our bedroom . . . on her dressing table under a scarf. It was off, so — I didn't realise, but that's why all the calls went to voicemail.' I reach into the drawer and produce it, handing it over like a fragile artefact.

He puts on a pair of gloves, then takes it from me. 'Do you happen to know the code?' His piercing gaze matches the tension in the air, each moment punctuated by the fear of what might come next.

'I do,' I reply automatically. '2-8-4-2. We share everything — nothing to hide.'

'Odd don't you think? Everyone likes their privacy. I take it you handled this?'

I nod. 'Yes, of course I did.' The DCI raises his eyes to me after punching in the code. 'It's not snooping! We have nothing to hide.' But the way he studies me sends chills down my spine.

He looks at me. 'Did she leave her phone the last times she vanished?'

'I . . . I don't know. No, she didn't. Sorry, I'm struggling to think straight. The first time it happened, I was too shaken to process it properly. I just assumed she'd be fine. She didn't answer when I called, but I never believed anything terrible had occurred. She has this habit of needing space after we argue. Sometimes, she'd retreat to one of the bedrooms and tell me not to bother her. But the first time she actually disappeared like this, I just thought she'd gone to stay with friends. Not that any of them admitted she was with them.' He gives me an odd look. 'When she returned, she told me she'd had her phone with her but had switched it off. She said she didn't want to tell me where she'd been — that it was private. Somewhere she didn't want me to find her. And since there were no charges on the credit card, I assumed she'd stayed with friends.'

'We'll have to take this,' he says, his voice resolute. 'How many times has she vanished this way?'

'I . . . don't know, half a dozen? Maybe. Maybe less. I can't think straight.'

The DCI nods and makes a note. 'Does Cat have a laptop?'

'Of course, take what you need. I haven't found her laptop. Maybe she took it with her.' But then I hesitate. 'Maybe I should have mentioned this earlier. We've been going through IVF, and it's weighed heavily on Cat. She's been . . . struggling. I may have pushed too hard.'

The chief inspector's demeanour shifts, and it feels as though the ground beneath my feet is eroding. 'And yesterday morning, everything was normal?'

'I thought so,' I reply, my voice cracking with uncertainty. 'Normal. Yes. She seemed fine before I went to work.'

'Tell me everything you did after arriving home last night.'

I recite each action, but as I do, the walls close around me, every detail peeling away a layer of the fabric of my life. 'And then I called everyone I knew she might have been in touch with, but nobody knew anything. They all said she'd been acting normal.'

'With Jason, how did he seem?' He nuances the tone, letting the weight of each word linger.

'Contrived, maybe. I don't know. I'm just feeling utterly confused. This whole situation is unreal.' I stand up and pace.

'And the other times she left. Did she take personal things with her, like clothes?'

I can feel the noose tightening, the desperation rising. My pulse races, and the dread threatens to swallow me whole as I consider how — how could I have let things get this far? 'I don't think so. Does that mean anything?'

'Maybe. William, I know this question might be sensitive, but is there a chance your wife was seeing someone else?'

CHAPTER 8

Jill

I park my car in the shadowed alley beside the B&B, careful to hide it from the landlady's prying eyes. I can't risk her spotting my new vehicle — if you come here, she might spill everything to you. Outside, the air crackles with the tension of an impending storm, a chill that crawls up my spine and tightens around my throat. I draw my jacket closer, feeling the weight of something dark and unshakeable as I walk, glancing nervously at the time on my phone. *Are the police looking for me? Are you?*

I can't shake the worry that security footage will betray me — where I've missed a camera, and you'll spot my car and be able to quickly track me down. I'm counting on the hope that you haven't started your search yet.

When I return to the B&B, the landlady's smile is cheerful, her eyes twinkling with a warmth that feels all wrong. Handing me my key, it feels like an invitation into a snare of confidences. I hurry upstairs, the walls feeling like they're closing in, and I can almost hear the low rumble of the storm growing closer outside. The sense of urgency, the desperation to escape this place before it's too late, drives me forward as I shower, change my clothes, and shove my belongings into my bag with trembling hands.

'I'd like to pay my bill, please,' I say, dropping my bag in front of the reception desk.

'All right, pet. Is everything okay? Room all right?' She looks at me but says nothing. I can see she wants to, but she refrains, for which I'm grateful. I don't want to get into a conversation. I just want to get out and move.

'Yes, but I decided to leave early. The room is fine, very nice in fact, thanks.'

'And did you find somewhere to rent?' she asks, remembering our previous conversation.

'Yes thanks.' I give a little chuckle. 'Don't ask me where, it's all on my maps with directions,' I lie, again. The least she knows the better. My heart skitters. I might drop myself in it and say too much if I try and make stuff up. So I stop abruptly.

She puts the bill in front of me for the two nights. 'Cash you said, pet? I'm afraid I'll have to charge you for both nights.'

'That's right. Yes I understand.' I reach for my cash that I've already counted out and slipped into the back pocket of my jeans, anticipating this would be the case, and hand over the notes. We exchange pleasantries and I leave with my bags.

'Take care of yourself now, pet, and good luck,' she calls out as I walk out the door. I don't reply but my stomach gripes. I need all the luck in the world. I grab her words and hold on to them tightly.

I walk to the end of the road and the small Co-op for food, ready-made salads, chocolates, bread, peanut butter, jam, tomatoes, cucumber to chomp on, yogurts, water. Anything that is easy to eat and requires no cooking or heating up. I pay with cash at the self-service till, making sure to keep my head down, baseball cap pulled low because of the cameras pointing right at me. Then on to Savers around the corner where I buy £2 eyeglasses with 1.0 percent magnification, hair dye and other bits.

In the car, with trembling hands, I stick a nose piercing I bought with the glasses on the side of my nose and slip huge loops in my ears. I change into baggy jeans, different hoodie, thick-soled ankle boots I brought with me, and you would never assume I would wear. The glasses sit on the end of my nose. I need to avoid looking through them to stop myself getting dizzy. I push them onto the top of my head until I need them.

The tension simmering beneath my skin gives my hands a permanent tremble I'm unable to shake off. I didn't want to walk out of the B&B looking like this. This way she can only give my description of how I used to look. When I get to my new stop, I'll dye my hair.

Each element of my disguise feels like both a shield and a shackle, and as I catch a glimpse of myself in the rear-view mirror, a stranger stares back — someone I barely recognise, draped in anxiety that constricts my chest constantly and has become a permanence I'll miss if it ever leaves me. The uncertainty of not knowing if you're already chasing me down lingers in the air like a spectre. I take a breath and prepare to step out into the unknown as I turn on the engine.

I head out of Carlisle on the A7 Georgian Way travelling north and head off east onto Brampton Road. From here I will continue to travel east a little way then head back north on to Houghton then Harker where I'll pick up the faster road north towards Longtown then west into Scotland — in total fourteen miles. It shouldn't take me more than half an hour on these winding roads.

The line that separates England from Scotland looms before me, a threshold that promises both sanctuary and peril. Crossing into Scotland, a dizzying rush of adrenaline washes over me — I've made it this far. I can't help feeling a little elated how far I've come. But I know you'll be looking for me. The thought sends chills down my spine of how much effort and how many favours you'll be calling in. I can't shake the feeling of being hunted all the time. Everything looks like your shadow trailing behind me, unyielding and relentless.

Gretna, the town I've chosen as my first refuge, is eerily quiet. The silence cloaks me like a second skin as I drive through. I know that I will stand out here, a foreign face among the locals. That thought gnaws at me. It's a mistake. I can't linger; I need to keep moving to get to Edinburgh to disappear into the throngs of people — a three-hour drive through winding back roads. Before I leave, I glance at the leaflets I grabbed from the B&B. On the back page of *What to Do When in Edinburgh*, there's a list of guest houses. I choose the cheapest and closest one — the photo looks decent enough. I call the number, relieved to hear they have vacancies and accept cash. I don't bother cancelling the booking in Gretna — less contact, less of a trail.

But safety comes at a price. The moment I reach the city, I'll have to really change — cut off my hair and dye it. The thought twists my stomach. I love my hair. How I despise that thought . . . yet how it may save me. I remember your hand laced through my hair, that perverse sense of ownership as you yanked me back into your embrace whenever I tried to break free. Each memory is a scar etched into my mind, pushing me to make sacrifices I never thought I would.

My eyes flutter, heavy with fatigue, as the white line in the centre of the road bends and warps, yet I wonder why — I haven't been on the road for long. Perhaps it is the weight of anxiety that drags me down, the fear whispering insidious thoughts in the quiet of the oncoming darkness and of what you'll do to me if you find me. To drown it out, I flick on the radio. Static crackles in and out. The signal is terrible around here, a ghostly companion in this unsettling journey. I listen, hoping for a distraction, but the music is a jarring reminder of the life I'm leaving behind.

You brought me to Scotland once, long ago, to St Andrews to show me your university. You took me to all the places you used to hang out as a student and told me all about the friends for life you made there. It was winter when we came. It tried to snow; we walked wrapped up in long down jackets. Holding gloved hands. We stayed at the Hotel Du Vin, where you first hurt me, yanking my long hair wrapped around your hand and bringing me to my knees. That's one of the stops I have in mind, later after I've led you a merry dance. You won't think I would go back there having left with a black eye and a body covered in bruises. Why would I ever want to return? Because that is exactly how you will think and precisely why I will be safe.

I come to a crossroads with no signs. The sun is nearly down; the days are shorter here. I look out at the landscape, at the outlines of the mountains on all sides. The air here is so much fresher I can almost taste it. I pull over and climb out of the car. My legs, stiff, my lower back aching. I marvel at the dense quiet around me, focus on the peacefulness of it all. Back inside, I study the map by the interior light and my torch. I'm at Blyth Bridge. Another thirty or so miles left. The storm that's been following me is here, unfolding like an angry god opening its bowels as rain explodes around me. I quickly close the door.

I'm booked in at another B&B on the outskirts, keeping away from Travelodges and the likes; those sorts of places are bound to have cameras everywhere. I still have plenty of cash and if I'm careful it should last me until I get some work.

Sometime later, it feels like hours and hours later on these winding roads, I pull up outside the B&B and my heart sinks. It's raining, big fat, heavy drops slapping the windscreen. The B&B looks grim; the outside light is fused and the stone is dark, no doubt looking darker without any light and in the rain. The garden is unkempt. I'm hesitant to leave my car. It looks nothing like the photo in the leaflet. Across the road two suspicious, hooded youths smoke and are soon joined by a few more.

I keep the car running as I go through my options. A, I have nowhere else to go tonight. B, I have no Google to search for another place. C, I could go inside and see if it's as bad as it looks. I don't want to do C or A or B.

A shiver crawls down my spine as the rain blurs the world outside my car, the windscreen wipers fighting a losing battle against the deluge. Eerie shadows distorted through the windscreen move in the distance.

As I glance through the rain-streaked glass, the figures across the road reveal themselves further — dark silhouettes whose faces are obscured, but I can sense their menace. They lean against the brick wall, watching. Smoke curling from cigarettes, the red burning end glowing like a beacon in the night, telling me that they're there, watching, deciding what to do.

My heart races as I slide lower in my seat, heart pounding against my ribcage like a caged animal. I feel their gaze, almost a tangible force, puncturing through the car's protective shell.

My heart sinks. They're coming towards me. I lock the doors. Another figure joins them from the side and another from the left. My hands on the steering wheel shake. I should go. Right now. One of them, one I haven't seen and who suddenly appears by my side knocks on the driver's window. Rat-a-tat-tat. The wipers thud back and forth battling with the rain. Five figures in hoodies, heads covered, hands in pockets, hunched over, look at me. Two in front. I look in the rear-view mirror, two behind. To leave I will have to mow them down. You taught me well.

'Hey there, wee lassie, are you lost?' the owner of the rat-a-tat-tat says, his face up against my window.

There's laughter. Another one comes close, grabs his privates and thrusts. 'You wanna bit of this, lass, plenty of it in here.' They all screech with laughter together. I'm reminded of the wildlife programmes we used to watch when a pack of hyenas gang up on their unsuspecting prey. I'm that prey right now and my heart, just like theirs, races. But I need to keep a clear head and not let the panic terrify me into paralysis. Another spits a mouthful of phlegm onto the ground in front of him.

I clutch the wheel tighter, knuckles burning. I can't let fear keep me pinned here. Not again. I push the accelerator down, feeling the car lurch forward.

They don't move. They will move or they'll be under the car. I keep moving forward, their hands on the bonnet push back. *Stand up for yourself*, I tell myself. A memory of our dark and visceral sparring sessions flares up and I straighten up in my seat.

As I keep rolling forward, the tension builds inside me. *What if they don't move?*

'Where you goin'? Come on, come on! There's no need to rush off!'

A thrill of panic surges within me, spurred on by their laughter, which carries a taunting edge. In the distance, a rumble of thunder rolls.

Suddenly, a tall figure with a twisted grin, leans in closer, smudging the window with his hands. His breath fogs up the glass. I refuse to look directly at him, but his presence presses down on my chest. Then he starts banging at the window, each thud resonating in my gut like a countdown. Thud! Thud! Thud!

'You needn't be afraid of us, lass. Come on, stop the car. Come for a wee drink.'

Thud! Thud! Each strike chips away at my will, a reminder of my vulnerability. Lightning fractures the sky, illuminating their grinning faces for a fleeting moment — zombie-like, grotesque in the electric glare. I feel my breath hitch in my throat. He bangs some more. Thud! Thud! Thud! Each bang feels like another punch in my gut. Lightning lights up the sky for a second. I clutch the wheel, tighter.

'Yeah, we're only joking. Let's go get a wee drink,' another says.

I drown out their mocking voices, repeating to myself, *Stand up for yourself. Stand up for yourself.* My fingers coil around the wheel as the pressure builds, my knuckles paling with frustration that simmers beneath my skin as I press harder on the pedal, urging the idiot in front of me to move, my leg taut with restrained power, ready to launch forward the moment the road clears.

Finally, they do, and I surge forward, the gears grinding as I hastily move up. I don't know where I'm headed — only that I need to escape.

The tears come fast, streaking my cheeks as my breath shudders, the last remnants of controlled fear giving way to sheer panic over what could have happened. My whole body shakes and quivers, overwhelmed by the near miss I've just had.

Before I even register where I've ended up, I spot a 24-hour Tesco car park and pull in, desperate for a moment to catch my breath and steady myself. I sit there, trembling, realising how lucky I've been — so far.

I could sleep in the car, but where? After that episode, it doesn't feel safe. I have no idea where to turn for help at this hour. The darkness presses in, and the last thing I want is to wander the streets aimlessly.

This is when I really miss my iPhone. Having no internet is the worst. It's useless to dwell on it now, though — I'll need to find a second-hand one somewhere. There must be shops in Edinburgh that sell them. That's a task for tomorrow.

I kick myself for not thinking of this sooner. How stupid was I to believe I could function without a phone? A second-hand one and a prepaid SIM card — that's top of the list for tomorrow, as soon as the shops open.

Sometimes, I swear, I'm a total moron. In this digital age, it's virtually impossible to go back to functioning without it. I'm too used to it.

Edinburgh, with its population of over half a million, feels like a place where I can disappear, just another face in the crowd. In the distance, I spot a sign for the Town Centre. That's where I need to go — find a bed for the night, somewhere safe.

I curse under my breath. I hate that I've run out of options. To stay safe, I need a place to lay my head. But if I don't find a quiet B&B and you figure out I was here, you might realise Simone was just a decoy.

Shit. Shit. Shit.

The best-laid plans . . . Well, there's no way around it. It's a risk I have to take. Right now, I need to find somewhere to rest.

The clock on the dash says 7.15 p.m.

I pull out my writing pad, flipping through the pages in search of anything I might have jotted down about other places to stay nearby. Every word on this pad feels like a risk, a gamble I took despite the constant fear you'd notice something suspicious.

I was always terrified you'd catch on, knowing how you'd rifle through my phone the moment you suspected anything. That left me with no choice but to do my searches elsewhere — at the library. And I made the reservations from the café.

Hiding my notebook became another layer of the game. Beneath the carpet, tucked next to my bedside table, with a stack of reading books piled on top — that was the only spot I could think of, the only place I believed you'd never think to look.

Staying shtum, watching what I said, careful not to let anything slip was the hardest part of the last few months.

But first I need to get a local newspaper and see if it can help me find a place for the night.

The store is busy; I note cameras as I walk in. I keep my head low, make my way to the newspaper stand just inside the entrance, glancing behind me, making sure you're not there lurking somewhere.

The fluorescent lights flicker above me as I clutch the newspaper, its pages crinkling under my tense grip. I take a step back, trying to blend into the group of people close by. The security guard shifts his attention elsewhere — thankfully — but I know better than to let my guard down completely.

I scan the community board next to the newspaper stand. Flyers hang in vibrant colours, promising everything from dance classes to book clubs, but all I see are opportunities for someone who can afford a normal life, one I'm no longer a part of. What would they all think if they knew the truth? If they realised I was a runaway, searching for a sliver of safety amid the chaos?

I open the back pages and search through the adverts for rooms to rent and local B&Bs. Bingo.

I make the call using my pay-as-you-go, moving away from the crowds. I can feel the weight of the security guard's gaze creeping back. I need to hurry.

'Hello? Caledonian Nights,' a gravelly voice answers.

'Hi! I'm calling to see if you have any vacancies,' I stammer, trying to sound casual, but the tremor in my voice betrays me.

'Are you looking for tonight?' she asks, her tone discerning. My breath catches.

'Yes, um, tonight, yes, do you have any?'

'We do. What's the name?' she says.

'Jill Hart. How far is it from the Tesco superstore?'

'About ten minutes.'

'Great, see you then.' I hang up without waiting for a response. Then realise I have no idea how much it will be. Doesn't matter — I need somewhere tonight. I'll have to scrimp some other place tomorrow.

I pay for the newspaper quickly, twitching because the longer I'm in here the longer I'm being recorded. The security guard is still watching me, making the hairs on the back of my neck stand up. I'm about to leave when a thought strikes me, and I go back to the newsstand, rifling through the nationals. There's nothing on the front pages so I flick through them all. There's nothing. *No, Housewife who disappeared.* Have you started looking for me yet? Why is it not in the paper? That doesn't feel right. The stories headlining the papers are generic or political. News about protest marches. Something controversial that some politician said. But I can't relax. Surely there'd be a photo by now.

Panic mingles with urgency.

I glance at the security guard. He's still watching. But I don't think he knows anything. He's just being creepy, I tell myself.

I need to go.

I'm about to flee when I stop again and see the signage pointing to upstairs and *electricals.*

I take the escalator to the next level and find a small supply of phones. These are new and very expensive. No. I can't spend my money so frivolously. I will go to the library in the morning and use the computer there to find a store that sells them second-hand.

'I know they're expensive but if you take out a contract with us for a SIM you can pay for it monthly,' a Scottish voice says, sneaking up on me and making me spin around like a Catherine wheel. I'm not used to the accent yet and a flashback strikes me for a moment of the men crawling all over my car. For a split second I think he's one of them, then logic rescues me. 'You can take out twelve- or eighteen-month contracts with great deals right now.' He sees my hesitation. 'If you get one of our Clubcards, or you might already have one, you get an even better deal.' He must be just eighteen, maybe pushing twenty — smart, eager and very smiley. My heart bleeds for him. Sales is not an easy job, especially in today's climate.

I'm perfunctory. 'No, no, thank you all the same, I was just looking, getting an idea for a birthday present for my niece. But thanks anyway. You've been very kind.'

'Oh, okay then.' There's a dejected tone in his voice making me feel bad but I can't dwell. 'Well, if you bring her in, she can choose the colour of the phone,' he continues, still trying and with a little more pep in his tone. 'That's always fun. Or you can take it out of the safety box, have a play with it. People like to do that sort of thing.'

Please go, leave me alone. I'm conscious how much time I'm here talking to him.

'I'm sure they do,' I say with encouragement. 'I'll be back with my niece some other time. Thanks anyway.'

I head out of the store, sit in my car, right at the end of the car park as far from the cameras as possible. I open the A–Z, and then starting up, I follow the directions as best I can all the time praying this B&B will be a million times better than the last. The cost is worrying me. I can't afford to be frivolous.

I realise the money is going to run out sooner than I think, unless I find a job to pay me cash in hand. Without an NI number I won't be able to get a job other than cleaning toilets or working in small shops, cafés that sort of thing. I can't let that stop me.

CHAPTER 9

Royce

After interviewing the husband, we're back at the station. Missing persons cases come in every day, and Camilla is more than experienced enough to handle them. She has an instinct for these things — a talent for sniffing out liars or sensing when something doesn't quite add up.

'If it looks like a duck, swims like a duck, and quacks like a duck, then it probably is a duck, boss,' she likes to say whenever I question her gut instincts. And most of the time, she's spot on.

That's why I brought my brilliant and trusted DS with me earlier to have a little chat with Mr Johnson-Smyth. While I asked the questions, I kept Camilla in the background, quietly observing, taking in the house, and reading him in ways only she can. That's her specialty — getting a measure of people when they don't realise they're being studied.

'Right, Camilla, what insight did you gain from our Mr Johnson-Smyth?'

'Aren't you supposed to be on annual leave, boss?' Camilla asks, her tone a mix of curiosity and something more perceptive, as if she can already tell something is off.

'I was. Now I'm not. They need me on this case.' My voice is flat just thinking about the cross words we've been having lately. I really don't want to be talking about this right now. I know I don't give her as much of my time as I should. But that's the nature of my job and she's always known that.

'Ouch. How's Natalie taken it? This isn't the first time you've cancelled a holiday,' she presses, sensing there's more to the story than I'm letting on. Natalie's anxiety is flaring up again and that's not helping things between us. But she's right, the job has caused me to cancel holidays before.

I grumble, unable to keep the irritation at her question out of my voice. 'I know. How do you think she's taken it?'

Camilla raises an eyebrow, leaning back in her chair. 'Wow. I'd be seriously pissed if I were her.' Her intuition picks up on the strain in my words. 'Ooh, sorry, maybe she's already told you how pissed she is.' She giggles knowing how I hate talking about my home life.

'Camilla, let's get back to the job in hand,' I snap uncomfortably. 'You were telling me your thoughts about our misper's husband.'

'Well, here's the thing: he admitted she's vanished a few times before, needing head space after they've had tiffs or arguments, hence not calling us — he thought it was the same thing again. Though he's no idea where she goes even though he's asked her. I think that's odd. But I'm not married. But you are, boss. How would you feel if Natalie did something like that? The brother, on the other hand, insists it's out of character and denies she's ever disappeared before, saying she'd never leave without telling *him*.'

'I don't think I'd be happy if she vanished like that, you're right.' I take a moment, my thoughts wandering. 'You have to wonder why she felt the need to vanish or needed head space like you said.'

'Those are my words, not his — it's how I interpreted what he said,' she says. 'She left her phone behind, which, according to the husband, she hasn't done before. He says they're in regular contact throughout the day, or at the very least, they keep the diary updated, but not when she disappears including this time. She left her phone and disappeared, and that's really thrown him. He wasn't lying about that — it genuinely unsettled him. I'm convinced he didn't know the phone was still in the house.

'Then there's the brother. He's aggravating the husband with accusations about their marriage. That's clearly rubbing the husband up the wrong way. While he's worried about her, I think what's bothering him just as much — if not more — is the fact that she's gone without saying a word, especially after assuring him she was fine. That reassurance came right after husband and wife had words about the IVF,' Camilla says.

'So, you think she's bolted?' I ask.

'I think the husband can't accept the idea that she's bolted because he had no clue anything was wrong. He still believes she might have had an accident or will be back in a day or so from wherever it is she likes to run off too. But that doesn't clear up why she left her phone behind. And let's be honest — if she didn't have her phone with her, what other ID would she have if something had happened to her?'

'Right. Get on to the hospitals, see if anyone matching her description was brought in last night or this morning. Let's also check local CCTV and see if we can track her movements after she left the house. There's a camera near the green that should've picked her up. And do some digging on Smyth — see what you can find. And check the phone for a tracker. Could be there's one on there and that's why it was left behind if she has bolted.'

'Got it, boss. What about the brother? The relationship with his sister seems . . . off, don't you think? I mean, I'm close to my own brother, but what they have — it's weird. I mean, the way he talks about her checking in with him all the time and how she wouldn't just go off like this without telling him. I think that's weird. I mean she's clearly done it before, the husband said so, if we believe him that is, and she didn't tell the brother then because he had no idea and denies it's ever happened. Talking of brothers, has Sid blocked you now for good?'

'Camilla, my brother is no concern of yours. Let's stay on track shall we? I'm not sure about Jason. I haven't fully sussed him out. Check him out too. I'm not ruling him out just yet — he could have something to do with this. And you're right, we don't know who's lying right now. Let's keep an open mind for now until we have more information. I don't want to focus on one person just yet.'

'Aren't you going to re-book your holidays? You know how fast those dates disappear. Bit unfair, don't you think, making you stay on and lose your holiday? I know it's all "you scratch my back, I'll scratch yours", but honestly? You know what I think? They wouldn't give a toss about scratching your back if they needed an excuse to let you go.'

I stare at her. 'You're so subtle, Camilla.'

'But you say all the time that I'm not subtle.'

'You're not. It's a joke. It's called sarcasm.' I sigh. 'I'm changing the dates, yes, but I've not yet got round to it.' Anyone else saying what she just did would get a flea in their ear. 'To be honest, Camilla, if this is a hush job like they say it is and they've requested me to handle it, I can hardly say no, can I?'

'Mmm.'

'What's that supposed to mean?' I narrow my eyes.

Camilla perches on the corner of my desk. 'Maybe you're just trying to convince yourself of that.' She pauses. 'Bit of a bummer though, right? Weren't you going bodyboarding with your nephews? Does Natalie do it too? I'd love to do that. But not in this country. Sea's bloody freezing here.'

My wife is used to the last-minute changes my job forces on me sometimes. 'Yeah, maybe it's a blessing in disguise. I wasn't looking forward to that trip at this time of year to be perfectly honest. Sid just mithered me to death. The sea is bloody cold, even in the summer. In winter? Probably unbearable. Natalie's been under the weather, so she won't mind.' I don't know why I just said that. We just can't seem to talk these days without it turning into an argument.

Camilla gives an exaggerated sad face. 'Oh poor Nat. You never said. You know she's not been in for a while.' She smiles. 'I miss her popping in with chocolates. I feel I have to eat them when the boss's wife brings them in. I hope you're looking after her.'

I smirk, remembering Natalie doing that for a while and enjoying coming in to see my unit. 'Of course I am.' But it's been longer than Camilla thinks, months in fact. She's getting worse in leaving the house. 'One thing's for sure — I'm handling this case like Smyth is just some ordinary guy — not some special VIP they want me to tiptoe around. No pussyfooting. If we need to go in hard, we go in hard.' I change the subject, done with talking about my personal life.

'Understood, boss.'

'So, what did you find on your recce of the Smyth home?'

'There were no shoe imprints around the perimeter. It rained yesterday, not a downpour, but enough that we'd expect some marks if this was a snatch job. The low-level windows all had locks — none had been tampered with. Everything was neat and tidy inside. No signs of a disturbance. No clothes taken. No drawers rifled through. If she'd run I'd expect to see something — like a sock or a pair of knickers dropped in the rush. Maybe a product or two knocked over. But according to the husband, all her stuff is still there.'

'What if she didn't pack?' I suggest. 'What if she left and took nothing?'

Camilla scrunches up her face. 'Maybe, but a woman walking out without taking anything? That's unlikely.' She taps her lip. 'Unless she wanted to vanish . . .'

'Exactly. If she wanted to disappear, she'd want to be invisible. Bringing anything could leave a trail.'

'That makes sense.' She nods. 'Are we leaning that way now?'

'Not yet. Let's clear the hospitals first, see what comes back from that search. I want to speak to her employer — call her and set up a time.'

'Will do.' Camilla heads back to her desk, closing my office door behind her.

A while later, I pull up Google Maps and plot a course from London — where would she go to get away? Her car was still in the garage, so she must've taken the train. I pick up the phone.

'Camilla, I know it's late, see if you can get DC Glennon to get me all the CCTV from the tube stations, trains, bus terminals and local car rentals between the times the husband says she disappeared . . . yesterday the tenth of October after 7.00 a.m. which was the last time the husband saw her and 8.00 p.m. when he said he got back home. We can check on ANPR and CCTV to verify he's telling the truth on that. Better still, take it back to the day before just in case.' It'll be a late one tonight.

'I'll look through them, boss, when they come in. Paul can help.'

'No. I want to do it myself. Send them to my email. You might have to wait till the morning for some of them to come through.'

'Really? You hate doing that sort of thing.'

'Different this time. If we miss anything, it'll be on my watch. You've got enough to do — interviewing her friends and that brother of hers. See if you can get more out of him about their relationship.' I sigh and fish out the phone from my drawer.

'Want me to chat to her boss, too?'

'I'll handle that. You focus on making sure Paul gets all the CCTV.' *I'll find you. You can't just vanish that easily. Not in London. Too many cameras. More than you think.*

I pick up the iPhone, punch in the code and scroll through all the messages. I check Maps for recent destinations. I search for Google activity — day trips, train timetables, bus schedules, airports, flights. Anything that could give me a clue, but nothing. Her passport was still at home, so she hasn't left the country.

CHAPTER 10

Jill

Caledonian Nights looms ahead, a beacon in the relentless downpour. It looks decent — no, better than decent — especially considering what I just escaped. I spot parking, too, a rare stroke of fortune. I manoeuvre my car in. I step out, pulling on my coat just as a sheet of rain cascades over my hood. I aim for stability but misjudge and step straight into a puddle. Damn it.

I snatch my rucksack from the boot and heft it against my thigh, my food bag clutched tightly in the other hand, which I use to wrap my hood snugly around my face and zip up, the fabric sheltering me as I tread across the dimly lit car park, each squelch of my boots echoing my apprehension at what to expect while the rain drums ominously above me.

Inside, the woman at the front desk draws my attention. She's probably in her late fifties — no, maybe her sixties — smartly dressed, with wispy platinum hair spun into a neat bun. Her long nails, fire engine red, dance dangerously in the air as she comes to greet me.

As I step over the threshold, the click of the lock echoes behind me. 'I presume you're Miss Hart?'

My eyes flicker around the room searching for cameras but there don't seem to be any.

'Are you Miss Hart?' she repeats, her gaze scrutinising everything about me.

'What?' I stammer, still preoccupied that she has a camera outside. I can't help wondering if it's all deleted after twenty-four hours. It must be. There'd be no reason for her to hang on to it for longer. I hope not, anyway.

'I said — are you Miss Hart?'

'Yes, yes, I am. I'm sorry, I'm just . . . tired.' I pull myself together. The truth feels like a stone in my throat. I was about to spill the harrowing details about the men who pursued me, but I choke the urge back — no need to etch myself into her memory. 'I just phoned, about half an hour ago. I have a room booked.'

She extends her elegant well-manicured hand. 'Welcome to Caledonian Nights, Miss Hart. I'm the one you spoke to. I'm Amanda McKay an' this is ma place — has been for twenty-eight years. You're lucky, we only have the one room available. I've just been freshening it up for you, opened the window a wee bit to let in some air, so it might be a wee bit chilly when you go up. Never mind, hey, fresh air is good for you. Just close it and it will soon warm up.' Her voice is warm, and welcoming.

I force a smile, shaking her hand; her polished appearance highlights how dishevelled I feel. I'm desperate for a bath and can't wait to get to my room.

'Is Jill short for Gillian?'

'No, just Jill.'

'Ah, just like Jack and Jill!' Her laughter vibrates too brightly beneath the heavy gloom of my thoughts. 'Now let's get you signed in. D'you have any more luggage?'

'No. That's it.' I hold up my rucksack. A wave of defensiveness floods through me. 'I asked on the phone if you take cash. Is that still the case?'

'Aye, we do, lass — nothing wrong with cash here. You booked for one night, but I could offer another at a discount.' She peers at her computer monitor. 'It seems we've just had a cancellation for tomorrow. What d' you say to another night?'

Tempting. Shivers travel down my spine at the thought of more driving in this weather; my instincts weigh heavy with caution. 'No . . . just the one night, thanks.'

Her narrowed gaze lingers, as if she can unearth hidden truths beneath my words. 'You look like you could use a good bath and a solid sleep. Have you travelled far?'

'A bit . . .' I wince as I consider my road ahead. 'Traffic and rain . . . a brutal combination.' *Not to mention what happened to me.*

'I could do that extra night for you,' she presses, her eyes piercing, 'round it up to one hundred and twenty for the two?'

Why the sudden kindness? My heart races with suspicion. 'Really, that's very kind, but . . . I just need one night.'

'Come now,' she insists, glancing at my modest bag. 'You seem a long way from home, lass.'

I force a laugh, but a chill settles in my bones. 'I'm fine, I assure you.' Something about her gaze makes me feel exposed, like she's managed to pull back the layers, revealing who I am beneath my facade.

'Breakfast is included,' she tempts, her voice unwavering.

'Yes, okay then,' flies from my lips, and before I know it, she's tapping my details into her computer.

'Let's get you signed in, then.' She smiles to herself. I think she's pleased she's convinced me. As we delve into the details, I hand over my money, internally screaming at myself for the decision. I need to keep moving. But the price for the extra night is too good to give up. I feel so tired. A part of me feels like a fraud after her kindness.

'There we go — room fifteen.' She presents the oversized key, its disc heavy in my palm. 'Breakfast is served between seven and ten, and tea and coffee are available by the television in your room.'

She seems ready to move on, but each word carries a weight as if she sees through me and it makes me feel ashamed. I don't even know why; I have nothing to be ashamed of. 'And don't hesitate to ask for more if you need it. So, are you on your own? Husband following? Boyfriend? It's a double room, that's why I ask.' I don't answer. 'You're not from around these parts, are you? D'you have friends, family nearby?' I shake my head. 'Oh, that's a wee shame. So you're visiting Edinburgh on your own, then?'

'Sorry, I'm really tired and I'd like to go to my room.'

'Aye and there's me gassing away. Don't mind me, I'm just being nosey.' She chuckles, amusement illuminating her features. 'You just call down if you need anything, lass.'

'Thank you,' I say quietly. 'This is all very generous of you. Are you sure it's no trouble? The extra night I mean.' Guilt and shame twist my gut horribly.

'Naw, it's no bother. It's coming up to Christmas soon after all. The season of goodwill. I like to share the love. We usually throw in breakfast for a two-or-more-night stay anyway.' Her laughter is cheerful, but underneath, I sense a probing nature of someone who likes to know everything.

'Well, it's still a way off.' I chuckle. 'We're only just into October.' I can't help it; she's so sweet and I wasn't expecting this sort of kindness. It does something to me.

She guides me through the hallway and up the ornate staircase, a reminder of a past when this would have been a private residence. The beauty is stunning, and I imagine in its day it was an opulent home, and for a heart-stopping moment, I wish I could admire it without the spectre of anxiety at my heels.

'It's been a quiet day. Most of my residents are foreign, and they keep to themselves. They're up at dawn and back at sunset, too weary for chatter.'

'Do you have Wi-Fi?'

'Aye, it's written on a sheet of paper in your room. We have the daily papers delivered too, only a couple of them and you're welcome to read them in the comfy chairs in the dining room or the snug, but not in your rooms. We find they never come back down and it's a service we provide for everyone not just the selfish few.' She roars with laughter again. 'You probably think I'm awful saying that. But believe me, lass, when you've been in this business as long as I have you get to know what people are really like. Now then, here we are.'

'That's a lot of stairs,' I say.

'You get used to them.' She takes the key from me, opens the door and enters, going immediately to the window and closing it. Next, she checks the radiator is hot by placing her hand on it. 'Well, this is nicely aired, don't you think? How does it look to you? Happy?'

I am, it's neat, clean and bigger than I expected. 'Oh, it's lovely and clean.'

She smiles, pleased that I've noticed. Her kindness shines in her eyes. 'Aye, I take pride in all my rooms. You won't find a cleaner room in Edinburgh. Leave your room as you found it, please. It's all we ask.'

I look at the bathroom and can hardly wait to get in the bath. I'm twitching to run the water, kick off my clothes and sink under the warm suds.

'I'll leave you to it then. Are you sightseeing? Is that why you're here?'

'Kind of.'

'Well, Edinburgh is a beautiful city. If you need any pointers just let me know. We have leaflets downstairs in a rack on the wall as you enter the dining room, help yourself. Where was it you said you've come from?' Her brow rises with expectation.

I hadn't. 'Newcastle.' My gaze lingers on the comfortable-looking bed and how desperate I am to climb inside.

'Well, that's not very far, lass.' She lifts a brow to suggest she's waiting for more and that I look like I've travelled much further than Newcastle. I don't elaborate.

I press my lips into a tight smile, the echoes of all those lies twisting through my mind — yours, mine . . . it's hard to keep track anymore.

Truth tangled with half-lies. It always seemed so effortless. Lying. The lies always lingered close to the truth, just enough to keep them steady — enough to make it hard to tell where one ended and the other began.

As thoughts about you begin to whirl inside my head, I pivot to stop them dragging me down. 'I'm moving here, well, the family is, you know how it is, husband, busy, busy, busy. So, I'm looking at houses, areas, that sort of thing.' I keep my gaze on her, not shifting it. I feel myself heat up and try not to react to how uncomfortable I feel right now, lying to her. *Look confident. Smile but don't over smile, don't be dramatic, don't chatter about it, keep it sweet and succinct.* I'm annoyed with myself that after holding it together moments ago now I've blurted out a story. You told me that was how good liars got away with lying by keeping things to a minimum. Have I said too much? If she asks me about areas, I'm screwed. Why would I not know what areas we're thinking of looking at? Nobody would do that.

'Well that's exciting, isn't it! Nice to have a change, I expect. To get away from the old and start new.' Her gaze lingers too long.

'Yes, yes . . .' I murmur; my voice trails off. Not everyone gets to escape their reality.

I sense she reads my discomfort as clearly as if I were plastered against a transparent wall. 'I'll let you go, then. Ye look tired.'

* * *

The moment the door closes I'm over in the bathroom, running the water, dropping in some of the bath salts by the side of the bath and stripping off all my clothes. I don't even wait for it to fill before I'm stepping in and sliding down, lapping the water over my body with my hands. *God this feels good.* And for a few moments, my mind is blank. My chest is loose, and my fear is gone. Until I remember something you said that at the time I didn't quite understand but now I'm frightened what you meant by those cryptic words, something about people knowing our business. You hated the idea of the outside world knowing what went on in our home. Why wouldn't you? The shame would destroy your life. So I never spoke about it, too scared about what you would do. I sink further down until only my nose is free and brush it off as paranoia of how you will react thinking that I've told people the truth of what's been going on in our lives.

I wake up some eight hours later and roll over in the comfortable bed to the sounds of footsteps on the stairs; they make me lie still and for a moment I think it's you coming for me, but then I remember and my heart slows as I hear the chatter of a couple talking in another language, Italian, I think, making their way down to the dining room. I check my Nokia charging by the bed for the time. My stomach tells me with noisy growls that it too needs some serious attention. I get up, stretch and look out the window. It's quite dark out with some of the streetlights still on. A few cars drive past; a handful of pedestrians walk by.

My money belt is under the spare pillow just poking out. My dwindling cash is my life raft right now. I can't believe how quickly it's going down. My rucksack is on the dresser, food bag next to it. There's nothing there that will spoil yet. I hear the rise of more voices below. The guests must all be up and eating in the dining room. I'm right above them.

I hear the front door open and close; Amanda's voice is recognisable; she's talking to a man. I lean out the window checking for your car parked on the street even though I know it's likely too soon and won't be you. Still, I can't help myself. You have all those connections with access to anything you need. You might have spotted me leaving and traced me to my car and . . . I can't bear thinking about it and shut my eyes, tight, forcing myself to stop.

Over the last eight years that we've been married there have been times when I could easily have gone nuts, let the depression that hovered on the fringes take me down or opt out altogether when the hopelessness of my situation seemed interminable. But you wouldn't let me. What stopped me was that I wasn't ready to let you control me. Crush me like an insect underfoot — that's how it felt, though I suppose feelings can be tricky things, hard to pin down or trust. I wanted to live *my way*. I thought I could do it, listen to you, follow what you said, and that was my reason for carrying on, to try and make it work or at least that's what I told myself. Letting go was easier, though, surrendering to the suffocating weight, letting it pull me deeper until there was nothing left to feel. But you wouldn't even let me have that. Numbness was a kind of escape. I've lost track of how many times I've stared into the mirror, whispering words to myself that might've been comfort — or maybe warnings. It was too hard. Exhausting. Miserable. Looking at my face and seeing the unhappiness within seeping out onto its contours. The ugliness hidden behind a mask of make-up day after day. The thought of one day being free of you was a battle with myself. Could I survive alone? I won't deny you so very nearly had me beat. So many times. Sometimes it was hard to get up and fight another day. But wallowing in my misery wasn't going to help me. When I got like that, I had to dig deep to find the steel I knew was in there. To grasp it with both hands and yank myself back out of the mire.

I hate myself for constantly thinking of you, having you still stuck inside my head every day. Every moment I stop concentrating you pop up like one of those hideous Jack-in-the-box. I need to keep thinking what you're up to. What steps you're taking to find me. I need to keep you there so complacency doesn't take over and trip me up. Keeping you in the forefront, no matter how much I detest it, keeps me strong; visualising how you're searching for me keeps me focused.

I leave the window and head to the bathroom. I open the shower cubicle and slip under the hot water. When I dress, I keep to my usual nondescript attire. And then my heart skips a beat when I hear loud, angry male voices in the street, the slamming of a car door. And for a moment my life stalls and judders to a stop. I imagine you racing up the stairs, two at a time, Amanda shouting you're not allowed to go up, but you keep going. My bedroom door flying open, crashing into the wall. And there you are, standing in front of me. Your eyes burn into mine, sharp and unrelenting, your expression twisting into something I can't quite name. The room feels smaller, tighter, the air heavy against my skin. My cheek burns, though I don't know why. Maybe it's the weight of your gaze. Maybe it's just me. Maybe it's something else. I flinch instinctively. I know it's not you. I know. But I have to take deep breaths to still my racing heart. I peek out the window to be certain. It's not you. The trouble with years of abuse is the terrible mental illness it creates. PTSD, the anxiety created by recollections, the stress of being found, the fear of discovery is no joke and can't be taken lightly. I fasten the laces of my boots, blow out a breath and breathe in again, slowly. It's just over two days that I left you. It will take months if not years before I can totally relax and feel safe. If I make it that is.

I head for the dining room, the smell of bacon guiding me. It's full. I stop at the entrance. There isn't a free table. I will have to share with that single male eating a cooked breakfast by the window. My legs twitch to turn and go back upstairs, but my stomach muscles clench demanding I stay put.

'Ah, there you are Miss Hart, Jill, lovely to see you. Did you sleep well? I'm afraid we're rammed right now. If you don't mind sharing, I've got one spot left or you can have a cuppa in the lounge or the snug, I'm never quite sure what to call it, until there's a table free. Sundays are always busy, lots o' guests checking out today.'

I want to say that it's okay and I will join the man. That it doesn't bother me. But the truth is that it does. I'm conditioned to be afraid of making a mistake. Amanda looks at me, at once detecting my discomfort.

'The lounge is lovely and cosy. Let me fetch you a drink. Tea? Coffee?'

'Tea please. I don't want to make a fuss.'

'Nae fuss. It's far too early for all that chit-chat, don't you think? I wouldn't like it, that's for sure.'

She guides me to the lounge, which is really a snug decorated in different shades of lavender with four club chairs. It is blessedly empty. I wait with my tea. Telling myself that was silly and I need to start stepping over that line you've drawn for me never to cross. I was never able to tell my friends what was happening at home. I hated they'd judge me. People on the outside don't understand. How can they? It's unimaginable to be controlled by another person. There's not always physical violence involved. Mental cruelty is sometimes more damaging than violence — because it's invisible.

I had to leave.

You'd never let me go.

You've never understood.

I'd rather kill myself than live like that again.

CHAPTER 11

William

My veins are humming. It's just over four days since you left. That DCI suspects me of being involved in your disappearance. Can you believe that, Cat? If you don't show up soon that's going to become a reality. I'm going to be their prime suspect. They're going to check the local CCTV to see where you went and with whom. *Is your wife having an affair?* What kind of heartless question is that to pose to a man whose wife has just vanished without a trace? I can't believe this; why must they jump to that conclusion? What kind of darkness clouds his thoughts to even consider asking me something so dreadful?

I drink the espresso I just made myself with that fancy coffee machine you made me buy, then make another. Jason already thinks I've done you in. I stare out of the kitchen window unsure what to do with myself today. I could go back to work, but they've given me leave for the week. I won't last though, sitting around wondering where you are. I'm going stir crazy as it is and it's only Monday.

They've asked me to check your bank account which I have access to. Nothing. And that's not good. If you've run away, then how the hell are you funding any of it? You've taken your cards, so you'll have to use them soon. You can't live on fresh air forever. But if you've had an accident that will be irrelevant. They asked for your social media and to check that too. You don't do social media, I told them, which was a surprise to them. I could tell from his expression. Then bloody Jason told them I don't let you. I don't let you my arse. Is that what you told him, Cat? I never told you I didn't want you to do it. I told you I'd prefer you not to do it. We don't need the world to see how we live. That's when you get burgled or scammed. I do not see the need to share our life with the world. You actually agreed with me. So why tell him something different?

I need to find a trail you must have left somewhere so I can find you. I need to know where you've gone and bring you home. I'm beginning to think you *have* left me and I still don't understand why? I love you so much. You know how much I love you. That last evening's conversation still haunts me. I remember you said you wanted to talk. I should have listened. But the IVF stuff and adoption was still bugging me. But we were going to talk about it. We were.

I know you, Cat, I know how you think and how you deal with stuff. You like to run away. Go to ground and lick your wounds. But where? Where do you go? The police asked if I'd found your laptop, but I hadn't found it then. They think you've taken it with you. I'll have to hand it over. If you wanted me to find you, you'd leave me a clue and if there is anything on the laptop, you'll have deleted it if you don't.

I must check it properly anyway before handing it over. Just in case you messed up and there is a clue I've missed. Although you're pretty savvy with technology, better than I am. I think of you on your laptop and on your phone recently, on the sofa, curled up like a cat, surfing you told me. Have you been planning this? I thought we had no secrets. Maybe you have run away. Maybe I'm being delusional thinking you wanted a baby with me when all the time you were screaming *no*, inside. But then why go through all that pain? It makes no sense to think that way.

I will find you and I will bring you home. Make no mistake. We will sort this out and if you don't want a baby then that's okay with me. I just want you home. I want *us*, Cat. God damn it, I love you. You're my wife.

I open your MacBook Air. I feel slightly wobbly thinking that maybe there was something wrong, maybe you're ill and you've been hiding it. Like cancer or something worse. But why keep that from me. From Jason. But why me? 'GOD DAMNIT,' I yell, frustrated with you. I snatch up the notebook with all our passwords. Remember when we decided it was a good idea in case something happened to one of us? *It's impossible to get into people's accounts without passwords*, you said. *Do you really need the hassle at that time?* I agreed because you were so right. I look and find the relevant one. Your mother's name backwards.

I sit in the lounge finishing the last of my espresso in one gulp, put the cup down on the coffee table and start to delve through. I punch in the password. The password box shimmers. *Incorrect password*. What the hell. When did you change this? And why didn't you write it in the book? I try something else. Still, it doesn't let me in. I check what you've written in the notebook. That's what I've typed. I take a breath and type it in again. Slowly. My fingers are shaking a little. Bingo! The screen opens.

I open your Gmail account, only to be met with another password prompt that catches me off guard. You never sign out of Gmail. This sudden shift makes my stomach churn.

I glance at the notebook. I find the password scribbled down and type it in; my heart races with anticipation or dread, I don't know which right now. The box shimmers mockingly at me. I try again, more cautiously this time, but still, the box shimmers, rejecting my efforts. Frustration brews inside me as I wonder why none of the passwords match. What secrets lie behind this digital door you don't want me to see?

I pause. Unlocking this will take hours — maybe days — if I ever even get lucky enough to succeed. The police wouldn't have a problem. Now I am even more certain that I need to read what's here before they do. In a moment of desperation, I decide to try my birthday. We always agreed never to use them as they're too easy to work out. To my surprise, the screen flickers and opens wide. Yes! I'm in.

But relief quickly turns to worry.

The first thing facing me is a message, *code, error*.

An error occurred when trying to delete files.
Please try again. Yes/no

My fingers hover over the space bar, hesitating as I realise what I'm about to uncover. You tried to hide something from me — something significant — yet in your haste, didn't complete the process before closing down and so you left your world open, and I can't turn back now.

As I gaze at the screen, dread coils in my stomach. I click, and suddenly your inbox swells before me, a chaotic sea of unopened emails — spam, advertisements, and names unfamiliar to me. Yet I am drawn in, compelled to pry into the secrets you wished to keep from my eyes.

As I sift through the digital clutter, I can't help but feel a growing tide of anger and betrayal. Unravelling the threads of your correspondence, I find familiar names, friends I thought I could trust. With every message I read, a jagged piece of my heart splinters. You shared our most intimate struggles — our attempts to have a baby, the tears, the heartaches — struggles you promised we'd face together, alone. How could you?

Then, there it is. The email that drives the knife deeper: one sent to Jason, of all people. My breath catches in my throat as

I read the words that shoot straight through me like arrows of accusation. You placed the blame squarely on my shoulders, claiming it's my fault you can't conceive. A lie, a cruel twist of truth, unwinding everything we've endured together. We got checked together; we were in this as a team. I want to scream, to shake you so you can see the cruelty in your words — but most of all, I want to understand. Why, Cat, why say such mean things?

With my heart pounding, I begin to wonder: *what other secrets are you keeping from me.* The pain of betrayal fills the room, and I feel utterly alone. *What's going on? I thought I knew you.*

Neither of us is to blame. I look at a photograph of you on the mantle. The fertility doctor said, his words echoing painfully in my mind, *You just might not be compatible. And, William, you do have a slightly low sperm count but it's nothing to worry about.* That sentence feels like a heavy weight pressing down on my chest. I turn my attention back to the screen in front of me.

The left-hand side of the screen displays several files, each one labelled with a generic title — nothing that sparks any sense of curiosity except for one: *Jack Russell.* A cold flicker of apprehension courses through me. I had a Jack Russell growing up who died, and it broke my heart; we always agreed we'd never get one. So why, in the midst of our attempts to start a family, is there a separate file dedicated to a dog?

As I hover the cursor over the file, goosebumps prickle all over me, warning me against what I'm about to uncover. Against my better judgement, I click, and a cascade of emails unfurl before my eyes, all from a mysterious address — Jake.stroud@gmail.com. The name is unfamiliar, and I can hardly breathe as panic mounts within me.

My heart races: this isn't just about compatibility anymore. It's about dishonesty, and as the truth begins to unravel right in front of me, I feel my world teeter on the edge of uncertainty.

A new email alert arrives. A message from Rita. I click on it.

Cat, can you get in touch. I've had the police and Jason calling me asking about you. Where are you? Are you okay? I wish you'd told me you weren't coming in. Why have you disappeared? I've had William on the phone, which is odd in a way if you have disappeared but understandable if he's being funny with you, again. He must be beside himself with worry. Jake came in asking about you, too. He said your phone's off and everything is going to voicemail. I'm worried. Call me. You went out on that delivery then to your appointment and never came back. Jake said you didn't turn up at his either. I haven't told the police that. But I'm going to have to unless you let me know you're okay.

What the hell.

Jake? Who is this Jake?

A few more emails drop like they've been stuck in the ether unable to deliver. I click on the ones from your friends. Elaine's first.

Cat? Cat, you need to get in touch. Jason's been on to me saying you've disappeared! What's he on about? And William. What does he mean, you've disappeared? Are you okay? I called round to the florist and Rita told me the same that you went to an appointment after a delivery and never returned. She said you've not even been in touch with Jake. Get in touch. Need to know you're safe. Where are you? XXX

Jake, again. I open the next one from Joanne.

Cat, listen babe. What's going on? Jason came over all flustered saying you've vanished. He was well worked up. He said William's hurt you? What's he on about, babe, hurt you? William? I don't understand why he'd say that. What's William been up to? I can't believe you never said. I won't say a word. Just get in touch, babe, please. Jason said the cops will be coming to ask questions. Sounds serious. I can't believe what he said about William! Bloody William! Goes to show you can't ever judge a book. Email me. Call me. Just let me know you're safe. PLEASE. XXX

I sit back. What the hell is going on? Why are you telling everyone I hit you? Why? What did that DCI know that I don't? *Are* you having a fucking affair?

I go back into the Jack Russell file and open the emails from him — *Jake* — going back eight months. I start with the first one eight months ago. All legitimate from what you've said to each other. He's a physiotherapist. Has his own practice in Chelsea. But how did you get to know this Jake Stroud? And where did you meet him? You never told me you were seeing a physiotherapist. I read more, then bingo . . . there it is . . . a slight change in the tone of your correspondence and an appointment at his practice *after hours*. What for? My mind wants to tell me but I'm not listening.

I read on. It seems you started to see him around the time you started to back away from wanting a baby. I move ahead to four months ago when I first felt your withdrawal. My breathing is fast now and loud. I can feel my nostrils flare. I sit upright. Bang my fingers down hard on the keys opening an email from last month that you sent him.

Jake, I can't go on. I can't stay here a moment longer. I want to tell him. It's going to be hard. I want to. I just don't know if I have the courage to. I'm scared.

I want to hurl the laptop across the fucking room. Instead, I lash out with my foot and clear the coffee table in front of me in one swoop. What's left of my espresso in the bottom of my cup spatters along the cream painted wall, shattering on the hardwood floor. Did you think, if you told me you were leaving me for this *Jake* that I would just let you go? Did you, Cat? Really? Are you truly so naive to believe that? No, I don't think you are. Not for one minute. I would fight for you.

I open his reply.

Cat, darling, you do have the courage. We'll tell him together. If you tell Jason, then he can be there too. What's William going to do, beat the three of us up? He's only a man, Cat. One man. And a weak one who likes to hurt women. When you come to the practice tomorrow, we'll find a date and set a time. We can do this. You can do this.

I want to fucking kill Jake Stroud with my bare hands. I check the date of the email. So you were going to see him the day you vanished? You told him I beat you? Why? I can't work out what's wrong with you for saying such things about me. If you really wanted to leave, I'd be devastated, but I'd never hurt you. I'd let you go. I'd only try to save our marriage. Never hurt you. You know that. So why say that stuff? But then his words come back at me, and I rage. *I'm only one man, am I? I'm more of a man than you, you prissy physiotherapist.*

You've played me for a fool, Cat. Pretending to want a baby. Did you even take the injections? Was that all a ploy? To give you time to spread your vile story? It makes sense now why you didn't want me to go with you for the appointments. Jesus, oh, wow, you really had me, didn't you. There was no doctor, was there? You relayed what you wanted to me. After that initial appointment which we went to together, you never went back, did you? What is it you want? My money? Maybe you're spreading these lies to set the tone and blackmail me. You know my family will do anything to avoid being dragged through the media.

Is this where you've gone now? To his place? Is that where you're hiding out? At his?

I thunder out of the lounge, my heavy tread as thunderous and dangerous as my rage. I grab the Aston Martin car keys off the sideboard, put in Stroud's practice address in Google Maps and speed out of my drive with no care or attention to other traffic.

CHAPTER 12

William

I arrive in a rage. I know you're not here, that you'll be at his home and right now I don't know where that is. It's mid-afternoon. There are a few cars in the parking spaces. I don't know whether Stroud works alone or if he has others he employs.

I park, climb out, slam the door and stride purposely to the front door where I barge in, the little bell over the door tinkling.

It's very clinical inside, white walls, minimalist furniture, calming music in the background, magazines on the oblong wooden coffee table in front of comfy-looking chairs. I guess he'd have to have those if his customers have back or hip pain. Two patients sit waiting and look up at my whirlwind entrance then go back to their magazines and newspapers.

There's a huge bunch of flowers in a glass vase on the reception desk, which is low and ornate with gold curved legs and black onyx top. It stands out against the white of the rest of the furniture and walls. The receptionist is young, probably in her mid-twenties, heavily made up with big ruby lips and nails to match. She's smartly dressed in a green silk blouse with large gold hoops in her ears. In front of her is a huge Apple iMac. She looks up and smiles. 'Can I help you?' Her voice is small and quiet.

'Jake Stroud. I want to see him.'

'Do you have an appointment?'

'No. Tell him I want to see him, now.'

'I'm sorry, sir, but you need an appointment for a consultation. Can I make one for you?'

I lean forward on the desk, lower myself down so I'm nearly in her face. She doesn't flinch. 'NO. Tell him it's William Johnson-Smyth to see him. I'm sure he will be willing to come out and speak to me.'

She stares me down, her voice harder now, firmer. 'I'm sorry, sir, he's with a patient. If you'd like to wait, you can take a seat over there.' She points to the comfy chairs. 'Otherwise, I can make you an appointment, as I said.'

'Look, you don't seem to be getting my message. Either you go get him or I will. Which do you think would be preferable to the both of you?' I stand back up to my full height. She registers the full force of anger in my face.

'I will go and see if he's available, sir. If you wouldn't mind waiting here. I won't be a second.'

Jake Stroud comes out behind the receptionist, who slithers back into her chair, watching me cautiously. He's taller than me by a head, good-looking with that confidence men who know they're good-looking carry. A full head of jet-black hair, strong nose, confident eye contact — and the colour of those Italian olives we like so much. Not an ounce of fat on him. Broad shoulders, slim hips. He's wearing a short white medical coat that comes to his waist. I hate that you've been naked with him. It makes my hands turn into fists. I hate that his mouth has been all over your body, in all your intimate parts, and I see you writhing on his bed while he touches, kisses and licks you.

Jake looks bored as he stands there, hands in the pockets of his white coat. 'I was wondering when you'd come over.'

'Where's my wife? Tell me your address. Or call her and tell her to come home.'

'Do you want to come into a private room, William?' He gestures to a room off to the right of him.

'No, I don't, *Jake*. You've been fucking my wife. Now tell me where the hell she is.' The two patients waiting in the seating area look up, agog at my language and the colourful saga opening up in front of them.

'If you prefer to talk here, in front of everyone, that's up to you,' Jake says not missing a beat, but I can see he doesn't really want that. 'Tell me, why would I tell you where Cat is? She's told me all about you and how you hurt her. Why on earth would I hand her over to you? Are you insane?'

His lies make me want to reach out and grab him by the throat and show him how insane I am. Instead, I say calmly or as calmly as I can manage with the adrenaline whooshing inside me, 'What Cat's told you! And of course, you believe everything she's told you.' There's real menace in my tone. I can't help it. I'm so confused right now. This *Jake Stroud* of whom I have known less than two hours is talking about you like he's your goddamn husband. What else have you told him about me? How we fuck? What you like me to do to you in bed? Does he know all of that? How honest have you been with good ole bloody *Jake Stroud*?

'Do you want me to call the police, Mr Stroud?' the receptionist asks, her eyes wide like saucers.

'That won't be necessary, Louise. William isn't going to hurt me, are you, William?' He puts his hand on my shoulder like we're friends having a good old chinwag. 'Let's take this into a private room.' He urges me along with pressure on my shoulder.

I shrug him off and stride into the room before us. 'You don't get the right to call me that! You think you can just waltz into my life and take what's mine?'

Jake follows, closing the door behind him.

'If you touch me one more time or talk to me with your conde-scending tone, I will put you in hospital and don't think I won't.' I don't know what's come over me. All I'm doing is playing right into your hands behaving like this.

'Well, yes I can believe that. Cat has told me how you like to — hit things.'

Jake stands insouciant in front of me, hands folded across his chest and looking at me like I'm something vile he's stood in.

'Where is she? She's my wife and I have a right to know. Do you know the police are looking for her?' The reality of my unrav-elling marriage smothers me like a thick fog. 'Fine waste of their time when all along she's been shacked up at yours. In your bed.'

'Calm down. First, Cat isn't at my house. This isn't about own-ership. This is about happiness.'

'Happiness? You think she's happy with you? How can you be so deluded? You think you know her? You think you have the right to take her away? You've disrupted everything she knows! You took her away from me, her husband, her home! We're trying for a family. Give me your address and let me go see for myself. I'll find it out anyway. Just quicker if you give it me now.'

'You're the one who drove her away. The fights, the distance — I'm not going to give it you in this state. I'll go with you if you like, and you can call the police if you'd like that too. But you won't find her there.'

'I don't know why she said those things to you. It's all lies.' I advance, fists clenching, trembling. 'You don't know a thing about our life. You see only what she's said to you, but you have no idea what's underneath.' A semblance of concern for his safety flickers in his calm demeanour. 'Where is she?' I struggle to keep my voice steady. Behind his confident facade looms a smugness that I'm begging him for my wife's whereabouts — it makes my stomach churn.

'This isn't how you were supposed to find out,' he replies.

'No? How was I supposed to find out? Were the two of you going to come over together, hand in hand, to announce it? Did you honestly think I'd smile and wish you both well? You're sleeping with my wife . . . and I don't know how to let her go. Or that I want to.' The words tumble from me quietly, heavy with a realisation that you want to leave me. Had sex with him. Pretended to want a family with me. 'I'm not just going to let her go without a fight. I love her. Christ, I didn't even know there was a problem with us?' The weight of knowing what you've done with him saps my energy.

'Despite everything, you still have that brute side to you, don't you?' he shoots back, indifference running through his tone as he dismisses my pain. 'A fortunate upbringing and fine education — yet here you are, acting like a street thug. She wants a divorce, and you have to accept that. It doesn't need to get ugly.'

I can feel the warmth of anger rise up, but it's different this time. It burns. It hurts. 'She's my wife,' I whisper, the cry of that simple truth resonating more painfully than a scream inside me. 'Where is she?' The question escapes my lips way too quietly, shrouded beneath layers of confusion and sorrow. 'If she isn't with you, then where is she?'

He hesitates, and I sense his fear creeping in after what you seem to have told him about me; he's scared now. Scared what I might do to him. Some of that indifference receding. It's all become very real to him very suddenly. 'You need to understand — I know how this sounds, but we're meant for each other. This is deeper than love. We're soul mates.'

A hollow laugh slips from my lips, in disbelief at his patronising words. My hands reach for the front of his coat, pulling him closer to confront the shock unfolding behind his eyes when he is right up in front of my face. *I'm not a violent man, Cat, but you're really pushing my buttons with your lies.* 'How can you say that to me?' I hiss, the words cold like steel, slicing. *God, how can you have betrayed me so completely?* 'She hasn't contacted anyone — her brother, her friends, her boss. The police are looking for her,' I implore. 'You've been corresponding in secret. You must know where she is.'

'I haven't heard from her,' Jake insists. The honesty in his voice results in a trace of doubt in my mind that maybe he's telling the truth. 'I've called her, but it all goes to voicemail.'

'I don't believe you. Today I find out on some secret email correspondence that she's been having an affair with you. So, I'm concluding that you must be the only person who does know where she is.' I slacken my hold on him. 'Then do you have any idea where she might have gone?' I take a breath to bring me back down. 'Please. I have to know. I need to find her.'

'I swear, I don't know,' he says, his voice shaky now, a little empathy mingling with his own fear for a change. 'I didn't ask her where she was going. She just told me she was leaving work early for an appointment, and would be in touch the next day,' he adds softly, almost as if he is now realising something he could not afford to before — that she might have dumped him too. 'But she never did and I've not been able to get in touch with her since.'

'So, she was meeting up with you the following day?' The revelation feels like a shattering silence. *You and I were going to have a cosy night in, talk things through. We talked about it that morning. But you had no intention of doing that, did you? You were planning to meet him!*

'So she said. Only she never called.' Each word deepens my dread that something might actually have happened to you.

You went to great lengths to keep things hidden; didn't you realise how much this would hurt me? 'Do you have any idea where she might have gone?' I strengthen my hold again. 'Please, you have to help me find her.'

'She mentioned the appointment after work but said nothing else. I don't know the details, so I can't help you with that.' His eyes reflect a genuine fear of the situation. He's coming to the same possibility. 'There's something more.' He raises his eyes to mine. 'We're having a baby.' Desperation cracks Jake's voice, sending my world into a disorienting spin. I let go of him. 'We had phones for each other. You know . . .' He tails off unable to finish his sentence.

'No, I don't know.' I step away from him. The revelation steals my breath. Shock scrambles my mind to make sense of his words. 'You can't be serious. Cat wouldn't . . . Cat is pregnant?' I reiterate, closing my eyes hoping the truth will disappear.

Time seems to freeze as my heart shatters into a million sharp pieces. I turn away, the room spinning with unrecognisable emotions — hurt, betrayal, and loss mingling into one painful cocktail. *You said you didn't want to keep trying. You've been building a future with him?*

In that moment, I let the anger wash away like footprints on the beach. I walk towards the door, but stop, turning back as a different impulse takes over. The pitiful sight of him, the man whose life intertwines with my wife, draws me back. I punch him — not for the anger, but for the sadness that overwhelms me, leaving nothing but an aching void in my chest.

CHAPTER 13

Jill

Monday morning, I leave the B&B and head into town. The bus is the safest option, so I take it. I sit at the back, far from the driver's gaze. I don't know these streets, and the fewer eyes on me, the better. A wrong turn in a car could cost me too much. The bus is nearly empty. I turn to the window, watching the city pass by.

How many people are walking around, carrying secrets or running from something? Probably a lot. But right now, I'm the only one who matters. And I can feel their eyes on me, even when they aren't.

Amanda, the landlady, is the one who makes me uneasy. She's too observant, too chatty, like she's trying to see inside my head. I don't think I'm her first *runner*, but I can't be sure. She wants to help, I think, or maybe she just wants to pry. Either way, I can't afford to let anyone in. Not now. Not ever.

The motion of the bus helps, though. It lulls me into a fragile calm, a temporary truce between my body and the world. My head leans against the glass, my eyelids growing heavy, and for a moment, I forget myself.

I'm walking down a street, and I know you're close. I can feel you, like a shadow. I turn, and there you are, just behind me.

Your voice calls my name, soft and pleading, asking me to stop. It sounds like you care. It sounds like you want to make things right, like you love me. But I *know* better.

I start walking faster, but my legs are sluggish, as if they're made of stone. The harder I try to move, the heavier they become. You're still there, getting closer, and my pulse races. My feet drag, my heart thunders, but I can't run. I can't move. I turn, desperate for someone to help, but the world is blind to me. Everyone passes by, like I'm invisible.

'Darling, come home,' you say, your voice dripping with false warmth. 'I'm taking you home.'

I can feel the heat rising in my skin, my forehead beading with sweat. My body screams to move, but it's like I'm trapped in place, suffocating under my own skin. You're closer now, your smile a cruel echo of the one that once made me fall for you.

Inside my mind, I scream — *run, run, run* — but my body won't listen. I turn, and you're there, right behind me, your hands reaching out to me.

I can't breathe.

I feel your hands on me. I can feel your fingers tightening, the pressure building. I scream — but it's too late.

I jerk awake, my neck stiff from the sudden movement. My face is damp. I can feel the wetness on my cheeks, the phantom grip from your hands still tight in my mind. I glance around. The other passengers are oblivious, caught up in their own worlds. Did I scream? I must have. I swallow, massaging my neck, and stare out the window, my breath uneven.

The city moves on, the people walking by, lost in their own thoughts. But something catches my eye — a man, someone who looks just like you. He's walking down the pavement, his gaze drifting upward, and for a brief moment, my world goes still.

For a moment, I forget to breathe.

Then the truth hits me like a punch to the gut: I'm truly alone. I've known it all along, but it's different now. There's no one here who could stop you if you find me. No one who would help.

That's why you can't find me.

That's why I must be careful. Everything I do, everything I say, it all has to stay buried. That's why I've not communicated with anyone back home. I can't risk it.

I can't let anything slip to anyone. Not even a hint of who I am, or who I was. Not even for a second.

* * *

I get off the bus a stop early. I need space to breathe, time to settle my thoughts. The weather's decent — no rain, but you can feel it in the air, just waiting to break. Amanda has given me directions to a second-hand phone shop, and I've already made the call to check the prices. No surprises there — more than I expected, but that's fine. I need a decent phone. I'll grab a pay-as-you-go SIM while I'm at it.

The street she mentioned is quieter, just off the main road. People move about, busy about their business, but no one notices me. I'm dressed down — tracksuit bottoms, trainers, a bulky puffer coat against the cold wind slicing through the city. Amanda said it was colder than usual for October, and they were due some early snow according to the forecast. My baseball cap is low over my eyes, just a habit. It's probably overkill. Who's going to look twice at me in this crowd? But that itch of exposure is still there, the sense that something's watching, something's waiting. Paranoia? Maybe. But staying aware isn't stupid. I remember what Simone told me and how I need to keep moving and disguise myself.

I find the shop at the end of the street, tucked between a coffee shop and a second-hand bookshop. It looks better than I expected. I push the door open, the bell above it jingling as I step inside. It's quiet — I'm the only one. The guy behind the counter is working on a radio, its guts spread out in front of him.

The shop's a mix of new and old electronics, cluttered but organised. My eyes are drawn to a vintage Swan Teasmade in the corner — just like the one my mum used to have. The one with the clock. That familiar ache hits my chest, sharp and sudden. I shake it off, focusing. I'm not here for nostalgia.

'Morning. Nice day, no rain for a change.' The guy's voice is soft, his Scottish accent warmer than I expected. He looks me up and down, then I catch myself going down memory lane and snap back to the present. My cap's still low. I pull it off.

He's got that clean-cut look, the kind you don't notice at first. Blue eyes, black hair short around the sides, a little longer on top. He's my height, maybe a little taller, and focused on the tiny parts of the radio, delicate fingers working without a hitch.

'Is there much of a market for radios these days? I thought everyone listens to stuff on their phones or laptops,' I ask, trying to keep the conversation light.

'More than you'd think,' he replies without glancing up. His glasses are thick, round — like the kind a jeweller wears when working on small objects. 'A lot of elderly people still like 'em. And retro ones? They're getting popular again. People are getting sick of their phones, they need a break.'

'I can imagine,' I mutter, not in the mood for a radio chat, but I get it. Phones are exhausting. 'Look, I was told you had second-hand iPhones?'

He glances up this time, eyes assessing. 'Aye, I've a few. What model are you after?'

I'm not picky. 'Not sure. What do you have?' I shrug slightly. 'As long as I can get internet and maps, I'm not fussy. You gave me a price when I called.'

He nods towards a locked glass cabinet at the back, hidden behind a stack of old Teasmades. 'Over there. They're locked up.

Had a break-in last month — lost a lot of stock. I don't adver-
tise them much anymore. Price I gave you is for the oldest ones.
Thought you might not want to spend more.'

I feel a flicker of sympathy. 'Got it. Are they priced?'

'Aye, underneath each one is a sticker. I can't promise much on
the batteries, but I charged them up myself. They seem to hold
okay. I don't refurbish 'em — just wipe them, sell as-is.' He raises
an eyebrow. 'You got a charger for your old one?'

'No,' I mutter, thinking of what I left behind. 'I lost everything.'
My throat tightens at the thought. I turn towards the cabinet,
making it clear I'm done talking for now.

He follows me, unlocking the glass. 'I've got chargers too, if
you need one.' He makes his way back behind the counter.

'Perfect, thanks.' I scan the phones, trying to gauge the price in
my head. The charger's extra. I hadn't accounted for that. Surely,
he won't overcharge me. I glance at him quickly. 'You trust me
not to rob you?'

He doesn't look up from his work. 'I reckon I could rug-
by-tackle you before you got out the door.'

I snort, a little amused despite myself. 'That's presumptuous. I
might be a kickboxing champion for all you know.'

'I'll take my chances,' he says, not missing a beat.

I flush a little, irritated but impressed by his quick response.
I pick a phone and walk back to the counter, handing him the
cash. I've pulled out more than I thought I'd need, stashing extra
in my pocket just in case the price was higher than expected. As
I pay, I feel eyes on me. I glance up. A man is peering in through
the window, cupping his hands to block the glare. I relax when
he walks off, but the tension's still there, crawling up my spine.

'Are you new in the area?' the guy behind the counter asks,
handing me my change. His tone is casual, but there's something
about its familiarity I don't like.

'Why do you ask?' I look down at my clothes, then back at him, my instincts kicking in to be wary of giving anything away. I don't like the way his gaze lingers — calm, but taking everything about me in.

He doesn't react. 'You look like you're new to Edinburgh.'

I can feel my muscles tense. 'And how do you figure that?' My voice comes out a little sharper than I intend. I snatch the phone and charger from the counter, my guard up now. I want to leave.

He snatches it back and plugs it into a charger on the back wall behind him.

'Hey, what you doing?'

He keeps his eyes on me, unfazed. 'Relax, it needs a bit of a charge. You've got that look you know.' I look at him questioningly. 'New to town, I mean. It's not hard to spot. And yeah, it is necessary, especially if you plan to use it when you leave. You don't want it going flat on you, do you?'

I feel a surge of irritation, but he might be right. 'And how is that any of your business?' I snap.

'I'm just being nice.' He shrugs, turning the phone over in his hands, wiping it down with a disinfectant cloth as it continues to charge. 'Don't need to get snappy. You're new, I'm just asking.'

I can feel my pulse quicken. My patience worn thin. My need to get out of here desperate. 'Yeah, I'm here looking for work. Do you ask everyone you think is new the same question?'

He shrugs again. 'No. Just you.'

'Why just me?' I raise an eyebrow, challengingly.

'I don't know,' he says, crossing his arms. 'Just did.'

I want to take the phone and leave. I can't help myself and I know he's right about charging it. 'So you're just nosey, then?'

He grins, the edges of his smile a little too sharp. 'Nosey, polite . . . same thing, right?'

I bristle. 'Well, I didn't mean—'

'Aye, you did,' he interrupts, his grin widening. 'Grumpy, but I get it.'

I feel my face flush with irritation, but I don't argue. I glance at the phone, weighing up whether to take it now or risk it running out of charge. He's waiting for me to respond, his stance relaxed but expectant. I know he's just being friendly, and I'm scared of anyone including my own shadow. He sees me looking at the phone.

'If you want to take it and leave, go ahead,' he says, his tone colder now, irritated by my lack of gratitude. 'But first, if you think I was rude, explain it to me. I thought I was being kind, just looking out for you 'cause you're new in town.'

I inhale, the weight of my frustration melting slightly. He's right — I was curt. But damn, I'm tired of people acting like I need protecting.

'I can handle myself,' I say, more harshly than I mean. 'It's not my first time navigating a city alone.' I can hear the edge to my voice, but I can't back down now. 'My phone was stolen, and it's thrown me off balance. So yeah, maybe I'm a little on edge.'

His expression softens, just a little. 'Aye, well, I can see that. It's a nightmare, right?' I move to the window and look out, waiting for a little while to let the phone grab some charge. Fifteen minutes later, he hands me the phone, and I take it with a nod, a flicker of embarrassment passing through me. The battery's at fifty per cent; it had twenty-five. It'll do.

'Thanks,' I mutter, feeling the weight of the awkwardness between us. I've had enough of small talk for today.

I turn and head out, the door closing behind me with a soft jingle. My steps are steady, but my mind's already running through the next move. I can't afford to trust anyone.

CHAPTER 14

Royce

The police station stretches across four floors; my office is perched on the top. I make my way down to the ground floor, where the interrogation room waits, along with the husband and brother of our missing person. My goal is to get them talking freely, so initially, I consider it's best to keep them together — neither can spin a story without the other checking him. But then I rethink it, deciding it's smarter to bring them upstairs to my office instead. As I head up, I reach into my jacket for a toothpick, a habit I picked up after quitting smoking.

I leave them to stew for a bit while I head down to the IT forensics team buried in the basement — a space thick with stale air and the drone of computers, where fluorescent lights and powerful air conditioning give it a stark, claustrophobic feel. Helen, who heads the unit with two trainees under her watch, is like a guard dog, quick to snap if anyone messes with her equipment. I push open the door.

'Hey, Inspector, word is you're on some hush-hush missing persons case, huh,' she says. Helen's always intense, with large, alert eyes that pop against her pulled-back dark hair, skin taut at the temples. She's a mix of quirks; I've never seen her in anything but long skirts, clunky boots, and a wool jumper to shield herself from the cold air. Her speech is a wild blend of British, American, and retro slang that catches you off guard. She's one-of-a-kind, though I wonder if all those hours down there are doing her any good.

'So much for hush-hush,' I reply dryly, annoyed how that information has got downstairs.

'Who's not turned up, then? Anyone fab or a bit dodgy? Go on, give us the goss — you know we're all confidential down here.'

'No, not famous. Just tied to old money — a powerful family, you know how it is.'

'Ah, the ruling classes, huh? What's this — *Men in Black* meets *Dynasty*?' She laughs, and I'd laugh too if it weren't so close to the truth. 'What d'you need, then? Want me to check something out . . . you know, off the books, so to speak?' She taps the side of her nose.

'No, keep it legal, Helen.' I keep it vague to stop her from digging. I check my phone; I'll need to wrap this up fast before the husband and brother start tearing into each other. I hear her typing, followed by the faint whir of a printer. There's a bank of computer monitors surrounding her. And it's freezing in here. I want to get out as quickly as possible. This place makes me feel claustrophobic with its low ceiling and lack of windows. 'Can you pull the CCTV from the local train and bus stations? She left her passport, so no airport. And get it sent up to me.'

'Reckon she's done a runner on him, then? DC Glennon already asked me for this,' she says. 'You want it, Inspector? Not Paul?'

'Yes, I want to go through it. Why's it taking so long? Can you get on it for me please? Also, check for Smyth's car in the vicinity of the house and the surrounding areas. I want to see if he came back at any time before he actually arrived at the house when he said he did at 8.00 p.m. on October tenth.'

'You don't believe him, do you? You think he's having you on?' She gasps, her eyes wide. 'Christ! You reckon he killed her and got rid of the body?'

'Please, Helen, just do what I ask and no speculating. And keep it legal.'

'Oh, blimey. You do, don't you? You think he killed her.'

'Helen — shut up. That CCTV information isn't to go anywhere other than to me. Got that?'

'I get it. But I have to wait for them to hand it over. I'll give them a shove. If I wait for a warrant, it will take longer.'

'Just get it asap and send it to me.'

* * *

I usher them into my office, gesturing to the two chairs across from my desk before settling into my own seat. As they sit, I chew on a toothpick and watch the tension settle on their faces.

'All right,' I begin. 'Here's what we know so far: Cat left the house at 8.15 a.m. on the tenth of October. That's her usual time, correct, William?'

'Yes,' William replies icily, his tone cautious.

'We have her on CCTV leaving the house and heading towards the green. But she doesn't appear on any footage after that — no record of her coming out the other side. Some footage comes from nearby street cameras, and some from Ring doorbells. We're having it rechecked for details and are covering possible blind spots with cameras further down. The camera near the green wasn't working and the cameras that did pick her up only had a partial view of her.' I see them questioning this. 'We can't see if anyone is with her, I mean.'

'Oh my God! Was she snatched?' Jason blurts out.

William's face tightens. 'Nothing else? You mean she's not on any other cameras?' He glances at me, voice strained. 'She can't have just disappeared. How is that possible?'

'Is that what you're saying? That she was snatched?' says Jason.

'She wasn't snatched, Jason — we'd have heard,' says William.

'We have no evidence of that,' I reply. 'There's a blind spot on your street corner, Mr Johnson-Smyth. She could have slipped into any of the small side roads leading off there, which makes tracking her tougher. That's why we're reviewing every camera in the area.'

'What does that mean?' William asks, the worry evident. 'Is it good that she's not been found?'

'What?' Jason snaps. 'Good? How the hell could it be good that she's vanished? It means one thing — someone took her.'

'Let's not jump to conclusions,' I interject. I don't make any positive or negative suggestions. 'At this point, we have no proof of foul play. We've checked the hospitals in case of an accident and come up with nothing. We're also still checking trains, underground and buses. You mentioned Cat's passport was still at home, so at least we know she's still in the country.'

'And what about this appointment?' William asks. 'She mentioned it to her boss — said she'd be leaving early for it. Didn't specify what it was or where.'

I get a sense there's something else he's withholding from me.

Jason stiffens. 'What appointment? Nobody told me of any appointment.'

William clarifies, 'She told her boss she had somewhere to be that day but didn't give details. She didn't mention it to me either. Neither did Rita mention it when I rang her in the first instance.'

Jason scoffs. 'I suppose *that* wasn't in your "precious" diary, then. Why didn't Rita mention it? Does she know something? I wonder why she didn't want you to know?'

William clenches his jaw. 'No, it wasn't. Cat must have just forgotten to write it down. And I don't know why Rita didn't mention it. You are going to ask her, right, Inspector? I mean that's wrong that she didn't say.'

'Forgot? Or didn't tell you?' Jason sneers. 'That must sting.'

'And you. Clearly, she didn't tell you either,' William retorts trying to contain his temper. He rubs his thumb over his forefinger — a nervous twitch that's either new or one I hadn't noticed before. I drum my pen on the desk, mirroring his tension.

'Something isn't right,' Jason mutters, shaking his head. 'Cat wouldn't just vanish. She knows I worry. And she'd have told me about an appointment.'

The idea flits past like a shadow at the things people are capable of when you least expect it.

'Why are you so worried, Jason?' I ask, watching his expression.

'Don't make it sound creepy,' he says sharply, addressing me. 'We're close. Have been, especially since she married . . . him.' He casts a resentful look at William.

'She's married; an adult,' I continue. 'She doesn't need to check in with her brother every time she goes somewhere. Maybe she's gone to stay with friends. Some neither of you know about.' I want to know what he means by *something isn't right*. That can have so many connotations.

William sighs, visibly weary of the accusations, but refrains from responding. I guess he knows it's not going to get him anywhere. Jason clearly hates his brother-in-law.

I lean in. 'Jason, you keep implying something about your brother-in-law. Do you have any proof he hurt Cat?'

Jason squirms. 'Not exactly . . . but I've seen bruises on her wrists now and then.'

'What sort of bruises? Did she say her husband caused them?'

'Yes. And I've seen the way he is with her — controlling, always hovering. She said he's hurt her but never gone into details.'

William shifts uncomfortably, crossing his arms. 'Inspector, this is nonsense. Unless he has proof, it's just hearsay.' William turns to Jason. 'You can't go on repeating accusations like that. I can sue you for slander, you know. Want me to?'

'Get stuffed. You won't. You know you're guilty.'

'You understand, Jason, we can't act without evidence. My team is talking to Cat's friends again to see if anyone else has seen anything concerning. If they back you up, we'll pursue it. But up till now there's no one who backs what you say.'

'And in the meantime, he gets to go free and live his life while my sister is dead somewhere. He's done something to her. You have to believe me.'

William leans forward, jaw tight. 'I don't hurt my wife, Inspector.' He turns to Jason. 'And stop saying she's dead,' he spits back.

I give William a long, hard look. 'Good. Then you have nothing to worry about, do you, Mr Johnson-Smyth? Jason, we only have your word that you think William has hurt his wife. There's nothing to prove that he has. We are looking into everything and if something has happened to Cat, we will get to the bottom of it.' This brother-sister relationship is not natural to my mind. I can't help but think there's more going on here than his brotherly love for Cat. I hope I'm wrong. I don't like where my mind's going.

Jason, visibly agitated, snaps back at William, ignoring what I said. 'And yet you weren't worried when she disappeared. You told me you'd check her route to work, see if she'd had an accident on that damn bike. Did you go out looking? No. Sat on your rich arse instead. Why? Because you know where she is. And you don't give a shit, do you?'

'You ignorant moron.' William finally erupts, getting to his feet.

'See?' Jason tenses, as if expecting a blow. 'This is what Cat was scared of. Always on edge, not knowing how he'd react to things. That's controlling behaviour.'

I turn to William. I haven't seen any signs of controlling behaviour from the husband, but the brother is oozing it. 'Did you try to find your wife after she didn't come home?'

He shifts uncomfortably. 'No, but I didn't think something terrible had happened. I thought maybe her phone died, or she'd forgotten to call. Who knows numbers by heart anymore? I assumed she'd show up. And besides, like I said, she's vanished before.'

Jason sneers, sniffing back tears. 'But you're not like that, William. You wouldn't just sit and wait.'

'You don't know what the hell you're talking about.' Wiliam buttons his coat that he'd never bothered to remove.

I can tell this won't get us any further right now. There's a missing woman — whether she's gone voluntarily or something more sinister is at play, we have yet to determine. The bickering doesn't help, though Jason's comments might make William crack if he is hiding something. 'We've issued her description, and every officer is watching for her. We're reviewing CCTV and checking rentals and banking activity. She'll have to use her cards eventually, and that'll give us a lead.'

Jason wipes his nose on his sleeve. 'If she's alive. If it's not too late.'

William cuts in. 'Inspector, isn't there a "golden hour" for finding missing persons?' He turns up the collar of his coat.

'There is, but we've missed it. That first hour's critical. We use it to capture evidence before it's lost or forgotten, to interview witnesses before they're out of reach. Your call came late, so we're a step behind. We've searched your house, Mr Johnson-Smyth. We found her phone, purse and passport left behind. No clothes are missing, as far as we can tell.'

'Exactly!' Jason stands, pointing at William. 'She wouldn't go anywhere without clothes or her phone. You know what that says.'

'We have her laptop now,' I say, noting the oddity that the husband brought it in today, claiming he'd *just come across it* after our initial search missed it. 'We'll see if there's anything on it. Up to now we've found nothing on her phone. We're going through deleted messages and photos presently but it's not looking hopeful.

'What if she's deleted everything?' William asks, hands twitching at his sides.

'Nothing's ever fully deleted, Mr Johnson-Smyth. Didn't you check her emails before bringing it in?'

His shoulders tense. 'No, of course not. I didn't touch it. I knew you'd want to see it first.'

'Really? I'd think that'd be the first thing you'd do if you were worried about her.'

William's face darkens. Jason opens his mouth to respond, but stops, shooting William a dark look instead.

'All right, Jason, calm down. This isn't helping.' I glance between the two of them. 'Go home, get some rest, and see if anything more comes to mind. We'll keep looking and contact you with any updates. And if you hear or learn anything, let us know.'

William makes a move for the door, then hesitates and turns to face me. 'Do I need a lawyer?'

I study his face. 'I don't know. Why would you think that?'

Jason sneers. 'Because he's guilty, that's why. Better get the best, dear brother-in-law. You're going to need it. And just for the record — what you said about Cat supposedly disappearing those other times? I still say they never happened.'

CHAPTER 15

Jill

The bench is cold beneath me, slick from the recent rain, but it's the safest place I know right now. I glance up at the heavy clouds. The forecast hints at snow — but I have a feeling rain is on the way. The park is nearly empty under heavy dark clouds. A fine drizzle begins, soaking me quickly. I realise I have no umbrella. I should have asked for one at reception when I left this morning. I tell myself I seek solitude and that's why I'm here, but deep down, I know — it's the need to escape watchful eyes and whispering voices saying . . . *you're coming.*

I pull my new phone from my jacket inner pocket. It's 2 p.m. It was too expensive, but worth it — at least I hope so. The pay-as-you-go SIM is supposed to protect my anonymity, if I don't contact you that is, and I don't intend doing that, shielding me from unwanted tracking — except I know that may be as elusive as sunshine on a day like today. You have all these people who can help you track me and that's what frightens me. Have you called in those favours yet?

I begin the setup, humming a tune I'd long forgotten. Once the setup screen fades, I breathe a sigh of relief and open the radio app I just downloaded. Music replaces my own hum as it sounds through my earbuds. I can only hope it manages to dampen the familiar prickling of anxiety in my mind and stomach that never leaves me. I picked up a pair of earbuds at the phone shop after buying my phone. They're an unknown brand — I couldn't afford better. Just a cheap Chinese knockoff.

I can't relax. I'm always on edge that you've caught up with me. It's exhausting. I haven't had a decent full night's sleep since I left. Not that I had many when I was living with you. I thought that part would change. I pull at a loose bit of skin around my nail with my teeth until it bleeds and hurts.

A few people pass by hurriedly to get out of the rain — a stream of life and laughter, as the fine, heavy drizzle overhead descends in force. I'm quickly soaked. My gaze drifts to a girl, nestled amid the damp grass and the tall trees leading to a path, her back to me, her handbag lying carelessly beside her, her phone casually on top. I think how uncomfortable she must feel sitting on damp grass. She draws her knees close, huddling into her puffer coat. A tight knot forms in my stomach; she looks vulnerable, lost in her own world. The sight of her unguarded like that makes my skin prickle. She has no idea how exposed she is. The weather doesn't seem to bother her either.

Just beyond her, a path meanders through thick bushes, a shortcut maybe back into town. I watch, fidgeting with my phone, unsure what to do. She's a lone figure waiting for a storm I fear is about to break when, suddenly, my attention snaps to a group of young men in hoodies, hoods drawn over their faces, emerging from the trail. They cut across the clearing towards her — a gang of five, their laughter clear in their faces and behaviour swelling as they approach, notice her, like vultures sensing their meal. Shoving each other and hooting. I hate that piece of clothing. Hate how it can make anyone look instantly threatening. My heart races, after my own experience yesterday. Glancing around,

I'm alone. I wipe the rain from my face with a scrunched-up tissue I find in my pocket. I'm cold and want to leave but feel I can't. I can't leave her out there alone. The cold is starting to penetrate my clothes and chill me inside.

They're not teenagers — older, early twenties maybe, with that cocky stride I recognise too well having witnessed it many times in London on the underground. I squint, lifting my phone's camera, zooming in. The girl doesn't flinch as they approach; she's got her earbuds in, I suspect. She doesn't see the threat, doesn't feel their eyes on her. And they're closing in.

What is wrong with you? I mutter under my breath, watching her remain blissfully unaware of the encroaching danger. *What is wrong with you? How can you not even sense they are there. In front of you. How the hell can you be so oblivious?* I pull my earbuds out and look around, dismayed to see how alone we are. Perhaps she's upset, broken up with a boyfriend/girlfriend. Had some bad news or lost her job. A myriad of situations could be the reason why she looks from the back like a lost and forlorn creature. Regardless of any of that, she is totally unaware of her surroundings. It makes me twitchy.

My fingers shake as I bring the camera up again, focusing on her expensive handbag lying on the wet grass. That annoys me. This feels like a ticking time bomb, her distraction a siren call for those who've already decided her fate.

Look up! I scream silently, resentment boiling inside me for her naivety and how I'm being dragged into this. This is not my problem. She should know better — keep one ear free, stay vigilant; that's what they tell you. My own self-defence training echoes in my mind: never let yourself be closed off to the world with both earbuds in. *Come on, look up!*

As the first man makes his move, moving in behind her, crouching, his fingers inching towards her bag, I can't look away. Her stillness, her vulnerability, churns something raw and furious in me. It makes my blood run cold. I slide to the edge of the bench ready to do something. The rain isn't just falling; it's like a shroud enveloping us. The park is now a ghost town. I'm rooted to my spot on the edge of the bench, unable to even call for help. What do I do? There's nobody here. I can't get involved. So what, she isn't my problem. Leave her to her fate? My conscience screams otherwise. She's practically handed herself over to them. I want to scream, to force her into awareness. I want to warn her — but I can't. I don't risk myself for strangers.

I put my phone in my inside pocket. Loop my handbag over my head so it's across my body. I can't let them hurt her. I stop.

I think back to the morons I came across surrounding my car. Their cocky attitude and intimidating behaviour still rattles me when I remember.

She's still unaware. She must have her eyes closed for there to be no reaction.

He moves in, slowly, like a cat with prey in its sights. I scramble for my phone once again. Watching through my camera I see them look at each other mischievously. Can't believe their luck, I bet. I don't like what's going through my mind. Not one bit. I have a terrible feeling something bad is going to happen and I'm the only one here who can help. *Shit. Shit. Shit.*

My hand pulls the tip of my baseball cap lower down. I edge further to the end of the bench, one foot in front of the other, ready to run towards them screaming if they do anything more than steal her stuff. I look up and ask the universe to help me out here, help her, because I do not need this in my life right now.

The man behind her grabs the phone and bag. I grip my knees with my hand; my leg is going like a piston ready to storm over there and kick his arse. *Fuck me, you dozy cow, open your eyes!* I did a course in self-defence a little while ago, because you wanted me to be safe. That was ironic, considering. You didn't like me walking about London when it was dark in the winter. I thought the course was a good idea. I'm grateful now that I did it. I feel a little safer knowing I can protect myself if I need to. Not that I've had any opportunity to use any of it. I tried it once on you, remember? The heavy bruising on my wrists stopped me doing it again. I get up then sit down. As much as I want to, I can't get myself to actually do anything about what is happening here, right now.

In a shocking moment, she looks up. I see the look on her face through my camera magnified to catch her expression as her world tilts on its axis as she clocks the danger surrounding her. She springs up, shouting for them to leave her alone. Her voice pierces the air like a siren — loud and desperate. I look around. We're alone. Not good. 'Give it back! Get away from me!' They surround her in a circle. But only laugh, a horrible cacophony that sends frozen dread coursing through my veins. The leader pulls out a knife, and I feel my body sway as if in slow motion. I drop the phone away from my face and look, feeling terrified. What the hell can I do now? Call the police? I should. I can't. I squeeze my eyes shut. Hell. I can't call the police. She stands her ground, fear morphing into fierce defiance. But the man lunges forward, catching her off guard, striking her shoulder with a brutal punch. She falls backwards. I drop back on the bench. No, no, no, no, this cannot be happening.

In that heartbeat, horror crystallises into sharp clarity. I can't just sit here, frozen in fear, while this unfolds before me. Not when I know how quickly a situation can escalate. She's not helping by standing up to them. *They want the bag and the phone. Let them have it. He has a knife, that trumps everything.*

Just as suddenly, the knife is at her neck. My heart races as chills cascade down my spine. She trembles violently beneath him.

Then, he and his gang scatter taking the handbag with them, abandoning her without a second thought. Rain pours anew, sending rivulets of anxiety coursing through me. I can't breathe as she scrambles onto her knees, screaming for help, her eyes darting around frantically.

'HELP! SOMEBODY, HELP, PLEASE!'

For a moment, her eyes lock with mine — an electric connection. I brace myself for her gaze to break through the invisible wall I thought I had built — but I don't move. A pack of students dash to her side, naming her like a lost treasure, their voices blending in a chaotic rush of concern and fear. I look around surprised, wondering where they've come from, where they've been sheltering.

I slip away, guilt clawing at my chest as I navigate towards the exit, feeling her eyes on me. I keep my gaze fixed ahead. I shudder at the weight of each pair of eyes that flit in my direction, anxious with questions about what I've witnessed. I mustn't get caught up in this. My only choice is to walk away. In that moment, the fear grips me tighter.

I can't help her. I won't.

CHAPTER 16

Royce

Later that day, I climb the steps of the stoop and ring the doorbell of the Johnson-Smyth residence. It's a very impressive Georgian stucco building. I read the latest email from Helen on my phone. I look up at the house's long windows, covered in fine voile to stop people seeing in. I can't imagine what these properties around here must cost. I look down the street and see Jason's van parked up. I rang ahead and asked him to meet me here after Helen got in touch. Another less formal meeting made to make them less anxious therefore less on guard. Smyth wasn't impressed having only been at the station a few hours earlier.

I imagine them bickering in the kitchen. A detective coming back to your home is always a worry. I'm sure they're both worried, whether I'm here with bad news that we've found Mrs Johnson-Smyth, or we found something on one of them. I picture the husband worrying whether we've discovered the wife's naughty little secret. And if the brother knows about it. That's going to be interesting; he thinks he's got his sister's ear, but I have my doubts about this one.

The husband opens the door just as I pocket my phone. A forced smile pinned to his lips. Unsure. Suspicious. He tries to read my expression as he ushers me in. He takes me to the lounge. I sink into one of the most comfortable sofas I've ever sat on. I take my time. Make him sweat. Stretch out my legs like I'm here for the afternoon. Jason is on the other side of the room, sat on another sofa facing me. His expression bland, the colour gone from his face. I watch them both. The room is cosy, 'double drenched' in shades of deep Atlantic Ocean blue. I got the term from Camilla who's decorating her house; it's effective and I could stay here all afternoon with a nice beer and the sport on the telly. The term means everything is painted in one colour or complementary colours and hues. The walls, skirtings, cornices, ceilings, even the window frames.

'Do I need to call my lawyer, Inspector?' William says looking me directly in the eye. I wonder why he thinks that right at this point and why he hasn't done so already.

I smile, pleased that I've managed to rile him a little more. Jason, I notice, bites his fingernails. 'If you feel you need one, be my guest. But you asked me this question earlier. I'd have thought you'd have been in touch with your legal team by now.'

'I'm asking you in case you're here to arrest me.'

'No, I'm not.' Interesting choice of words though.

'Then why are you here? Calling us in to your office earlier and now again, here at my home. Are you toying with us? Playing your silly police games?'

'I can see you're impatient to hear what I have to say.' I don't let him get under my skin. His type is all the same. Unfortunately, I've come across them way too often.

Jason can't control himself and shifts to the edge of the sofa. 'Have you found her? Is that it? Is she dead? Oh God, she is, isn't she? I can feel it deep in my bones.'

'No, Jason, I haven't come to tell you that. We still don't know whether your sister is alive or not. She's vanished right now, and we have no leads. We're doing our best to try and find her or establish what's happened to her.'

'Is that it? Is that what you've come to tell us? That you can't find her? What sort of crap police are you? Couldn't you have said it over the phone instead of all this goddamn drama?' William's nerves are making him antsy.

'William, would you mind answering another question for me?' I stay seated. He gets up and hovers, thinking what is the best thing to do, then sits back down.

'Sure, I've nothing to hide.' That's not what his body language is telling me.

'Yeah, right,' grumbles Jason sarcastically and lets out a snort. He continues chewing on his finger.

'You said you left work at the usual time the day your wife went missing, which was 5.30 p.m., and came straight home, but the CCTV at the end of your street says you arrived at the house at 8.00 p.m. Does it take you two and a half hours to come from your office in Allen Street to your home in Upper Addison Gardens? By my reckoning that's a nine-minute drive, give or take half an hour for traffic. Half an hour to three quarters if you walked. And you did drive home that day, didn't you?'

'I did. Yes. You know I did. I already told you that.' William's voice is solemn.

'Why did it take you two and a half hours then?'

'Did you meet Cat somewhere? Did you find out where she was going on that appointment and lost it with her for not telling you?' accuses Jason, looking at him without blinking. Hands turned into fists at his sides.

'Well, let me see,' William says ignoring Jason and clearly struggling to recall the events. 'I did drive as you know, and I stopped at the off-licence on the way. There's a good one halfway home on Turner Green. I found somewhere to park. I bought the wine and went next door into The Hammer and Chisel for a drink while the traffic died down. There was a lot of traffic, Inspector.'

'And you didn't think to mention this when we first questioned you at home or even earlier today?'

'No, I didn't,' he says gravely, his gaze drifting to the floor, as if searching for answers. The weight of his words hang heavily in the air. 'You didn't ask me specifically. You asked if I came straight home, and I did . . .' He exhales, his voice trailing off before continuing quietly, 'Via the pub. But I was only there a short while.'

His brow furrows, as if wrestling with his thoughts. 'What difference does it make?' His tone is laced with defeat, as if he is presenting evidence of a crime he didn't even commit. He takes a moment, collecting his thoughts, though they seem scattered and reluctant to return. 'I forgot, if I'm truly honest,' he says at last. 'I was stressed, worrying about my wife, Inspector.' He speaks each word slow and deliberate.

'Is it worth driving that short journey? Stressful, I imagine. Why would you drive in this city if you didn't have to? I'd walk everywhere if I could. Nothing like gridlock to raise your stress levels.'

'I drive because sometimes I have to go and see clients. Is that acceptable to you?' He folds his hands on his lap and does that thing with his fingers. 'I like to drive, Inspector. London isn't safe especially at night. I don't like not to drive.'

As far as suspects go, William is ticking all the boxes as a prime one, but we don't have enough, if anything, yet to bring him in. I write down the name of the pub and the off-licence. 'What did you buy from the off-licence?'

He sighs like he's weary of tedious questions and I'm an annoying fly buzzing around his head. 'I told you a bottle of wine. Barolo. It's our favourite.'

'Your favourite. Was there a special reason why you bought that wine that night?' Damn, I love a good Barolo. The pricier the better and I'm guessing his was top shelf.

'Inspector, do I really have to go into all the reasons why I bought a bottle of wine?' I mentally wonder if he drank it or it's still kicking around the kitchen some place and I can take it with me — as evidence, of course.

'Yes, actually, you do. Unless there's a reason why you wouldn't want to share that information with us. Is there, William, a reason?'

'We had a tiff the night before and I wanted us to sit down and talk.'

'What sort of tiff?' My antennae prickle to attention. 'Is this the tiff about the IVF you mentioned?'

He sighs heavily collecting his thoughts. 'Yes, I told you already. She wanted to stop the IVF, and I didn't, and we had an argument. I've told you this.'

'Why didn't you tell me that you stopped on the way home?'

'I thought I did.' His hand trembles slightly, the movement of his fingers rubbing together intensifying. 'She told me she really wanted to have a baby, and then . . . suddenly she didn't.' He pauses, a hint of regret softening his voice. 'And — well, yeah, I got angry, kind of, but you know this — this is why we were going to have a night in the next day and talk it through. I've already told you this.' His eyes drop, the weight of unspoken words heavy in the air. 'She wanted to talk. So I thought a bottle of our favourite wine would set the right tone.'

'Did you hurt her, is that what happened?' Jason accuses. He is suddenly on his feet. 'And went too far and had to get rid of her?' His hands clench and unclench as his words spit from his mouth like bullets.

William narrows his eyes. 'Don't be so ridiculous.'

I can see he wants to say more but holds his tongue. Keeps composed.

'Do you think your wife left of her own accord, William?' I see him flinch like the words are darts hitting his flesh. He turns away to look out of the window. 'It's not out of the realms of possibility that she might have felt under pressure from the IVF and needed to get away. So, she leaves her phone, laptop, everything personal to her that might track her and just goes.' I leave a beat, watching him carefully as he snaps his head back to me, shocked. 'Is it possible your wife has another phone that she recently bought?' I suggest, wondering if he will be honest.

William squirms. I've clearly touched on a sore point. 'I wouldn't know. Why are you asking?' There's a tremor in his voice. Is he wanting to see how much I know in case he drops himself in it? I spin it out. Let the quiet fill the space. Let him sweat a little. He looks genuinely upset, like talking about it hurts too much. I can't make out if it's for real or an act.

'Another phone?' splutters Jason, coming back to life, stepping forward within an inch of William, bearing down on him, angry he might know something he doesn't. 'For what?' He turns to me accusingly for the inference on his sister. 'No. Cat does not have another phone. I would know if she did, Inspector,' he says, winding himself up till he's nearly fit to burst.

William says nothing though. He just watches my face trying to read what I'm going to say next and whether he should come clean or keep his trap shut. I know he's hiding something. His poker face gives nothing away, but I've seen hundreds of blokes like him, cool on the outside, but inside the mind is churning like a goddamn tornado.

Jason whips around to face his brother-in-law, sensing he's out of the loop. His anger all over his crimson face. 'Did she have one?' he demands of William.

There's another beat of silence in the room. A slight sheen covers William's top lip. Waiting for the big reveal I know is coming. I can hear all of us breathing in the deafening silence. Jason, quickly. William, agitatedly but trying to show calmness, and me, steadily. There's one thing people who lie tend to do and that is try very hard to look as calm as possible. They think that is the key to getting someone to believe them. They're wrong.

'Yes, it would appear so,' William finally says defeatedly. The words crash into Jason the same as if William had punched him in the solar plexus.

'You're lying,' accuses Jason, expelling a lungful of air. He starts to hyperventilate a little.

William turns slowly to his brother-in-law, a bitter smile tugging at his lips. 'Sadly, I'm not,' he says, the sarcasm thinly veiling the hurt beneath. He takes a moment, letting the weight of his words sink in as he studies Jason's face. 'It seems your perfect sister has been having an affair,' he continues, his tone laced with pain. 'Using her identical phone to text her lover — right under my nose.'

Jason slumps back in his chair, stunned. William tilts his head, a sad, mocking edge creeping into his voice. 'So, what do you have to say to that? Looks like she didn't tell you everything after all, did she?' His words are sharp, the mix of betrayal and sarcasm unmistakable.

'I don't believe it,' Jason grumbles through gritted teeth. 'You're trying to soil her name. Cat would never — no, she'd have told me.'

'Yes, smart, she bought the exact phone to her everyday one so I wouldn't notice her texting him. If it weren't true, then I would have seen the messages on her everyday phone, wouldn't I? So, what do you make of her now? Honest? Trustworthy?' He turns to me next. 'I'm not going to insult your intelligence, Inspector. I'm guessing you already know who she's been shagging because from the all-knowing look on your face I take it you already know his identity. It was him who told me of the phone.'

'We do, yes—'

'Wait, how long has she been seeing him? I mean, how long has this been happening?' Jason asks, his voice trembling with disbelief.

'About six months, right around the time she chose to turn her back on our dreams of having a baby together. Then she goes and sleeps with another guy. Truly a wonderful woman your sister, don't you think?'

'Who is he?' asks Jason pathetically.

'Jake Stroud, physiotherapist. He's based in Chelsea,' I tell him. I watch them both without a shadow of discretion. I feel for Jason; he looks genuinely hurt by his sister's actions while William shoots me a glare.

'So, what now?' William says, his voice raw and hollow. 'I guess this just makes me even more guilty — that I might have hurt my own wife, right?' His words slice the air, a confession and accusation all at once.

Jason leans back in his chair, his expression frozen like he's just been shot with a tranquilliser dart. Whatever last thread of hope he had about his sister seems to be fraying, unravelling right before him.

'But I thought Jake was a friend not her lover,' says Jason.

I listen and watch Jason's reaction to this new discovery. A secret she hadn't shared with him.

'You knew about him?' demands William.

'She mentioned him in passing, that's all.'

'It seems, brother-in-law,' William says, with a slow, bitter smile he can't quite suppress, 'that my wife played us both.' The enjoyment in his voice is unmistakable, and the twisted satisfaction at watching Jason's pain flickers across his face. There's no love lost between these two — only layers of dislike.

'So anyway,' I continue, giving Jason time to recover himself, 'we've checked her bank over the last twelve months and noticed she has been withdrawing chunks of money. Did you know this?' William shakes his head. 'She did it randomly, sometimes fortnightly, sometimes weekly or monthly. There was no regular pattern. I guess that was her point.'

'How much did she take?' William asks, seemingly unbothered. But this is the tip of the iceberg that he's not seen coming.

'Just over ten grand. Did you not notice this going out of your joint account?' I know the answer. There was so much money in their current account it hardly made a dent. They had more floating in there at their disposal than will be in my pension pot when I retire.

'No, I honestly didn't. I don't check it regularly. Money goes in from the trust, that's what I see, I don't bother with the rest.'

Nice, what a way to live, never having to balance you bank account. I look at my notebook and open it at the page I want. 'Her bank cards still haven't been used. I think it's a good idea to leave them open just in case she slips up and uses them. We just need the once for us to see where she is.'

'Wait a minute,' pipes up Jason. 'You're suggesting she's run out on us. But you're wrong, she wouldn't do that. What if someone was blackmailing her? What if they knew she was having an affair and blackmailed her to take out the money? Then she says she isn't doing it anymore and they kidnap her. You're assuming she's run away. You're assuming she's withdrawn that money for herself.'

'Because it's the most logical way to think,' William snaps back through gritted teeth. 'Nobody has kidnapped Cat. She's run off because she's fucking pregnant with this other guy's baby. Two and two make four, not five. Can't you see it? Can't you *fucking* see she's a liar?' he yells, the emotion raw in his words.

William's shoulders are so full of tension and so is his face. I brace myself in case he leaps on Jason and starts battering him. I wonder what he really wants to do right now. I know it's not sit in front of the TV and chill. He thinks he's coming across as the crossed husband or at least that's what he's curating for me, but I see hidden depths to this man. Some I cannot read.

'Did your wife have any accounts in her own name?' I continue unmoved to try to keep them from killing one another.

William's shoulders deflate; the tension in his face dissipates slowly. He falls silent as if reining himself in before speaking again. His words hitch in his throat. 'No, we just had the one joint account.' He thinks this is a certainty. And because it wasn't on the laptop, he won't have thought she had anything else to hide. I can see what he's disclosed about Cat being pregnant is hurting him.

'She might have an online account. She told me she was thinking of getting one,' offers Jason meekly. 'I don't know though if she ever did.' He looks sheepish.

'What the hell for?' William says, astonished.

'I didn't ask her, she just asked me if I knew if it was difficult to open one, what she needed etcetera because she was thinking about it.'

'What, you didn't ask what for? That would be novel for you. You want to know every time she sniffs. You're lying. Why did she want another account?'

'You sound shocked,' I say, flicking through my notebook.

William sneers as if this whole ordeal is odious to him, not to mention bewildering. So many emotions cross his face I can't keep up. 'So, when did she open this online account then?' William directs this at Jason like he wants to rip the information from him with his bare hands.

'Seven years ago,' I inform him.

They both freeze and stare at me flabbergasted as if I've just stripped naked right here in front of them. The surprise on their faces is very real.

Neither respond. But I can read William's face battling with the fact his wife had a secret bank account he knew nothing about on top of everything else. And if it's true what her brother says, that he likes to control her, then this will be sending his blood pressure sky high. I flick again through my notebook finding the page I was looking for with all the information, making it seem like I'm looking for it when in fact I have it right in front of me. I want to draw this out as much as possible. I want to see how each piece of information I'm throwing at the husband slams into him and his reaction. 'She opened the account under her maiden name — Catherine Riley. Why d'you think she did that?' I wait to drop the next colossal bomb. It's not quite time yet. Timing is everything.

'I don't know,' William says, his voice breaking. He starts pacing, running a hand through his hair. 'She had everything she could ever want. She had access to our joint account, spent what she wanted. There was no reason for her to . . . to do that.' His gaze drops, lost and hollow. He pauses, swallowing hard, looking utterly bewildered. 'It was just one year after we got married,' he whispers, as if he's trying to understand how it all went so wrong. The disbelief and hurt in his eyes are unmistakable.

'No idea why she opened it in her maiden name? D'you think it was on purpose to hide it from you?'

'Obviously. But I don't know why.'

'Arsehole, you could never see her, could you? She used to work, have a job. She wanted to work again, but you wouldn't let her. You thought it was best for her to stay at home. She had no independence of her own. You knew everything she bought, how much it cost, how many times she spent money. Don't you get it?'

William throws his hands up in the air. 'Clearly not. I don't get why she needed to work. She never said, she never told me she felt that way. I don't get why you think different?'

Jason laughs having come around now and found his voice again. 'You'd have talked her out of it if she'd told you she wanted to go back to work. She enjoyed being a lawyer. It wasn't her choice to stop, not really. You didn't want her to work when you married. Oh, wait, she did talk to you about going back and like you always did if she asked you for independence, you told her she did have independence and there was no need for her to work. Control again.'

'I never stopped her from working — I simply told her I'd prefer if she didn't. The choice was always hers. Not once did she say she missed it or wanted to go back. Not once. No matter what you think you know, Cat hated working. She despised the pressure. She was working at a florist, for God's sake. So tell me, how does that fit into your ridiculous theory of control? Try thinking for once, it might make a nice change.' William turns away from Jason. 'Look, Inspector. I have no idea why she did that or what for. How much was in the account?' He's regained his composure and looks irritated more than angry, like he wants to pack up and get out of here. Like it's all too much for him right now.

I sit back in the comfy sofa and read from my notes knowing this will take the legs from under him. I know the figure, but I make another point of pretending to look for it in my notes a little while longer. 'One hundred and twenty thousand pounds.'

The blow floors him. He staggers back, bumping into the arm of the sofa in front of me. 'One hundred thousand pounds? Cat? But . . . how did she get so much money? I would have noticed that much going from the account.'

'She put in an initial amount of twenty thousand pounds and for the last seven years she's played the markets. Your wife has a remarkable talent, William.' He looks dumbfounded. They both do. 'Recently though she gave away ten thousand pounds.'

'Who to?' William asks.

'To a local women's refuge. I take it you know nothing about this.'

'That twenty thousand she inherited when our parents died,' Jason tells me. 'She wanted security, she told me once, but I never knew about this. Everything they have is in her husband's name. She owns nothing. She did tell me, Inspector, that she felt she herself had nothing. If something happened to him, she'd be out on the street. It's all in trusts you see.'

123

'Wait a minute, she gave ten thousand pounds to a women's refuge? D'you know anything about this?' William asks, turning to Jason. He shrugs and shakes his head.

'So, if you died or divorced, she'd get nothing?' I clarify.

William nods. 'Yes, the money is given to me, that's how the trust is set up. I don't own the trust, I just get an allowance. The house belongs in the trust for me to live in. It cannot be passed down, only to a child of mine.'

'Doesn't sound very kind. I mean your wife would end up on the streets then. Doesn't that bother you?'

'I'm not going to die, Inspector. And plus, there's money in our account. As you've seen, lots of it, and some in a savings account which would be hers. She would not be destitute like Jason is trying to make out. I have personally made provision for her. But I cannot change the trust. I have put in place money and provision for her.'

'Still, I find it hard to understand that even if you were together for fifty years she'd have to leave her home unless you both had a child and said child lived in the house,' I say. 'My wife and I have everything joint. She'd bring up the family, if we had one, and I work. That was the plan. We have one account out of which we both have access. What's mine is hers and hers mine. I couldn't bear the thought of suddenly she having to move out because the house belonged to a trust.'

'No disrespect, Inspector, but we're talking a lot more money here than in your situation.' William's tone is mocking that I have even put us in the same breath.

'I agree, but all this tells me is that you didn't trust your wife from the beginning.'

'That's not true. Besides, it's always been out of my hands. It's how it was set up by my parents. Nothing to do with me. And like I said, I have made provision for Cat.'

'Hmm,' I say. 'And does your wife know this?'

'Look, despite what Jason is trying to convince you of, we were happy. She had times when she was depressed or down, but don't we all. Our situation worked for us. And no, I didn't tell her. I thought it was morbid to discuss it. It's only recently with the IVF that there's been a bit of tension in our relationship. But as I said, she was putting adoption on the table — and it's something we were going to talk about.' He sighs. 'But maybe what she wanted to talk about was to tell me she was pregnant with Stroud's child.'

I move on. 'Okay, let's get back to her affair. You were very intimidating to Mr Stroud when you paid him a visit?'

'Intimidating? What was he expecting me to be like? Did he tell you that the two of them were going to come over and tell me how much in *love* they were? Wouldn't that have been sweet?' He gives a mocking laugh, his pain turning to anger quickly. He sits back down, runs his hand through his hair. He wants to be anywhere but here right now having his life laid out in front of Jason this way. It's clear to me William is a very private man.

'At least they were going to tell you and not just leave you,' says Jason.

'Yeah, that was big of them,' William says with a tone like he's stood in something unpleasant.

'And she was pregnant. According to Mr Stroud, they were very much in love and looking forward to the baby.'

'Very much in love, of course they were.' The sarcasm drips like molten lava. 'She hardly knew the man, for God's sake,' he says through curled lips. 'It was an infatuation, I'm sure of it.'

'You two couldn't get pregnant, is that right?'

'Not compatible, apparently.' Shame colours his face. He throws me a look for bringing it up again.

'Shooting blanks more like,' says Jason.

'Idiot. You know nothing of our lives despite thinking you know a lot. Why are you still here? In my home?'

'Really? Can't imagine you admitting you had an empty tank though, can you? So not being compatible is the more polite version, is it?'

'Did you want to harm him? I mean really beat the shit out of him? After all, he was fucking your wife, and she was having his baby,' I say to see if he will show his anger to me.

His face turns beet red. The tick in his fingers working overtime. I can see he wants to lash out at me and is doing all he can to rein himself in. Poor sod having his love life opened up like this.

'I'm going for a glass of water. Does anyone else want one?' says William.

Jason and I shake our heads.

I check my phone for messages and send Natalie a quick one.

I read the texts that have come in from Sid. I wondered when he was going to get in touch. I wince at the tone and let out a deep breath. Damn. I start to write a polite reply to explain then delete it. Instead, I just send *sorry*. I'll make it up to them as soon as all this pressure I'm under comes to an end.

CHAPTER 17

William

I never thought it was an issue for you. You never let on you weren't happy. I mean, my God, you had everything you could want. What more was there? You had been as eager as me to start a family. I just don't get why you had an affair. I return to the sitting room and sit back down.

I want all this to be over, for him to go and that brother of yours, too. I want a drink. I want to be by myself and think what to do about finding you because I bet I can even if these idiots can't. I shoot the inspector a hard look.

'So, let's get back to your wife and her lover,' the inspector says. 'Jake Stroud says they were in love and making plans for the future. They were even looking at houses. I guess she was going to use the money she had in the bank as her contribution.'

I grunt. 'That's not going to get her much in London. I suppose they'll pool their interests, yes. She always knew how it was. I should have told her I had made provision for her.' Maybe it is my fault she's left me. But I truly believed she wasn't interested in the financial side. I did tell her I'd always take care of her. Clearly, she didn't believe me, which added to her insecurity of what might happen if she didn't have a child. I've messed up.'

'I suppose she loved you a lot at the time and it didn't bother her to start with or so she said,' says the inspector with what sounds like a lack of sympathy. 'She never thought she'd want to leave you, maybe thinking she could get you to change things, but things change, don't they, and she thought ahead maybe when she realised that wasn't ever going to happen. Planned for her future while she could.'

'She was planning to dump me for that idiot, that's for sure.' There's a sinking certainty that makes everything around me seem dull and grey.

'She even told me herself that you dazzled her with all the glitter, and she fell for it,' Jason adds. 'Honestly, Inspector, it's infuriating that you're not grilling him about how he deliberately hit my sister, time after time. It's like you're so blinded by his charm that you can't see the monster lurking beneath!'

'We don't have any proof that he did, Jason, only your say-so. Her girlfriends never mentioned it; they actually spoke highly of your brother-in-law.'

'Bullshit. I can't believe she didn't speak to them about it. I can't.' Jason curls his lip. 'Spoke highly of him, yeah, right,' he adds mockingly.

'But her boss, Rita Armstrong, did mention that she came into work one day with a black eye and said she'd walked into the door. That was about a year ago. She didn't believe her, but Cat wouldn't talk about it, and it was never mentioned again.'

'Ha! Well then, what more do you need?' Jason shoots off the sofa, fired up. 'He hit her and gave her a black eye. I told you so,' Jason says rolling back and forth on the balls of his feet. 'I bloody told you. There's your proof.'

'Did you see the black eye? It's not enough, Jason.'

'Course it fucking isn't, it never is with this lot. They have money and get away with everything. But you have a witness now, surely that's enough.'

'We don't. Nobody saw it happen. For all we know it could be true, and she did walk into a door. It's hearsay, Jason. Nobody saw William hit his wife. No one else can corroborate this. We can't use it. There's only your word for it.'

I feel my blood drain from my face at the memory of that day. And unable to help myself, I stand up and shove Jason away from me. He crashes into a coffee table, losing his footing, and falls sprawling on the sofa.

'Jason, please take a seat,' the inspector says, his tone leaving no room for argument. 'Let me clarify something for you: if it is determined that William is responsible for your sister's death, he will face the full consequences of the law, regardless of his social status or influence. Justice will be served.'

I look at them both and try to calm down.

'Now the other thing I want to say is that we ought to put out a reward for Cat. Don't you agree, William? It might help bring in anyone that's a bit reluctant to come forward with information.'

I know the family won't like our lives splashed in the tabloids. Of course, that will reflect badly on me if I say no, so I have to agree and encourage it along that it is a good idea. It is. Only the family won't be happy. I'll have to speak with Mum and prepare her for what is coming. Still, how do they think you'll be found otherwise?

Jason finds his voice again. 'Nothing less than thirty thousand.'

* * *

'Sure, sure, that's what you say now. But she did have a black eye.' Jason crosses his arms over his chest and scowls but remains seated.

Seething, I jab my finger straight into Jason's chest, furious that he thinks he can spread this ridiculous lie about me like it's some kind of truth. He stands up to face me. I poke him hard with each point I make, practically daring him to deny it. 'First of all, that was an accident!' I exclaim, punctuating my words with another poke that makes him stumble back into his seat a bit. 'We had an argument, that's all!' The irritation is boiling over.

'What! You seriously think it's okay to hit a woman just because you had a little spat?' Jason shoots back.

'It was an accident! And honestly, it's none of your business,' I fire off, feeling fury surge through me as I recall how I hurt you without ever intending to. It's like I can't believe you'd even try to make anything more of it than what it was.

'No, but it is my business,' the inspector asserts with certainty. 'Now, can you explain why an argument would lead you to believe it was acceptable to physically strike your wife?'

'I didn't! I swear, I keep telling you that!' My voice trembles with panic that it's all sounding too horrific. 'We were just arguing — seriously, I don't even remember what it was about — it was years ago! Please, you have to believe me!'

'One year to be precise,' says the inspector, 'according to Rita Armstrong.'

'Look, I know it sounds bad, but here's what happened. I was about to walk away when she threw a glass tumbler at me. It struck me on the side of the head, and in that moment of anger, I turned around and slapped her. I never meant to hurt her. It was a rash reaction, and I felt absolutely terrible afterwards. I regretted it instantly. We made up, and I thought we'd put it behind us. I loved my wife then, and I still love her now.'

'Despite her having an affair?'

'Despite that, yes.'

'Her boss said she had a real shiner. It must've been a hell of a slap.'

'Yeah, well maybe it was. How would you react if someone threw a tumbler at your head.'

'I doubt I'd slap my wife if she did.'

I narrow my eyes. 'Easy to say here and now but very different in the heat of the moment.'

'So, tell me, what was the reason you didn't let your wife work? I mean if she wanted to, why not? Were you jealous she might meet someone at the office? Didn't you trust her to stay faithful?'

'You know my wife is stunning, and yes, she would turn heads, I'm sure of it. But no, that was not the reason why. Haven't I already explained all this?'

'So, why didn't you let her?'

'I didn't want her to work. That's it. Very simple, Inspector. And neither did she. Weren't you listening earlier? It was Cat's decision not to work. She now works in the florist, like I said, I have no problem there.'

'But you're jealous now, right?'

'Yeah, just a bit.' My heart is breaking as I speak. 'I just found out she's been having an affair right under my nose, and now she's pregnant with his child. So, yes, you could say I'm feeling a bit of jealousy — more like a raging storm of betrayal if I'm honest.'

'And there's your motive, Inspector. It's as clear as day,' shouts Jason.

'Do you ever hear yourself?' I can't resist. 'I only just found out about it! How on earth can you think that's my motive?'

I swallow, dragging the fear down into my stomach as to what this could imply. The inspector watches me. Considers what's been said.

'Your wife certainly concealed a great deal from you,' he says, maintaining a steady tone of authority. 'It raises the question: are there any other hidden secrets lurking just beneath the surface that could come to light? What was her connection with the women's refuge?'

'I can't answer that question,' I say, my voice trembling a little with panic. I look at Jason and he's unable to look me in the eye. But truthfully, it's something I've worried about too, other secrets being kept. I mean, they must be discussing this at the station, tearing apart every detail of your life, searching for anything else they can dig up. It's probably safer if I just don't say anything more. They're making it obvious that they're trying to pin this on me, and I can't shake this fear.

'D'you think she's spoken to a lawyer about leaving you?' the inspector says.

'Well, I mean, why bother asking me? Clearly, I'm the last person to get any updates about my wife around here,' I say with a heavy dose of sarcasm. 'Why not ask him?' I nod towards Jason, staring at me with those narrowed eyes of his. Fantastic — just what I need. I really wish he'd just disappear, but starting another argument isn't going to help our situation with the police, so I try to remind myself to keep it together. It all looks pretty sketchy, and the last thing I need is to give them more fodder.

'She did mention she was thinking of going and talking to someone, yes,' says Jason.

'With Jake?' I ask, leaning back in the chair, the tension inside me pulling me taut as I think of the two of them walking hand in hand into the solicitor's office.

'Yes,' says Jason. 'She mentioned in passing about wanting to know what to expect. I don't know if she ever went through with it.'

I nod slowly, my fingers tapping a restless rhythm on my leg as I try to process the crushing weight of what he said. I don't believe him. He knows more than he's saying. The inspector's gaze is locked on to me, searching for some kind of reaction, maybe hoping for anger or disbelief. But how can I possibly muster those feelings when the reality sinks in and all I feel is hurt? She was willing to throw everything away — for a physiotherapist of all people. A wave of pain washes over me, and I feel a bitterness rising in my throat. 'What? Don't you have anything to say, Inspector?' I finally manage to force out, a mix of confusion and hurt blending in my voice. I just want him to stop staring at me that way.

'I'm wondering how you feel knowing she was planning to see a lawyer.'

'Come on, how do you think I feel?' I say, emotion tight in my throat. 'Honestly, it's just another betrayal, isn't it? I mean, I've already had the biggest shocks. This is just yet another wound to add to the growing list. She wanted to leave me because she's found someone else, and it wasn't even about the money.' My voice is sharp, every word laced with the pain of her deception, a heartache I never saw coming.

'Hmm. All right, let's clarify a few things. What exactly transpired that day during the altercation that resulted in her receiving a black eye?' The inspector's tone is firm, steady. 'You mentioned that you two reconciled afterwards and decided to move past it, but I need a complete account of the incident. So, what really happened?'

'We did, yes. It'd got out of hand. We both realised that.'

'You say that, but do you genuinely believe Cat actually forgave you?' The inspector's tone is steady, authoritative, cutting through the tension in the room. 'Rita mentioned that Cat struggled to hold back tears when she was asked about the incident. She refused to share any specifics.'

I lose my patience. 'What are you suggesting?'

'I'm just curious as to why you neglected to mention that the very next day, you resumed communication — this time through email with aggressive tendencies,' the inspector states firmly, his tone leaving no room for ambiguity. 'The authority in his voice unmistakable, and the weight of the situation hangs heavily between us.

I stare at him as heat rushes through me. Oh God, the emails. I mustn't have deleted everything.

'What are you insinuating, Inspector?' I say steely.

'Look, William, we need to get to the bottom of this,' he says, his tone authoritative but measured. 'And let's be frank, sometimes women can hold on tighter than a dog with a bone. They can be relentless, can't they? You think you've settled an issue, but there they are — banging on about it like it's fresh. I can't say my wife doesn't have her moments of being pedantic — I can relate to that. So, did she keep pressing you, which is why your email came off as, well . . . bullish?' He studies me, his instincts homed in on every twitch, every reaction from me, looking for the truth he thinks is buried beneath the surface.

'No. I don't. Care to clarify?' My body twitches. 'You can interpret anything any which way you want when you don't have the full story, *Inspector*.' I spell it out to him that I will not be put in a box of his making.

He's relentless.

'Well, they want all the T's crossed and all the I's dotted for clarity and then that just rehashes the whole thing again and you find yourself back where you started. Don't you find that?'

'No. I don't. And we didn't *re-hash* it and we didn't *go back to where we started*, either.' I rub my hand over my stubble, aware he's getting to me, and it shows. I glance at Jason watching me intently.

The inspector nods, seeming satisfied, but I'm not so sure it's how he's thinking.

'So, when you punched your wife—'

'I never claimed I punched my wife, Inspector, or slapped her or hit her intentionally in any way,' I hurriedly explain, my heart racing with the weight of the accusation he's throwing in my direction. 'It was an *accident* — a reaction to her *throwing* the glass at my head. It was instinctive, primal, that's all. You wouldn't be trying to twist my words, would you? I slapped her only after she threw the glass tumbler at me, and it was purely a reflex, a defensive action. Look, you have to understand how it was that night. You can't pick out a frame and make up the story either side so it fits your way of thinking,' I say cautiously, every word carefully measured, but pointed and fearing that one misstep could seal my fate if he decides to.

'So, when you slapped your wife after she *threw* a glass tumbler at your head, did you genuinely forgive her? I mean, did you *truly* forgive her, or was there a part of you that wanted her to suffer for what happened? Here's what I'm getting at, William: did you feel wronged? Aggrieved that her actions could have seriously harmed you? Because I'll be honest — if I were in your shoes, I'd find that difficult to reconcile. It's a lot to process and could undoubtedly leave a person feeling angry and betrayed.' His gaze is unyielding, searching for sincerity as he waits for my response.

'Are you playing good cop now?'

'No, William, that's not what this is about,' he says firmly. 'I'm trying to get to the heart of the matter here because I believe you're an intelligent man — sharp, even. You give me the impression that spontaneity isn't really your style, that you like to keep things under control. But then we came across that email you sent to your wife, dated the day after the incident. For your information, we've uncovered that email thread between you both. In it, you wrote, *If you ever do that again, I will fucking murder you, and nobody will ever find your body.* Now, it's troubling, to say the least. So, I need to understand. What was going through your mind when you hit send on that message?' His tone is steady, deliberately probing, ensuring I feel the full weight of his words.

CHAPTER 18

Jill

Back at Caledonian Nights, Amanda McKay, the landlady, intercepts me on my way to collect my key.

There's a bunch of girls cleaning the place — vacuum cleaners, brushes and the smell of pine and disinfectant hangs in the air. She keeps it nice and clean; I can see she's proud of her establishment. One girl is polishing the windows with vigour. The net curtains used to keep the outside world from looking in are being taken down for washing.

'It's wash day, and spring cleaning although it's more autumn cleaning than spring. I always go in for a big clear-out this time of year!' Amanda's dressed impeccably — tight black pencil skirt, a red silk blouse tied in a neat bow at the collar, high heels clicking against the floor with every step. The desk she uses as reception is awash with papers and detritus. 'Aye, and that includes me.' She chuckles, the corners of her mouth lifting. 'I'm a terrible hoarder o' wee bits an' bobs that only ever end up in the bin on days like this. I think they might come in handy someday — but they never do!' She speaks sagely, her words tinged with wisdom. Her gold necklace swings lightly as she leans over her desk, a locket bobbing against her chest. It catches the light, but the inscription is unreadable as she bends and straightens, digging in and out of her drawer. She finally sits down on her chair, lets out a small sigh and straightens her spine; there's an audible click — like something being put back into place. 'Ah, that's better. Right,' she murmurs as if the motion somehow settles everything as it should be. 'Your key, is it? And how's your day been, then?' She reaches into one of the pigeonholes behind her to retrieve it. 'There you go!'

'Yes, good thanks. It's going to feel even better to get out of these soggy clothes,' I say, peeling off my damp jacket. 'I went for a walk into town and ended up in the park when the rain hit.'

She clicks her tongue in disapproval. 'Did you no take a brolly? A wee bit of advice — never step out in Scotland without one — especially at this time of year.'

'I'll make sure I have one next time. Thanks.' I grab the key, the heavy disc swinging from it, and head to my room.

I shed my wet clothes and turn on the shower. As the water warms, I spot the hair dye I bought earlier. I set it on the counter and lay out fresh, dry clothes on the bed. Once the steam fills the bathroom, I take a long shower to warm up, then dye my hair. After I rinse it off, I wrap my hair in a towel. Feeling warmer and more relaxed, I flop onto the bed and pull out my phone, scrolling absentmindedly.

I'm desperate to know if there's anything out on social media about me. But I can't bring myself to look. I could open an account under a different name . . . but I don't dare. What if it somehow leads back to me? I'll find out soon enough, though. I'll probably end up in the news before long, whether I want to or not.

A sick feeling churns in my stomach at the thought that you might already be on your way, hunting me down. I still don't understand why there's been nothing in the news. Have you told the police? My thoughts begin to race, my mind scrambling for the next step. Should I stay here for another day? What if someone's looking for me already? You've probably hired someone to track me down.

Restless, I head downstairs. I need to move, to shake off this uneasy energy. The coffee machine in the lounge is calling me. I stand in front of it, scanning the pods available, trying to focus on something mundane. Then I hear my name. My spine stiffens.

'Jill, nice to see you. I was wondering if you had any plans for dinner tonight. Are you going out?'

Dinner? I hadn't even thought about it. I'm not in the mood to go out, especially not alone. I turn to face Amanda, my heart still pounding in my chest. 'Oh, you startled me! I didn't hear you come in. I think I'll just grab a takeout. Is there somewhere around here?'

She smiles, unfazed. 'Aye, plenty. Chinese, Indian, burgers, Greek . . . We've got them all.'

I drop the pod into position, place the cup beneath the spout, and press the button for a cappuccino. 'Well, I guess I'll go with one of those,' I mumble, not turning to look at her.

'Aye, that's a grand idea, but most of them only take orders online. You'll need a card for it!' Her voice lingers, and I can almost feel the weight of her gaze, though I don't dare glance at her. What's she thinking? Curiosity? Suspicion?

Who doesn't have a bank card these days?

'Oh, right. No problem, I'll sort it.' My voice is tight with forced calm. 'Thanks for the heads-up.' I can't believe I didn't anticipate that. Looks like I'll have to go and pick it up in person.

'Your hair looks nice,' she says casually, and I give her a quick side glance, instinctively touching it with my hand. I try to make the gesture look natural, even though my heart is suddenly in my throat. The cappuccino is ready, and I grab it, forcing a neutral expression as I turn back to face her.

'Thanks, I like it,' I say, taking a sip.

'Aye, it looks grand on you!'

'Do you really think so? I was worried it might be too dark.'

'No. Just makes you look a bit different, that's all.'

'Oh! Does it?' I feign surprise, keeping my voice steady.

There's a brief silence. 'Aye, maybe that's a good thing?'

'Or not.' I laugh, but it sounds tight. I want to snap at her to mind her own business, but she's been kind to me, and I know she means well.

'Aye . . . or maybe no. D'you think your man will like it? It's quite the change!' I shrug, the thought of you, twisting something inside me. 'Huh, I guess I'll find out soon enough.'

'Oh, is he coming up then?'

'Uh, no. I mean . . . when I get back.'

Another silence. Amanda sighs, walking over to the coffee machine, dropping in a pod. Her long nails click against the machine as she closes the lid and presses the button.

'Look, tell me to mind my own business if you want, and I won't bring it up again. But I've seen a fair few folk come through my doors over the years, and I reckon I'm not too bad reading them. I'll say no more, but if you need a place to stay while you sort yourself out, this is as safe as any place you'll find.' She pauses, and I feel the weight of her words. 'You know what I mean, lass?'

I don't answer right away, my heart pounding. 'I . . . I don't,' I lie. My instinct is to look away, but instead, I meet her eyes, focusing on them. You once taught me that if I look at someone's nose when lying, they won't know I'm avoiding their gaze in a lie.

Amanda stirs her cappuccino, the clink of the spoon against the cup unnaturally loud in the quiet room. 'I think you do,' she says gently. 'You know what I'm saying all right.' She spoons some of the froth into her mouth, leaving a red lipstick mark on the spoon. 'You're not the first to come through here running from something or someone. I can always tell.'

I lower my eyes. I feel like a beacon, glowing red, visible to everyone. What's wrong with me? Why does everyone seem to notice?

'I . . .' I start to speak, but the words stick in my throat.

Amanda sets the spoon down with a soft clink, then turns to me. 'I could be doing with a wee bit o' help around here for a few days. One of ma lasses called in sick — she usually helps in the kitchen and sees to the laundry. If you're staying, I could put you to use. You can keep your head down for a while, give you some space to get yourself sorted. How does that sound?' She sounds so sincere.

I hesitate, feeling a mix of gratitude and confusion. She doesn't know me. She doesn't know why I'm here. For all she knows, I could be running from the police — maybe I've done something terrible.

'I'm not sure it's any of your business why I'm here,' I say. The words slip out sharper than I intend, tinged with a small tremor. I feel a pang of guilt. I shouldn't have snapped. She's been kind. I could've been more gracious.

Amanda doesn't flinch at my tone, just smiles, nods gently. 'Huh. Maybe you'll come round after you've had time to dwell on it.' She sets her cup and saucer down on the counter and clicks off towards the door, her heels echoing on the wooden floor like a countdown or something. When she returns, I'm staring at the newspapers on the coffee table next to me that I hadn't noticed when I first walked in.

A jolt of fear shoots through me when I see the front page of one of the tabloids. My heart begins to race, the cold grip of dread tightens in my chest when I see the headline.

MISSING:

Catherine Johnson-Smyth. The wife of millionaire venture capitalist, William Johnson-Smyth, went missing four days ago after leaving her home in Holland Park . . .

I can't tear my eyes away from the picture. That face smiling, her hair blowing in the wind, staring back at me from the page. There's a hollow ache in my belly as I stare at it, my throat constricting painfully like I'm suffocating.

I grip the sideboard, my knuckles going white as the room begins to spin, and I cling to the edge to steady myself.

I catch Amanda glance over when she returns, following where I'm staring. 'Do you ken that woman?'

'No, no I don't,' I reply too quickly.

She picks up the paper, her face thoughtful as she reads and says, 'Her husband is desperate to find her. They're saying she might've had an accident, lost her memory or been kidnapped.'

Her red nail taps the page, drawing my attention to the next line.

REWARD: Thirty thousand pounds for information leading to Catherine Johnson-Smyth's whereabouts.

She lets out a low whistle.

My chest tightens knowing that will make people take notice.

'So,' Amanda says after a long thoughtful pause. She puts the newspaper back on the coffee table. 'You want to ken what I think?'

I stare at her waiting.

'You need a job for a wee while, I ken you do, and you've got one here *if* you want it.' Her voice is firm, not unkind, but there's a no-nonsense quality to it that tells me what she wants to say is to stop being so damned proud when help is offered. 'The offer's still on the table if you want it.'

I swallow, nodding, slowly quelling my flight response that's kicking in right now. 'Okay, maybe you're right. Maybe I should stay for a little while. A couple more days.' I glance at the fireplace, watching the flames dance.

* * *

In the kitchen I pick up an apron that's lying around. I look for some rubber gloves but can't find any. There's a lingering aroma of cooking fat that makes me wrinkle my nose. What I do find are lots of cleaning products and cloths in a cupboard by the kitchen door that when I open most of the products fall out. A magnitude of tins and plastic bottles litter the linoleum floor.

'Hi,' a young woman's voice says standing beside me. She laughs looking at the clutter on the floor. 'Aye, er . . . that happens all the time. There isn't enough storage for all that crap, and Amanda keeps on buying products, whatever! She really needs to stop. I ken she's obsessed with cleaning, duh. I'm Sarah.' She sticks out her hand. I take it and shake.

'I'm Jill.' She must be anything between eighteen and twenty; it's hard to tell. 'I'm new. Amanda has me cleaning the kitchen.' Sarah is part of the cleaning crew that comes in regularly. I don't want to step on anyone's toes.

Sarah wrinkles her nose. 'Aye, better you than me doing that shite job. Murder on your hands all that crap.' She means the products. 'So, where you from, then? Obviously not Scotland.' She giggles. 'And don't say England, I ken that much. I mean, like, where in England?' She tilts her head to the side and smiles and chews gum. 'I went to Manchester once.'

'D'you know if there're any gloves anywhere?' I avoid answering.

Another laugh. 'Like, no, she used to provide them, but people kept taking them home so she stopped bothering.' She shrugs like it's not important.

That makes sense, but now I have none to wear, and this stuff is going to damage my skin. All the products say *wear gloves*.

'Sarah, you coming out here any time soon?' another Scottish female voice calls out from the dining room. 'I can't stand like this forever. Hurry up, will you!'

'Aye, that's Martha. Left her holding the curtain pole that came off the wall while I went to find a screwdriver.' She laughs, rolling her eyes. 'She pulled the curtain back too hard and it came away from the wall.' She stands there looking around, wondering where she might find one and in no hurry whatsoever.

'There's a box of tools over there by the back door. I saw it when I came in. You might find one in there,' I volunteer in the hopes she'll find what she's looking for and leave.

'Aye, great. Thanks, Jill.' She beams at me, rushes over, looks through the box and picks up one she wants. 'Bingo! I ken this is what she wanted, huh. She asked for a Phillips, no idea what that is, do you? She said it had a star shaped end, so why not just call it that instead of a Phillips? Who the hell kens what a Phillips is, anyway? Whatever, this looks like what she wants.' She rushes out and leaves me picking up all the detritus off the floor. I pile it on the end of the worktop. First, I fill the sink with hot soapy water. Choose a can of Grease Attack then spray it over the tiles behind the cooker. Within a few minutes it starts to streak down the walls in a yucky brown colour. I grab the stepladders, step on the first step, lean over the cooker and begin to wipe down with a damp cloth. Then I rinse the cloth in the hot, soapy water and begin again, and on and on I go. I get into a rhythm and drift off thinking about Amanda's kindness, knowing that as much as I would like to stay here, it wouldn't be conducive to my health to stay too long.

Sarah comes back a little while later making me jump when she suddenly appears beside me. 'You scared me,' I say, startled, dropping the now disgusting looking cloth on the cooker. I start descending the ladder.

'Sorry, mind yourself off the steps. Jill, this is Martha, the one with the foghorn who was holding up the curtain pole and the one who pulled it off the wall.'

143

'Hi,' I say and smile remembering not to make conversations with anyone. This isn't going to plan. I wish they'd leave me alone.

'Hey. Shite job you got there. You with the agency, aye?' Martha asks, pulling out a roll-up from a small tin in her apron pocket.

I pick up the cloth again. 'No, no. Um . . . passing through. I asked Amanda if she knew anywhere to pick up a bit of cash and she offered me this.' I screw up my face, wringing out the grubby cloth that was once yellow but is now brown. The water is disgusting and has gone cold as I plunge my hands in. I pull the plug and re-fill the sink.

'Huh,' Martha says looking me up and down. 'You look a wee bit upmarket to be looking for pin money jobs like these, eh?'

'Well, you know, it is what it is.'

Sarah rolls her eyes but doesn't speak. She's sneaking a look in the fridge and shoving a cooked sausage in her mouth while at the same time keeping an eye on the internal door. Shovelling the last of it in, she unties her apron, rolls it up, and tucks it into a bag hanging on a clothes peg with the coats in the room next to the kitchen. Pulling out her phone she starts to scroll and leaves the room. As far as I can tell, Martha is just making polite conversation. Maybe being a bit nosey but that might be because she thinks I'm going to steal some of their work. I try to appease her of that notion and maybe she'll back off a little. 'I'm only stopping for a couple of days.' Martha walks to the back door, opens it, lights up the wrinkled cigarette and smokes it. She has a round face that's flushed but it's not hot in here and I wonder if she looks that way all the time. She's leaning against the tiled kitchen wall, half in and half out of the kitchen, blowing smoke out of the side of her mouth to avoid it coming inside. Her inky black hair is tied up in a scrunchy, pulled off her face which makes her look hard. It looks dyed and doesn't suit her. Her thick, dark eyebrows knit together as if she's trying to recall something from memory. It makes me nervous.

'Are you Amanda's regular cleaners, then?' I try to sound friendly. I carry on spraying, wiping and rinsing, moving my stepladder a little further along each time. It's gone cold now she has the back door open. She should be grateful I'm doing this minging job and Amanda doesn't ask them to do it.

'Aye, we are. She's used us for the last four years. We do all her cleaning for her. It's ma mum's company.'

I can see how I've stepped on her toes. I don't want to start anything. 'How nice to have someone so loyal like her.'

'What's that supposed to mean, eh?' Martha says, a little spitefully, like a child in the playground. I re-evaluate her age. I thought she was the same age as Sarah — maybe she's younger than she looks, by a lot.

'It wasn't supposed to mean anything.' I gauge that Martha is one of those women who can start a fight with little encouragement. The ones who like to make drama all the time, just for the sake of it.

'Pack it in, Martha, will you,' Sarah hisses, walking back in, sliding her mobile phone into the back pocket of her jeans. 'Act yer age, not yer shoe size, you daft cow! C'mon, let's get outta here.' Martha sizes me up more intensely, her gaze sharp. I try not to wince and look troubled. 'You look a wee bit posh for a job like this. Where you from then?' Her scepticism hangs heavily in the air. Openly suggesting she doesn't believe me. She straightens her spine and puffs on her cigarette, squinting at me. She tilts her head to one side.

Martha's brow furrows as she weighs something in her mind. 'You seen the papers today? That English woman that's gone missing? You're not her, are you?' My heart skips. Why would she ask that?

'No, of course not. She doesn't even look like me,' I say.

Sarah chuckles. 'Martha, are you mad? She looks nothing like her!

What's in that ciggie, wacky baccy or something?'

'Huh. I dunno you know. I mean if I narrow my eyes a little like this and tilt my head, you kinda do have a look of her.'

'You're an idiot, Martha Fraser, she looks nothing like her.'

'Aye, I dunno. There's a huge reward, did you ken?'

'Aye, for information leading to finding *her* not for someone who looks like her just 'cause you can *narrow* your eyes and tilt your fucking head to one side and pretend, she has a resemblance.'

'Might be worth a try, you never know where it might lead. I mean, she's English, isn't she?'

I carry on cleaning, but my hands have begun to shake. I don't look at her nor acknowledge what she's saying. If they call the police — my time here is limited now that she's talking this way. I need to fade into the shadows.

'Come on, let's go. We're no' getting paid for standing around, are we? Put that ruddy ciggy out and let's get out of here. Our shift's done. Let's go grab a coffee and a bacon sandwich down the road. I'm bloody famished. Oh, aye, Peter MacBride might be in the café today,' Sarah says enticingly, giving Martha a shove in the shoulder. 'Maybe today he'll buy you a sticky bun or give you a sticky bum.' She roars with laughter.

Martha strikes a pose of hands on hips. 'You're a filthy bitch, sometimes, Sarah McColl, does your mother ken you talk the filth?'

'Oh, aye, but does your mother ken you *do* the filth?' Sarah moves quickly away from Martha's outstretched hand which only just misses her.

'Right, well, if yer no' coming then I'm off on my own. What's got into you?' asks Sarah, flinging her handbag over her shoulder and pulling up her hood. 'It's started raining, again. C'mon, can you come on before it buckets down, and we get soaked.'

'I'll no' get soaked, I've an umbrella.' Martha takes off her apron, shoving it in her handbag that Sarah has brought over for her. Sarah throws Martha's coat at her; she puts it on slowly.

'Stop being an arse and let's get out of here. I'm gasping for that bacon sarnie. C'mon, let's just go! We're wasting time,' Sarah urges. I clutch the cloth tightly, my breath shallow. *Yes, get lost, Martha, go.*

'Wait. No . . . hold on! I ken. Why not come with us?' Martha declares, stepping closer to me. My stomach twists at her words. 'C'mon. It'll be fun. You're not from around here. You'll be okay with us, won't she, Sarah? C'mon.'

With every moment that passes, I can almost feel the panic converging inside me, wanting to spill out. My voice remains trapped in my throat, silenced by fear. I do not want to go with them. Neither do I want to bring myself to their attention for being difficult.

'I have to finish this, sorry, maybe another time.'

'Okay then.' She turns away following Sarah out of the back door. 'Wouldn't it be great to get hold of that thirty grand, eh? God, what I'd do with that money.'

'Like what?' asks Sarah.

'Leave Scotland for sure. Go travelling. Go around the world maybe. You coming with me?'

'Maybe. Let's get out of here before it pours!' Sarah cries, looking up at the greying skies.

As they bicker, I seize the opportunity to sink further into the mundane task at hand, praying for oblivion, praying for freedom.

But the moment lingers, suspense drapes the room almost suffocating me, while I struggle against the weight of the inevitable.

With a growing dread, I realise that hiding has its price. As their voices fade into the distance, I am left staring at the door, waiting. I can almost hear the clock ticking, counting down to a moment when the truth surfaces, and I can no longer remain hidden in the shadows. That moment will transform everything, and when it does, I need to be ready to run.

CHAPTER 19

William

It's the fifth day now that you've been gone. I pull your pillow from under my head, the one I've been sleeping with to keep you close, to trick my mind into thinking you're still here. The scent of myrrh and orange lingers on the fabric, and for a moment, I mourn the space you've left behind. But then, I remember what you've done. The betrayal. Anger floods in, sharp and bitter, and I hurl the pillow across the room. It crashes on to your dressing table, sending everything — your perfume, your brushes — tumbling to the floor in a clatter of broken things.

I get up, the morning light dull and grey, just after seven. Inside me, there's this heavy, empty feeling, like something's been hollowed out. I drag myself towards the shower, every step like lead. The water's scalding when I turn it on, as hot as I can take it, until it's almost unbearable. But still, I stand there, letting the steam and the heat envelop me. The cramp in my belly tightens again, deep and unforgiving, each twist making me wonder where you are, what you're doing. And what the hell happened here.

You're not dead. I know that. I would know it; I just know I would. But you've gone, and that's almost worse. You've run. You're hiding. What's the plan, Cat? Are you with Jake now? Are you going to change your name and disappear, start over somewhere far away?

I'll find you.

Does that inspector genuinely believe I've killed you? Or harmed you in some way? I can hardly wrap my head around it. But, then again, with your moronic brother whispering melodramatic fantasies into his ear all day, can I blame him? If I had been the one to do you in, would I be foolish enough to leave myself with no alibi? Unlikely. They've torn this house apart and found nothing to suggest I've harmed you. Honestly, if I'd taken that route, would I really have committed the act here? That's beyond stupid.

Still, the detective's presence unsettles me — not just his scrutiny, but his knowledge of those emails from a year ago. He'll be piecing together my movements from the pub and the off-licence I visited. Losing my cool with him yesterday certainly didn't bolster my defence. The lash of sarcasm I threw his way certainly wouldn't be benefiting me, either.

What bothers me most is why he keeps bringing your brother along. The last thing I need is Jason's inflammatory commentary on our relationship. I expressly told you not to spill the details of our lives to him. I recounted parking at the off-licence the evening you vanished, buying the wine and lingering in the pub, all the while knowing he would dig up some gap in the timeline when he checks the CCTV. My panic surged in that moment; I could have come clean, but I refuse to lay bare my private life in front of him. I can explain the gap later; I'm sure the detective will come to understand. But why should I let that moron know about my affairs?

I can only guess what Jason imagines has happened to you — maybe he thinks I tossed you in the Thames. I wouldn't be surprised if divers are soon dispatched. But right now, you've simply vanished. No evidence of foul play exists, so I assume the diving operation is still a proposal in the minds of the authorities.

From my window, I see reporters lurking outside, eager for any glimpse or scandalous titbit. The moment your photograph hit the media, the vultures descended like a ravenous tempest. Working from home is hard enough without having to fend off those mercenaries. My boss said to take the week off, but I need to do something to stop my thoughts driving me mad. I can feel their lenses shifting towards me, seeking a moment of vulnerability. I hastily draw the curtains shut, muttering curses — bloodthirsty leeches, each one yearning to unearth your corpse for ratings.

The police have canvassed the neighbourhood, just as the press have done, their reports spewing across the internet like lava from a volcano, feeding an insatiable click-bait appetite for sordid details. Clever girl, Cat, how you managed to evaporate so seamlessly — almost as though you turned a corner and simply ceased to exist.

But the most damning evidence is that you left your phone behind. Did that pretty boy, Jake, suggest you leave it so we couldn't track you?

I just don't get it. You looked happy, Cat. *Why? You had it all.* The thought shrouds me in anxiety as I pass your dressing table, swiping the rest of the clutter on to the floor in a fit of frustration. The fragrant, shattered bottle of Jo Malone Orange Blossom floods the air. I bought you that. I'm suffocated by memories, the scent almost mocking me.

I think about maybe going back to the office to get away from the claustrophobia surrounding this house. Even the short ten-minute drive to Burkes & Hardwick seems unbearable with this entourage following me. I don't think they'd appreciate me dumping them on their doorstep.

I change into a T-shirt and running shorts, leaving my phone behind — each notification lighting up the screen with a bombardment of new messages. It never stops. But I daren't turn it off in case you try to contact me. The tally on my email icon says over one hundred emails, and I suspect most won't offer the sympathy I need.

I peek out the back door. It's drizzling, overcast and miserable out there. Good. Let the reporters get soaked. London feels like a grey blanket over my heart, but I need to break free, to gather my thoughts away from here. I slip on a hoodie, jogging down the long garden path, typical for a property like this, and surrounded by a high brick wall with a wooden locked gate in the side. I unlock it and step out into the passage separating us from the next property, hoping not to bump into a rogue reporter lurking close by. To my relief, it's empty.

I stride out and jog, dodging the crowd outside gathered on the stoop, finding temporary refuge in the anonymity of pedestrians and my hood pulled down low. I get a whiff of bacon sandwiches and coffee as I cross the street, turning onto Holland Park Avenue and finally into the peace of Holland Park, hoping to clear my mind.

Half an hour later, the return feels like slipping back into a spotlight, yet no one seems any the wiser that I even left. In the kitchen, I grab a bottle of water, only to be assaulted by a flood of overlapping messages when I check my phone. Concerned notes ranging from *Are you okay?* to *Call me!* drown me in a cacophony of worry telling me we are all over social media. I refuse to engage in social media, so I won't be looking at those.

After washing my face, drying it with a paper towel and tossing it in the bin, I wander back to the window and peek through the drawn curtains; the chaotic scene outside remains unchanged.

Once I'm back upstairs I take a quick shower, returning to the kitchen, dressed in jeans and T-shirt under a pullover. I pull eggs, bacon and bread from the fridge, making a mental note to do a food delivery order — anything to avoid the circus out there.

As I prepare breakfast, throwing a teabag in a mug and a couple of bacon rashers into a pan with a couple of eggs in another, thoughts of you flood my mind. I can't shake the nagging suspicion that Jake might have stayed here while I was away — my weekend golf trips to Scotland, business meetings in New York and LA. In the kitchen, I glance at the huge granite island with four stools tucked beneath one side, haunted by the image of you sprawled across its surface, fucking him. *I bet you let him stay the night and made him breakfast in our kitchen. Fed him our food.* I grasp the pan with the bacon, toss the food on my plate then shove the pan aside, clinking it noisily in the sink. I plate up the eggs.

Suddenly, there's a noise by the back door — the sound of keys scraping against the lock. I freeze, half-expecting a swarm of reporters to rush in, capturing my every reaction or even you returning full of apologies. Instead, my sister Lucy slips through the door, silently closing and locking it behind her. Surprised to see me, she laughs. 'Will! You scared the hell out of me! What on earth are you doing standing there, staring at the back door?'

'Where else should I stand? This is my house, after all. And my kitchen.' I don't tell her I thought and prayed it was you walking in.

'Not like that. I thought you'd be at work or something. I came over to make you some food. I bet you're not eating properly.'

'As if. I can't focus right now. You do know what's happened, right?'

'Not from you, thanks to your silence.' She snatches a slice of bacon off my plate. 'Why did I have to learn about this through social media and the TV?'

'Do you think it's easy to call you up and say, 'Hey, my wife is missing, and everyone thinks I killed her?'

'Right. So, Jason is behind this rumour mill, I take it?' She grabs another slice and drapes her coat over a stool leaving me with no bacon. 'It's a mad crowd out there. Have you left the house at all?'

I grab a glass of water, sit down and pick at my food — or what's left of it.

'It wasn't bad until the press got involved. We released her photo hoping to find someone who'd seen her — that's when they descended like hyenas.'

She furrows her brow. 'You have no clue? Really?'

I push my plate away, wipe my mouth on a napkin. 'No, I really don't. But that doesn't matter to anyone. Jason insists I harmed her. Can you believe it?' I drink some water.

'Does he really think that?'

'Not sure what he really believes, but he's doing his best to have me arrested. But without a body what can they prove? They're ready to convict me with no evidence, at least that's what it feels like. The police are coming on hard, and the press seem to have made up their minds.' I wince, remembering what's being written about me. 'Jason's lost it. He's insisting something's happened to her. He won't even contemplate that she might have run off, left me. I hate thinking that.'

'But it's not true. You couldn't hurt her. I know you.'

'The detective is convinced I've done her in. He's a problem. If he latches on to that idea, who knows where this ends? You hear such horror stories.'

'You spoke to Mum and Dad?' I shrug. 'They said you can stay with them. The press won't reach you there,' she says.

I ponder it, wondering how inviting that would be knowing what I do. 'I might have to. What do I do about Jason? He's lost without Cat.'

'How can you think about him like that after what he's saying about you? He's not being very nice about you to the press.'

I sigh. 'I know, but she loves him and he's family. Besides, he's not all there is he, I mean, to be so obsessed with your sister that you have no life of your own. Don't you think it odd he's never

153

married? Or has a girlfriend or boyfriend? Cat wouldn't ever talk about it.'

She shrugs, pulls a face. 'Loneliness can twist people. They were always close. Really odd though, I agree.' Walking to the fridge, she retrieves an open bottle of wine. 'Want a glass? It's five o'clock somewhere.' She pours one for herself as I shake my head.

'My lawyer said to ignore it for now. Going to battle with him over his stupid allegations just makes things worse. Do what the Royals do, never complain, never explain. They've told me not to talk to anyone about it. You know how easily things can get twisted.'

'Brilliant plan,' says Lucy with a touch of sarcasm. 'But in the meantime, surely if you don't say something or stop his lies, he's just going to escalate it, make more wild claims. And mud sticks, William.'

'True enough, I guess. But the less I say, the less he can use against me. My lawyer says that, in time, he'll just come across as a man with an axe to grind. And once the press catches on to his obsession with Cat, the tide will turn.'

'Or maybe not. Depends how the press spins it. They'll do anything for a story — trust fund husband, missing wife . . . that alone is enough to feast on.'

'Fantastic. So glad you could drop by,' I reply, my tone heavy with irony.

'Always here to help. So, what have you found out? Anything new?'

'Something like that,' I murmur, rolling my eyes as I recount the madness of your secret life — and how frenzied the press would be if they ever got their hands on any of it.

CHAPTER 20

Royce

I get a call from Helen as soon as I'm back in the office.

'We got a ping from William's phone the night of October tenth, between seven and eight p.m. He was exactly where he said he was.'

'Really? I could've sworn he was lying.'

'I haven't finished. He was in the vicinity of the pub and the off-licence.'

'Vicinity? What does that mean? Can't you be more certain?'

'You know it's not an exact science, but he was definitely about. Can't say for sure if he was down the pub or at the offie, but he was in the area.'

'Well, that blows my theory out of the water. I could have sworn he was lying. Got anything else?'

'Yeah, after he left Turner Green, he popped over to Fairhurst Street for about half an hour. Had a look around the area — loads of private businesses there. You've got a private GP, massage parlours, nail salons . . . and, well, it's not exactly quiet when it comes to hookers, if you catch my drift.'

I'm taken aback. 'You think he was with a call girl? What if his wife found out? Maybe she got angry and threatened to expose him?'

'I knew you'd jump to that conclusion,' Helen says, waving it off like it's scandalous I'd think that. 'Why? He could've been at the private GP, for all you know.'

She's right. 'Guess that's just how my brain works.'

'Oh, you mean like how all men are stuck on one track, is that it?'

'Something like that.' I chuckle. 'Anything else?' So now we know he was where he said he was that night — not at the house — but he's not being honest about where he was all that time. Why?'

'After that, he went straight home, just like he said. Never left — well, not with his phone, anyway,' Helen adds. 'And the misper's phone doesn't have a tracker on it.'

'Okay, thanks. So, he's got an alibi for being late. Thanks, Helen. We just need to know where else he went. By the way, did you get my email about those bank card numbers? I was hoping you'd check on them.'

'Got it. We're already monitoring the accounts through the bank. Any activity, and we'll be alerted. We have the various names, married, maiden — and this other card that—'

'Just track all the cards I gave you.' Camilla is walking towards me but gets sidetracked by DC Glennon. 'Let me know the second you hear anything.' I hang up and shout, 'Camilla?'

'Boss?' She turns around. She has a coffee for me and sets it down in front of me on my desk. 'Thought you could use one.'

'I need you to visit a private GP clinic on Fairhurst Street — two streets away from the pub Smyth said he was at on October tenth. Seems like he went into the wider vicinity. See if he visited any of the doctors there. We might need a warrant, but at least try and confirm whether he was there. If that doesn't pan out, check out the businesses a few doors down. If that leads nowhere, check the rest of the businesses in the area.'

'Got it. I'll take Paul with me.'

Once she's gone, I close the door and call Helen back. 'Did you get that CCTV footage I requested from the bus and train stations?'

'Didn't see anyone who matched our misper.'

'For Chrissakes. How many times do I need to ask for this? I said to send it over to me. Can't anyone follow instructions around here? Send it over now.' She's only doing her job but still.

'Understood. Sending it over now,' she responds tersely.

'Fine, just hurry up. You know how Butterworth will be breathing down my neck.' I see the email pop up and hang up.

* * *

It's late — past midnight — and my eyes feel like sandpaper from looking at all the CCTV. I check my phone again, though I can't quite say what I'm expecting. Natalie hasn't replied. The silence feels strange —maybe pointed, maybe not — and I can't help wondering what it might mean. I hit pause. Part of me wonders if going home might make a difference, if there's anything I can do to fix this. But another part hesitates, unsure whether I'm chasing hope or running from the truth. The pile of CCTV footage is endless, and I think I might go blind trying to get through it all. I shake the empty packet of crisps, hoping for a stray crumb, and tell myself it's time to call it a night. Not that it matters much these days what time I get home — would she even notice? That argument still weighs on me, tangled in a haze of unanswered questions. How are we supposed to fix this when she won't talk? Or maybe she's waiting for me, again, to make the first move . . . but what if I've misunderstood everything. Then I change my mind and decide to give it another fifteen minutes.

I'm about to stop when I catch a glimpse of something. A figure rushing out of the gate of a nearby green space, heading straight for a car parked on a building site. *Got you.*

* * *

The next morning, I wake up to the soft buzz of my phone on the nightstand. The dim light sneaks in through the blinds as I blindly grab for my phone, my head still sunk into the pillow. I let out a breath, rubbing my face before rolling onto my back. The other side of the bed is empty. Nothing strange about that. She's always up early for her morning jog. Her shampoo still lingers faintly on the pillow.

I sit up and glance over at the bathroom, then the dresser. Her phone and watch are gone — she never runs without them. Maybe she'll surprise me and come home before I leave for work.

I think about sending her a quick text but change my mind. Sometimes she just needs her space. This probably isn't the morning for a chat. With any luck, this cold front between us will warm up soon. For now, though, I've got work to do. My finger hovers over a notification from Helen that just popped up on my screen.

I open the message — there's been activity on the cards. I spring out of bed. I don't waste a second, dialling her number as I roll the tension out of my shoulders before standing.

'Helen, what do you have on the bank cards?' I'm already moving towards the kitchen for a coffee where I see the corner of the granite countertop shattered.

'Good morning to you too, boss. We've got two hits — two different spots, nowhere near each other.'

'Where?' About time, the search is shifting to a positive direction at last.

'First one's for twenty-two pounds forty at a service station on the M6, probably food. The second, for sixty quid, is for petrol in St Helens about half an hour later.'

'Find that petrol station and get me the CCTV. Now.' We're getting closer.

'Will do, but, boss, there must have been a time lag or something — they're all coming through now from the last couple of days. A restaurant in St Helens. A B&B. A coffee at Nero. Tesco. A pub.'

'Great, now we're talking. I'll be in soon.' I hang up and run upstairs to get dressed. I focus on the petrol station — those might be our best leads. I shoot off a quick email to Helen.

Get the footage for the petrol stations. Prioritise those and send me the footage as soon as it comes through. Rush it. And keep this between us, Helen. There's no point alerting everyone to what's going on. I hit send, setting the phone down beside my coffee, and I jump in the shower. Whatever is on there, I want to be the first to see it.

I make it to the office and dive back into the CCTV footage from last night of the car the figure got into. Zooming in, I manage to catch the number plate. I'm on the phone before I even think twice.

'Helen, run this plate number for me. Don't share anything until you've got the info.'

'Got it. Oh, and we've had a few more pings — cash withdrawals in Manchester, one for a hundred quid, another for fifty in Didsbury.'

'Did you get the footage from last night's petrol station ping?'

'Still waiting on it.'

'Get on to them, will you? And from the hole in the wall in Manchester, too. Do we know how long the lag is?'

'A day or so max is my guess.'

That means she's been doing some weird driving. St Helens. Manchester. Didsbury. As I'm processing everything, Camilla sticks her head through the door. 'Boss, Helen said you had the CCTV. Want me to take a look at it with you?'

I'm about to say no when my phone rings. I pick up. 'Sid? Everything okay?' I shake my head at Camilla. She takes a pause before leaving my office.

'Surprise,' Sid says, 'I didn't think you'd pick up. Thought I'd catch you off guard and half expected it to go to voicemail.'

I chuckle because that had crossed my mind. If only I'd checked the caller ID before answering. 'Is everything okay?' I don't have time to go through, again, for the millionth time why my job takes priority. He just doesn't get it.

'Don't worry, we're not about to descend on you, panic not. Your short, sharp text was enough to put us off.'

I groan, realising how that would have come across.

'We're sorting out dates for going away in the summer school holidays next year and seeing as how Mel can't get any reply from Natalie, I thought I'd ring you. I know it's a way off but, well with kids you have to think ahead, and anyway, we wanted to check if you were both actually intending to come back down before then?'

Well, I'll look forward to an opportunity to talk to my wife about that. So, I'm not the only one she's ignoring.

'And, well, bro' why not take some time over Christmas, it'll do you both good to get out of the city. Make it happen, Royce, I'm forgetting what you look like.'

I frown; he's not wrong. 'Probably. Sounds like a good idea. I'll run it by Natalie. But you know the nature of my work and all that.' I can feel the disappointment coming through the phone. 'Listen, you sort yourselves out and if we can we'll fit in around you. And I'll speak to Natalie about Christmas and get back to you.'

* * *

I spend the rest of the day chasing down leads. Camilla had no luck with the private GP clinic — they won't release any information without a warrant. We did have better luck at Cat's doctor's office, though, where we obtained what we needed with a warrant. Turns out she's four weeks pregnant like William said. I think he thought maybe Jake had lied to hurt him. The reality his wife was pregnant by him too much to handle right now.

I pull up outside the marital home and find myself wondering why William's family thought it necessary to put everything into a trust. Maybe that's just what the wealthy do to protect their assets. If they divorced, Cat would certainly be entitled to a sizeable share, so maybe that's why. It looks like no one's home. I call his office having no response from his mobile and find out he's decided to go back in and forgotten to mention it to us. So I turn the car around and head over there.

His office is nothing short of plush — it screams money, the kind that has no problem flaunting it. The staff are all dressed to the nines. I look like I've just rolled out of bed compared to them, and I'm wearing one of my good suits. From the looks they give me, they want to make sure I know it.

'I'm here to see William Johnson-Smyth. He's expecting me. DCI Royce Benedick.'

The receptionist gives me a polite smile, clicks a few things on her computer, and then speaks into her headset. 'DCI Benedick is here. I'll let him know.'

She looks back at me. 'He'll be down in a moment. Please take a seat by the coffee machine. He won't be long.'

'I can go up to his office—'

'That won't be necessary. Mr Johnson-Smyth will be down shortly. Help yourself to a drink. There's a small fridge under the coffee machine with a selection.'

I take a bottle of water from the fridge and settle into a chair facing the bank of lifts. The lift doors slide open, and a flood of people pour out — all of them wearing serious expressions, scattering in every direction like ants. William is the last to step out. He scans the room briefly, then meets the receptionist's gaze, who gestures in my direction.

'Inspector, this is a surprise. Have you come to arrest me?' His face is tight.

'No, to ask you more questions.'

'More? What more can I tell you? I don't know any more.'

'There's always more, William. The thing is, I'm wondering why you would keep some information back from me.'

'I haven't. I told you everything I can remember. If you're going to try and intimidate me then you can talk to my lawyer. He's already told me not to speak with you.'

'Oh, really? Now why would you say something like that when all I'm trying to do is find your wife? It makes me question very seriously what I'm about to ask you next.'

Johnson-Smyth blinks, looks over his shoulder at the receptionist who isn't looking our way and sits down next to me. I look at his hands and see his fingers rubbing together. 'Look,' he says. 'I don't know what you're talking about.' He keeps his voice low. 'If I've forgotten something, then you can put it down to stress. I'm worried to death about Cat, you know I am, so why are you trying to make me out a liar?' His voice breaks.

I have three options to mention here: the GP, the office with all the businesses or the hookers. I have to choose. I look at him, see how nervous he is. A film of sweat forms on his top lip. 'Fairhurst Street.' He takes out his handkerchief to wipe his lip.

'What about it?'

'Do you know it?'

'Yes, of course I know it, it's not far from where I live. So what of it?'

'Were you there visiting the hookers?'

He pales. 'How dare you.'

'So is that a no?'

He eyes me suspiciously. 'I don't have to answer that.'

I let the silence stretch. 'I don't give a sod whether you were seeing hookers or anything else. I want to know why you lied to me. You were there for thirty minutes. That's a long time with a hooker, isn't it? And besides, I thought you were trying for a baby. Why would you go there? Did Cat know? Did she find out? Was she following you and caught you one day? Is that why she started having an affair?'

'You're disgusting. My lawyer told me I don't have to talk to you. If you want to continue this conversation, bring me to the station, and we'll speak with my lawyer present. You're sick, do you know that?'

'Just doing my job, William.' I let the silence drag out again. His face is shiny, and his fingers move faster. 'If you've nothing to hide then just tell me what you were doing there. Otherwise, I have no choice but to assume the worst. And you don't want me to do that, do you? Imagine' — I gesture towards the lavish office surroundings — 'what the press would do with a story like that. It wouldn't be good for your reputation, and it would cast a long shadow over you.'

William shoots to his feet, his fury flaring. 'Go ahead! And while you're at it, get out of here! Stop coming to my home. If you want to talk, we'll do it at the station with my lawyer. If you say anything to the press that could be construed as libel, I will sue you! I keep telling you. I didn't hurt my wife.' There's deep sorrow behind the words of a man pushed to the edge and burdened by secrets.

CHAPTER 21

Jill

I know how cunning you are, so I have to be careful. I won't be staying here much longer. After work, it's already time for lunch, and I'm drained. I take a long shower, scrubbing away the grime that feels like it's sunk into my skin. Exhausted, I collapse onto the bed, the weight of the day pulling me under.

I fall asleep, but it's not peaceful. I wake up from a nightmare, disoriented. You've found me, tracked me down somehow, bumping into Martha along the way. Another nightmare follows: Martha calling the information line for Cat Johnson-Smyth, suggesting I might be her. You rush over, grilling her before heading straight for me, banging on the door until it nearly comes off its hinges.

I glance out of the window, wiping a sheen of sweat from my chest with the duvet. The daylight is fading. I check my phone — it's only 4 p.m. Voices float up from the hallway. I strain to hear if any are familiar. I catch Amanda's voice but no one else. Then, heavy footsteps pass my door and stop. I wonder if she's had the same thought as Martha. I squeeze my eyes shut, knowing it isn't you, and breathe a sigh of relief when the footsteps move on.

Later, when I head downstairs for a walk to stretch my legs and grab a takeaway, Amanda calls me over. 'Jill, before you go, would you give me a wee moment?'

I turn and head back to her. She's sitting at her desk, talking on the landline, tapping a rhythmic beat of annoyance with her nails on her desk. I feel heat rise in my face. My mind races, searching for the reason for her irritation.

'Thanks for waiting. I don't want to keep you, lass.' She hangs up the phone, clearly agitated, and it's contagious. 'You off somewhere nice?'

'Me? Oh, not really,' I say, trying to sound casual. 'Just picking up a takeaway. Nothing exciting.'

She hesitates, then speaks again. 'I hate to bother you, but did you happen to notice a pendant I was wearing this morning? It was gold, on a long chain. Thing is, I've lost it. I'm such an idiot.'

I try to keep calm. 'No, I haven't seen it. I remember you wearing it, though. It was beautiful, really heavy. But no, I haven't seen it anywhere else. Did you take it off?'

'Aye I did. George, an old friend, came by for coffee. I mentioned feeling tightness in my shoulders, so he gave me a neck massage. He's got magic hands so he has. He does this for me regularly, such a dear. I always take the pendant off for that as it gets in the way otherwise.'

'Where did you put it?' I ask, uneasy.

'On my desk. In the wee Chinese box where I keep my stamps.' She gestures to the black-and-red lacquered box on the desk. 'He can't work on my neck with it on. I always put it there, so I ken exactly where it is.'

I glance around the desk, now cleared of the clutter from earlier. 'Do you think you might've accidentally swept it up with the rubbish?'

She smiles, but there's a faint edge to it. 'No, lass. I wouldn't have done that. It's too valuable. Belonged to my mother. My father gave it to her when they married. She told me it cost him a small fortune, and he worked for weeks to pay it off.'

'That's really sweet,' I say, though it sounds distant in my own ears. 'But sorry, I haven't seen it around.' My voice feels cold and detached. My heart races at the thought of the police getting involved. 'The last time I saw it, it was around your neck.'

This isn't something you predicted, did you? I hear you whispering in my ear with your hand wrapped around my hair. *If she doesn't find it, she'll have to call them to get a crime number to claim on the insurance. They'll ask awkward questions. Maybe want to see your ID. But the one you gave Amanda is the one you used to buy the cars. They'll be onto that name by now. If you run, she'll have to give them your details. When they type it into their computer it'll come up as a stolen identity. Then I will hear of it. Then I will come for you. Me and the cops after you. Together on your trail. Like bloodhounds. How far d'you think you'll get then, Jill Hart?*

She looks at me, her eyes narrowing slightly. 'I see,' she says slowly. 'Well, if it doesn't turn up, I might have to call the police, George says. To get a crime number to claim on the insurance.' My heart drums quickly. 'But I'd rather not have to deal with that. It was priceless to me. No amount of money can replace it. So, no point in claiming.' She shrugs, looking frustrated. 'I'm sure it'll turn up. I'm sure it's me forgetting where I put it. Don't fret about it, Jill. I just thought I'd ask on the off-chance.'

My heart pounds in my chest. If the police get involved . . . I try to steady my breathing, but the heat in my face intensifies. 'What if other things go missing?' I ask, barely able to keep the words in check. Does she think I'm a thief?

Amanda looks at me, her gaze calm but searching. There's no accusation in her eyes. 'I'm sure they won't. I'm pretty sure I've misplaced it. I'm just in a tizz about it now. I saw you and thought of asking, if you'd seen it by chance. Don't read anything else into it.'

My heart sinks that she thinks it's me. I can't shake the tension in my body that she might change her mind and call them. Then she surprises me and asks, 'Do you want to tell me something, Jill?'

I quickly shake my head. 'No,' I answer quickly. 'I was just thinking back, trying to remember if I saw anyone come in. But I was in the kitchen washing down the walls when Sarah came in looking for a screwdriver. She said Martha had pulled down the curtain rail or something in the dining room and was holding it up while she found one.'

'I see,' Amanda says, standing up and going to inspect the curtain pole. 'Looks fine to me. Martha did a good job.' She nods, satisfied.

I can't help but feel like she's missing the point, or maybe she just doesn't want to go there. I smile awkwardly and nod. Will she be asking them tomorrow or is it just me she's questioning? I wait for her to say more.

'What if it doesn't turn up? What then?'

Her eyes pause on me. A smile. I'm right — she thinks I took it. I feel the money belt around my waist, grateful I thought of bringing it with me. I have a powerful feeling she'll be in my room the moment I step outside. 'It will, I'm sure of it. I'll have put it down somewhere silly.'

I leave and head for the nearby takeaways, the weight of her words and the sense of unease still pressing down on me.

CHAPTER 22

Royce

I pull up outside Jake Stroud's house on Conduit Mews, a charming, cobbled street of rainbow painted mews houses. The ivy creeps up the primrose-yellow brickwork, and every house is immaculately maintained — one of the prettiest streets in London. I can't help but wonder what secrets lie hidden behind those pastel brick walls. The rain has let up today, slashes of blue intermittently visible with a promise of brightness on the way, possibly.

I'm not implying that Jake Stroud has anything to hide, but he's certainly kept a low profile since everything blew up. Then again, a visit from William Johnson-Smyth likely wasn't very enjoyable. Stroud's name's been plastered all over the tabloids too, thanks to his affair. I can only imagine the toll it's taken on his practice.

My boss isn't thrilled either. What should have remained low key has now spiralled into a spectacle of Schadenfreude on social media since we released her photo. The press is hounding Stroud, forcing him to seek an injunction to keep them away from his home and workplace.

I ring the bell, and after three attempts, I hear footsteps approaching. He looks like hell — unshaven, wearing pyjama bottoms and a T-shirt. From the smell, it's clear he hasn't showered in days.

'Inspector, nice to see you. Here with bad news?' There's a crack in his voice. A darkness hoods his eyes, masking the flicker of fear beneath the surface. The space around us seems to shrink.

I say nothing at first, letting the silence hang in the air like smoke. 'No, no news yet, Jake. Can I come in?' My words drop into the space between us like a heavy stone.

He steps aside, and I walk into the tidy, light hallway. It's bigger than I expected. He leads me to the kitchen, where he pulls out a pine chair from beneath a varnished pine table and gestures for me to sit.

'Drink? Tea? Coffee? I'd offer you something stronger, but I'm guessing you're on duty.'

'Tea will be fine, thanks.' Despite his dishevelled appearance, his house is surprisingly neat — clean surfaces, organised bookshelves, even the clutter of old papers stacked in neat piles. It's not what I'd expect, given the man standing in front of me. I can't help but comment. 'Looks like you're either good at housework or you've got someone cleaning for you.'

He raises an eyebrow, a sharp, almost defensive gesture, as he drops two teabags into mugs. 'What's that supposed to mean? You think I'd look like this if Cat were hiding out here?' His voice is light, but there's an edge to it, something about the way he words it that leaves a mark. The room is almost too perfect, the kind of place that looks lived in but never actually feels it.

I smile to myself, impressed by how quickly he picked up on my hint. 'You never know, Jake. You never know. I've seen it all.' I take the mug of tea from him, letting the warmth seep into my hands. The temperature has dropped outside quite a bit and there's snow in some parts of the north of the country.

His eyes flicker up at me, the briefest flash of annoyance before he looks away, but it's gone too quickly to be sure. 'You think you've seen it all?' His voice is light again, but there's something calculating in the way he watches me.

I raise an eyebrow, deciding not to bite back immediately. 'I've had my fair share of surprises,' I say, taking a sip of the tea. It's strong, just the way I like it, but the heat in the back of my throat from the tea is like the tension in the room, which is slowly building between us.

I set the mug down and look at him. 'We still don't have anything on her. The camera near her home was broken, so we've struck out there. All we have is her leaving the house and then nothing. We think there could have been somebody with her. We caught a trace of something but it's not enough for us to be certain it was a person. We've mentioned it to William, and he doesn't know of anyone that might have come to the house.'

'What about the brother?'

'Likewise, though he was a little skittish when we asked him. And now I'm asking you.'

His lips press into a tight line. He mutters, almost under his breath, 'Brilliant. No, it wasn't me.' He leans back against the counter, looking out of the window with a faraway gaze. 'This country's going to the dogs. What's the point of cameras everywhere if they don't work when you need them?'

I can't argue with that. It's hard to deny. The way things have been going lately, it's hard to shake the feeling that nothing's working anymore. But there's no time to dwell on it.

'Just unfortunate,' I say. It feels empty, even as the words leave my mouth.

'Unfortunate, is it?' He doesn't bother to hide the bitterness creeping into his voice. He turns sharply towards me, his tone rising now, the edges of frustration starting to show. 'And none of the hundreds of spy cameras around caught a glimpse of her? Not one?' His hands gesture vaguely. He shakes his head, incredulous, his voice heavy with disbelief. 'Unbelievable. Totally unbelievable how she's just vanished.'

I don't respond right away. I sip my tea, letting the silence settle around us. He's right — it is unbelievable. But I'm not about to say it out loud or what's bothering me about this whole thing.

I let the words linger in the silence. The mug of tea feels suddenly too hot in my hand, the steam rising in the quiet kitchen. Jake's shoulders tense, his gaze shifting for just a fraction of a second, but it's enough for me to notice.

'What do you think happened to her?' I ask, the question coming out sharper than I intended. 'You keep saying you don't know, but honestly, she was pregnant with your baby and leaves you? That seems odd.'

His eyes dart to meet mine, a glimpse of something — anger, disbelief, maybe, both pass fleetingly across them. He takes a step back, his posture going rigid, as if the space between us is suddenly too close. The quiet hum of the house fills the silence. I hear a washing machine at work somewhere close, changing cycle.

For a moment, he doesn't speak. Then, in a voice that's almost too calm, he says, 'I don't know what happened to her. You think I'm some kind of expert on women running off?' His laugh is hollow, a dry sound that doesn't reach his eyes. 'She just . . . disappeared. One day, she was here planning a life with me, and the next — nothing.' He turns away, pacing towards the window, his back to me. I watch him closely, the tension in his shoulders telling me more than he's willing to admit. I just don't know whether that's a good thing or not. 'It doesn't make sense,' he presses, his voice lower now, more insistent. 'You don't just vanish like that — pregnant, in a relationship, and just . . . walk away.' It feels like there's more behind his words than their utterance.

'She had lots of money,' I say. 'Money she'd made herself on the quiet that nobody knew about. Her brother suggested she thought if she ever left William, she'd get nothing. She was planning a nest-egg. Maybe she thought this was the time and wanted to be alone.' I sip my tea waiting to see if he'll comment. 'Is there something you're not telling me, Jake?'

He doesn't turn around, but I can see his jaw tighten from his side profile. He takes a deep breath, like he's preparing to say something he doesn't want to. 'We were going to leave together,' he says quietly, almost to himself. 'But perhaps she had reasons why she went alone. Maybe I'm not the one to tell you what they are. She told me stuff about William like she told Jason, but then nobody else knew about that. What if he threatened her and the baby, even me? What if he did know about us? And she ran to keep us all safe? Have you thought of that? He could be lying to all of us.'

I don't reply immediately. Something about his tone of voice, the way he avoids meeting my gaze, makes me question whether he's hiding more, or if he really doesn't know and is grieving for the life he's lost and his child. 'You're not giving me much to work with here,' I say finally, frustration slipping through my words. 'We are looking into William very closely. We just don't have anything on him apart from one email suggesting he'd kill her after an altercation they had. But his lawyers could get that thrown out of court.'

'Why? Surely—'

'We need more. It's not enough. I've already told Jason the same. I was hoping you'd have something you might have remembered. And why give money to a women's refuge. So much money and not tell anyone? Jason says he doesn't know anything about it.'

'You believe him? They're close you know. I know she was worried about him.'

'I don't believe anyone right now.'

'I'm giving you everything I have,' he responds, voice tight. 'Look,' he continues, his voice softer now, 'I don't know where she went or why. But I know she didn't just leave because of me. She . . . had to have her reasons. And I wish I could figure it out.'

Convinced the man across from me knows more than he's letting on, I put down my empty mug, then stop, my hand frozen in mid-air. Something about his earlier words linger in my mind.

'You said that maybe she had her reasons why she left alone and that you're not the one to tell me what they are?' I repeat, narrowing my eyes.

Jake, standing across from me, shifts uncomfortably. His hands grip the edges of the worktop. He knows I'm onto something.

He takes a breath but doesn't respond right away. I wait, sensing the opening I've been looking for.

'Go on,' I urge, leaning forward slightly, lowering my voice. 'What's stopping you from telling me what happened? You seem to know a lot about her reasons, and I know you still haven't told me everything. What is it you're withholding?'

He shifts again, the muscle in his jaw tightening. Then, after what feels like an eternity, he speaks. 'She wasn't running from anyone, Inspector,' Jake says, his voice careful now. 'She wasn't running from me, either.' He glances up, catching my eye. 'She was running to . . . someone.' His words hit like a cold, unsettling gust of wind.

I tilt my head, my heart beginning to race. There's something in his tone now, something subtle that suggests he's trying to make me believe *I'm* the one who's looking in the wrong place. 'What are you talking about?' I demand, my frustration starting to show.

Jake interrupts me, his voice taking on an almost grim quality. 'She wasn't having my child, Inspector.'

The words suspend there for a long moment, as if the room itself has frozen. I blink. 'What?'

'Cat was pregnant with William's child,' he says, his voice laced with a hint of bitterness. 'Not mine.' He opens a drawer and pulls out a letter. 'I found this in the bedside table yesterday. I think she wrote it for herself. I'm sorry I kept it from you . . . I was in shock. I'm still in shock. She was going back to him. I was going to tell you.'

The room falls silent. 'You mean . . . the IVF worked? Then why not tell William?'

Jake doesn't flinch. 'Read it yourself,' he replies, his voice flat and resigned. 'She was shocked it was William's baby. She'd stopped going for IVF because it had been so difficult for them to get pregnant, she never thought it would actually happen. She didn't tell William though. She was scared. She didn't give me a chance to prove to her that I was okay with it — that we could get through it together. It's all there in the letter. She was struggling, trying not to hurt William.'

I stare at him, incredulous. 'What would you really have done? Pregnant with William's child? That's a big ask.'

'Nothing but support her. I loved her,' Jake says quietly. 'She never gave me a chance to show her that.'

'How could she be so sure? I mean, she was sleeping with both of you, right?'

'The dates,' Jake explains, his gaze steady. 'I was away abroad at a conference when she got pregnant. She worked it out on her own. She didn't know how to tell William.'

Maybe the reason Cat left wasn't because she wanted to be with her lover, but because she feared William might take the child from her once he found out about the affair. 'You said it was your child,' I say, a new realisation dawning. 'You withheld information from the police. This changes everything.'

'It's what I believed at the time. Like I said, I only just found the letter yesterday.'

'Just one thing. You said you loved Cat in the past tense.'

He looks shocked. 'Figure of speech, that's all, Inspector.'

As I leave, I say one more thing. 'Oh, and stop going on social media or forums discussing the case. You're not helping.'

As I get into the car and drive away, I pass a supermarket and think about a meal tonight and wonder if I'll be dining alone again.

CHAPTER 23

Jill

After breakfast the next day, it is six days that I've been running and they've flown by. I don't need to be a genius to realise that the gossip has started. The air feels thick with it. As soon as the cleaning team arrives, I sense it — the subtle shift in their behaviour. Sarah's and Martha's eyes avoid mine, their glances sharp and wary. There's an edge to their movements that wasn't there before. They don't say anything, but it's in the way they move around me, a cold distance that wasn't there yesterday.

I don't want to talk about it. I don't want to acknowledge it. But I know that the moment I open my mouth, it becomes real. I'm already a target.

Today's task is miserable. I'm assigned to empty every cupboard, wipe it down, and restock it — simple, thankless work that's starting to feel like a punishment. My knees burn with the strain, the ache creeping up my legs. It's mind-numbing, but it's the only thing I can focus on, the only thing distracting me from the pressure building in my chest.

The kitchen feels different today. The staff all give me a wide berth, the silence heavy between us. Clive, who used to banter with me and make me toast or offer a cup of milky coffee during breaks, doesn't even glance my way. It's as if he's trying to pretend

I'm not even here. The kitchen porter — silent, ever-present — moves around me, going about his work, but he's no comfort. His indifference feels colder now.

And then there's Martha. She's acting strange. She keeps looking at me out of the corner of her eye, her expression unreadable. Every time our paths cross, she shifts away, as if I'm somehow toxic. It's subtle, but it's there — something simmering underneath. The way she glances at me, like she's trying to figure out if I'm guilty. I can feel the judgement in the air.

Finally, when the kitchen clears, Sarah slips in. She looks over her shoulder, making sure Martha isn't close, and then steps closer to me. She doesn't meet my eyes at first, but when she does, there's something fragile about her expression.

'You know everyone's talking about Amanda's pendant going missing,' she says, her voice barely above a whisper.

'I know,' I say, my voice tight, every word scraped out with effort. I don't want to talk about it, but I know I have no choice. It's already all anyone can talk about.

She chews her nail nervously, her gaze going from side to side. 'They say it was you.'

The words land like a punch. I try to keep my face neutral, but inside, I'm reeling. The accusation is sudden, raw, and it cuts deep. I can feel my chest tightening, a cold sweat breaking out across my skin. I keep wiping down the cupboards, the motion mechanical, trying to bury the panic rising in my chest.

'I know,' I mutter again, not sure if it's resignation or deflection. It doesn't even sound like me anymore.

'Is that all you've got to say? *I know?*' Sarah presses, her voice tense. She takes a step closer, eyes searching my face, desperate for a response.

I drop the cloth into the water with a sharp slap. The liquid splashes over the counter, a small mess that matches my chaotic mind. My heart thuds in my chest. 'What do you want me to say?' I shoot back, unable to keep the edge out of my voice. 'Are you going to believe me if I say I didn't take it?'

She hesitates. It's like she's weighing her next words, not sure if she's crossing a line. 'If you didn't, then why not just say that?'

I laugh, but it's bitter, harsh. 'Because it doesn't matter,' I hiss. 'I'm the new one here. The one who doesn't belong. This kind of thing never happens, not here, and now the obvious scapegoat is me.'

Her eyes widen, and for a moment, I can see the guilt flash across her face. She's not as sure as she was before, but she's still afraid. 'You need to stand up for yourself, though. What if she calls the police?'

My breath catches in my throat. The words hit me like a knife. *The police.* My heart races. The thought of them coming, investigating — turning my life upside down — makes me dizzy with fear. If Amanda calls them, I'm screwed. But maybe not. If I can get out before they get here — if I can stay ahead of them . . .

Sarah's face softens, but it doesn't comfort me. 'She loved that pendant,' she says quietly. 'You ken that, aye?'

'I know!' I snap, the anger bubbling up before I can stop it. 'I *know!*'

Sarah chews her nail some more, looking more nervous than ever. 'Martha — she really thinks you're that woman from the paper. She wants to call the police. She's convinced you're the one they're looking for. I keep telling her she's wrong, but she won't listen. All she can see is the reward money.'

The idea of Martha calling the police, of her thinking I'm the woman from the paper, sends a chill through my bones. It's absurd. Completely ridiculous for her to see that is a possibility.

We look nothing alike.

At least, that's what I tell myself after changing the colour of my hair.

But then I think of the photo they used. Grainy, low quality. The kind of picture that could warp details, blur edges. Her hair is lighter than mine — but lighting can do strange things. And people see what they expect to see.

A face that seems familiar, features that line up just enough — that's all it takes for someone to be sure they recognise you.

Martha is sure. And that alone makes her dangerous.

If she calls, it'll be a disaster. They'll show up, they'll want to see my ID, and then they'll know it's not me. You'll know it's not me. But Martha — she's too blinded by the reward money.

CHAPTER 24

Royce

My mind ablaze from what I've just learned, I pull out of Conduit Mews and drive, trying to get out of the traffic building up. I see the notifications on my phone from my Ring doorbell of someone walking down the side of the house. I hit traffic. Great. I need to get home. The way Natalie is shutting me out is seriously getting under my skin. I take a right then a left, cutting through the back streets then shooting down a one-way street and back onto the main arterial road that will take me home. My workload is already overwhelming, and the last thing I want is my private life dominating my thoughts any more than it already does. Natalie, Sid and the damned holiday requests for Christmas and next year. Je-sus, who thinks that far ahead? I've got enough pressure going on. I send a quick text via Siri.

> *On my way home. I'll be home in twenty minutes. We need to talk.*

I hit send, too impatient to wait for Siri to read it back to me. A whoosh tells me it's gone. Ironically, I get a text from Carole, Natalie's friend, and ask Siri to read it.

Hey, Royce, thinking of doing a surprise party for Natalie, you know how she said she wanted no fuss for her thirtieth? Well, the girls have decided to ignore that. Can you make sure she's around for the twelfth of next month. It's the day after but it's easier on a weekend. Xx

I reflect how damned work has swallowed me whole of late — and I've let it. I can't believe I've forgotten her birthday. I should have made more time for the important things in life — like my wife! I slam the steering wheel with my palm. Well there's no time like the present. We *will* sit down and talk. And listen to each other. Truly listen. Sort everything out. And put the world to rights when we are about it.

My grip tightens on the steering wheel when a sharp thought hits me — what if she's at home, right now, making some kind of decision? The idea feels both uncomfortable and tangible, and it won't stop gnawing at the edges of my mind.

'Come on!' I snap at the driver ahead, who's just waved another line of cars through like we have all the time in the world.

The moment I see the house my heart hammers. I climb out.

My hand hesitates on the door, caught between the weight of what might await inside and the resolve I'll need to face it. Whatever comes next, I'll take it. Whatever I have to set aside, I'll swallow it — if that's what it takes. I push open the door and step inside.

The house is silent.

Of course it is. That's how it's been for days now. Not a slammed door, not a raised voice — just this unbearable quiet, thick enough to choke on.

I step inside, shutting the door behind me. I listen for movement upstairs. Nothing. Maybe you're in the bedroom. Maybe you're ignoring me all over again.

I call your name, but it sounds strange in the stillness.

I take a breath, force my shoulders down. I won't let this turn into another fight before we've even spoken.

In the kitchen, the mug I left in the sink this morning is still there. A faint coffee ring on the counter beside it. A knife, half out of the block, like it was grabbed in a hurry.

Signs of her presence, everywhere. But no sign of *her*.

I check my phone. Nothing from you. Again.

Upstairs, the wardrobe door is shut, but a dresser drawer is open, a sweater draped over the edge. Maybe you got changed and went for a walk. Maybe you just needed space.

Maybe I should give you that.

I swallow hard, my throat dry. 'Natalie?' I say again, quieter this time.

I half expect a reply. I don't get one.

But I tell myself that doesn't mean anything.

I think of the Ring doorbell going off, the faint echo of it still lingering in my mind.

CHAPTER 25

Jill

'So, what are you thinking?'

I'm nearly done when Martha appears beside me. I jump, and she smirks like she knows something I don't.

'Jesus, you scared the life out of me. You can't just sneak up like that.'

'Aye, maybe you're right.' Her tone's too casual. 'Worried about something?'

'Just wondering what everyone thinks of me,' I say, keeping my voice even.

She leans in, her grin sharpening. 'Aye, I'd be worried too — with all those eyes on you.'

I focus on the sink, pouring out dirty water, shelving supplies. Anything to stay calm. Martha picks up a jar, sniffs it, grinning.

'You ken, I went to the police.'

Heat floods through me.

'So you still think I'm the woman in the photo. What did they say?'

She tilts her head, letting the silence fill the space between us. 'What do you think?'

'They're on their way, right?' I counter, doubt worrying at me. What if I'm wrong?

'Maybe.' Her smile is airy, her gaze razor-sharp. 'Strange, though. Amanda's pendant is missing. And you're the new face in town.'

'Plenty of strangers pass through here. Ever thought of that?' My voice is tight.

'They were all out that day,' she says, eyes glinting.

'Still. Someone could've slipped in.'

'Who'd risk that?'

'You're quick to point at me. Why's that, Martha? What bothers you so much?'

She smirks. 'Amanda's kind, letting you stay here for free. We don't like seeing her taken advantage of.'

I stiffen. 'That's none of your business.'

'Oh, it is,' she says. 'Amanda loves strays. None of them stole from her before.'

Her words scrape under my skin. I keep quiet, but she presses on.

'You're secretive. Saw you looking at that missing person story the other day.'

I slam the cupboard shut. 'Why don't you leave me alone?'

She steps closer, voice dropping. 'Why did that story rattle you? Tell me, and maybe I'll tell you if I really went to the police.'

Her smile needles at me. I scrub my hands at the sink like I can rinse her off.

Martha says lightly, '*You* know that woman in the paper, don't you? If you ask me, I'd go as far as to say you know something about what's happened to her.'

I glance over my shoulder, my expression cold. 'So now you've jumped from the woman in the newspaper being me to claiming I know something about what happened to her? That's quite a leap.'

She shrugs again, her grin widening. 'Is it, though? People tend to talk when they're guilty. I heard that in a film once.'

I stiffen, gripping the edge of the sink to stop myself from snapping back. 'Are you just trying to stir up trouble for everyone, or is this your idea of fun?' Her smile doesn't waver, but her eyes glint with something sharper, more dangerous. 'Or maybe both.'

'Everyone? No,' she says, her voice calm but cutting. 'I'm not trying to cause trouble for anyone — anyone who hasn't done something wrong.'

I grab a sheet of kitchen roll, drying my hands slowly to keep them from trembling. Then, I walk to the door. 'But you are,' I say, keeping my tone even, 'and you will be if the police come here looking for a thief. That's going to cause problems for Amanda. People will think the staff are stealing, and they won't want to stay here, feeling uneasy about it. So, yes — you are, and you will be.'

She laughs, the sound grating and smug. 'No, you're wrong. I'm not talking about that. I'm talking about telling the cops you know this woman or you are this woman — and, let's face it, you are kind of shady.' She saunters up to me just as I reach for the door, her steps slow and deliberate. 'I bet when they come, they'll find out you're up to something. Or maybe—' she leans in, her voice dropping — 'you're not who you say you are? And that reward? Very tempting.'

Get out. Now.

I pull open the door, but before I can step through, she's already there, slipping outside and cutting me off. Her movement is quick, unhurried. I freeze. My heart pounds. Is she blocking me because she knows something? Because the police *are* already on their way?

This is it — the net she's been weaving, cast wide and waiting to tighten.

She leans in closer, her breath brushing my cheek. Her proximity makes my stomach churn, her smugness pressing in on me like a weight. Being this close to someone sets my nerves on edge.

I think of you and how things used to be — lines crossed, tensions rising, waiting for someone to break.

'Don't rush off,' she whispers, her voice dripping with mock concern. 'Let's talk some more.'

It hits me like a blow. The police *are* coming. I can feel it now in her tone, her confidence, the way she blocks the exit like she owns it.

I don't think. I just move.

I shove her out of my way, harder than I intended, and stride towards the stairs, my steps fast but controlled. Don't run. Don't panic. Not yet.

Upstairs, I move quickly, shoving things into my bag with shaking hands. A nauseousness comes over me I can't control. I rush to the loo and vomit. Feeling my money belt for security. My mind races as I double-check I've left no trace; then I'm out the door again, heading downstairs with measured strides.

Once I'm outside, the air is cool and sharp. I don't stop to think. I just keep walking.

CHAPTER 26

William

I've gone into the office today. I worked from home for the last two days after the police collared me even there, but being at home since you disappeared is unbearable. My boss keeps telling me to stay at home; they don't realise how difficult that is for me. Even if I can feel their eyes on me — colleagues stealing glances, whispered conversations that halt when I walk by. The lift ride to the eighth floor feels longer than usual, each floor ticking by like a countdown.

Not long after I sit at my desk, the phone rings. My stomach knots when I see the name on the screen: Pete Drummond, the powerhouse of Burkes & Hardwick. My boss.

'William, do you have a moment?'

'Sure,' I say, trying to sound steady. 'Do you want me to come to your office?'

'If you could.'

I hang up, already sensing this won't be good. They've been the ones pushing me to stay working from home, saying it would help me. I told them it wasn't the right move, that I need to come in to be around people, not cooped up at home.

I knock on his door, a grand glass-walled office perched high above the city like some modern throne room.

'William, come in. Take a seat.'

The chair I sink into is impossibly soft, buttery brown leather that feels almost too indulgent given the circumstances.

'Is something wrong?' I ask, unable to mask the apprehension in my voice.

'Wrong? No, not with your work.' He leans back, studying me with that unreadable corporate smile. 'I know you've been working from home, taking time for yourself. How's that been for you? I heard you came in a couple of days ago.'

'It's . . . fine. Coming in helps keep my mind from unravelling.'

'That's good. That's excellent,' he says, but his tone is clipped, transactional. 'So, we — by we, I mean the board — have been discussing whether it might be best for you to continue working remotely.'

His words land hard. My idea in the first place, dismissed back then, is now suddenly their solution. I stare at him, trying to process.

'You don't look pleased,' he says, misreading or ignoring my shock. 'I know I asked you to come back in when you felt up to it, but here's the thing. The board is concerned. You're in the news, and by extension, so are we. Being linked to the disappearance of your wife . . . well, it doesn't reflect well on the firm. I heard the police were in to see you a couple of days ago.' He pauses as if expecting me to agree. 'I trust you understand where I'm coming from.'

'I do,' I say slowly, my throat tight. 'Which is why I suggested working from home to begin with.' That was before the press got involved.

'Yes, yes.' He sighs, brushing that off with a wave of his hand. 'But now, there's . . . this fresh information. You know, the rumours about . . . well, about you hitting your wife.'

Something shifts deep in my core.

'Are you firing me?'

'Good Lord, no!' He looks almost offended by the suggestion. 'You're one of our best brokers, William. We don't believe the rumours. But we do have to be careful. You understand that, don't you? It's about perception. We want you to know we're behind you, but we can't have you on the premises right now. Just keep your head down, work from home, avoid interviews or statements — anything that might bring attention back to us. You see where I'm coming from?'

I nod, though his assurances ring hollow.

'Good,' he says, flashing a grin that doesn't reach his eyes. 'We're counting on you to be discreet.'

'I'd prefer it that way,' I reply stiffly. 'I have no intention of speaking to the press.'

He nods, visibly relieved, and with that, I'm dismissed.

I leave his office, my jaw tight with anger. His words of support were nothing more than a corporate formality, empty and rehearsed. Of course they're not standing by me — they're protecting their image, as they should. Why would they risk their reputation for someone like me?

* * *

I slip back home through the narrow passageway down the side of the house, pressure builds against my ribs. The press — now only three or four diehards — remain stationed out front, but they haven't noticed this little escape route.

My phone rings. It's Mum. Christ, you'd think she was telepathic.

'Hi, Mum.'

'William, at last. How's it going. Is the reward helping?'

'Sorry, I know you didn't want this to blow up in the press and I was trying to handle it on my own. But no. Nothing yet.'

'Bit late now don't you think, worrying about the family name? I'm using the old papers in the litter tray. It was disconcerting having Cat's face under Bernard's arse.' Bernard being the cat, a fat black and white that one day just arrived and never left. 'Sorry, darling, that was insensitive.' I laugh, despite the inappropriateness. She doesn't really mean it — she's trying to cheer me up. 'Why not come here to Bristol? I told Lucy to tell you to come.'

'She did, but I can't. I need to be here in case Cat comes home.'

She sighs. 'Well, I suppose, but maybe for a day or so to recharge.'

'Thanks, but I'll be okay.'

She senses I'm about to hang up. 'Quickly, darling, will you call your father? He's very worried. He knows you're bottling all this up on your own. He won't make the call because you've not responded to his.'

'Okay, okay, yes, fine. I will. Have to go now, Mum.' I terminate the call and fetch myself a glass of water. What unsettles me most about all of this: the accusations you've whispered into Jason's ear. You told him I was violent towards you. Him, of all people. Not Joanne, not Elaine your closest friends. If it were true, wouldn't you have confided in them? But they've reached out with nothing but warmth and sympathy, completely unaware of your claim. It's sickening, really, this game you seem to be playing. Testing the waters, perhaps? But testing for what? I can't figure it out, and the not knowing is driving me mad.

Lucy calls out from the lounge as I step inside. 'Hey, that was a short day.'

'Yeah. They told me to work from home.' I toss my bag down by the door. 'Apparently, I'm bad for the company image.

'Right . . . well, at least you still have a job.'

'Oh, for now.' I force a smile, trying to change the subject. I glance around the room. She's made herself at home, as usual, with her mess spilling out of every corner. 'I see you've been settling in nicely.' She smirks cheekily. 'Just had Mum on asking if the reward has brought anyone forward.'

'Still nothing I take it?' I shake my head. Only the cranks and losers trying it on. 'Well, that police inspector came by earlier. Wanted to talk to you. Listen, don't hate me here, but he said something that got me thinking and I was asking myself the question why she would go all silent on you like this. Have you considered that she might be pregnant with Jake's baby?'

The words hit me like a splash of ice water. I don't look at her. I make my way to the sofa, but not before pouring myself a generous scotch and drink it in one. 'What?'

'You okay?' I keep my eyes averted and pour another before sitting down. 'I know it sounds terrible, but it might be why she's vanished. She can't face you. Something like that. Haven't you even considered it?'

'Yes. But we both have problems in that department.'

'Yes, I know, and together they're multiplied. But with Jake . . . maybe they're not problems.'

I take a long time replying. 'That never occurred to me. No.' I give her a small smile and look away. I don't want to talk about it.

'Well, look, I'm probably barking up the wrong tree, you know. Forget it. It was only something I thought of. Brought on by something the inspector said that I can't quite recall. She probably wasn't. Sorry, Will.'

I really don't want to talk about it.

'What did the police want?' I ask.

'Didn't say. Just that he'd call back.' She eyes the glass in my hand like she can't look at me. 'You're drinking a lot these days by the way.'

'I know. And?'

'Nothing.' She puts down the book she was reading, her gaze shadowed with concern. 'Just saying.'

'Well, don't.' I take a long sip. 'So, did the inspector have any news?'

'Not really. But Jason came by too. God, he's so weird.'

My fingers tighten around the glass. 'Jason? What the hell does he want now?'

She shrugs. 'He kept asking if the police had told you anything that they hadn't told him. Then he accused me of lying. Said I was keeping things from him.' She hesitates, biting her lip. 'There was a bit of a scene at the front door. The photographers caught it. Sorry, I forgot they were out there.'

I sink back against the cushions, the scotch burning down my throat. 'Fantastic. Another delightful headline tomorrow.'

She frowns, her tone softening. 'It's strange, though, isn't it? That the police haven't found anything? Not a trace of her. You'd think with all the cameras around, one of them would've picked her up.'

'That's what I thought at first.' I run a hand through my hair, my voice dropping. 'But what if someone picked her up knowing exactly which cameras wouldn't catch them? The broken ones. It's not impossible.'

Lucy looks sceptical. 'That's a hell of a gamble. What if the camera had been fixed?'

'It's just a theory.' I glance towards the window, my mind spinning. 'There are so many theories running through my head, none of them good. Do you think we should mention Jason's visit to the inspector, I mean him asking if we'd been told something he hadn't? I think that's odd. He's fucking odd.' I get up, pour another drink and sit down. 'Don't even say it, Lucy. Just don't.'

She hesitates, her brow creasing. 'Maybe. I don't know . . . There is something about Jason, William, you're right. Something more than just weird. I feel uncomfortable around him.'

'What do you mean?' I lean forward. 'Tell me what you're thinking.'

She folds her arms, her voice dropping to a near whisper. 'It's a hunch. Like . . . he said Cat told him you hit her. But why just him? Why not Joanne? Or Elaine? Girls confide in their friends, especially about things like that. But Cat didn't. Doesn't that strike you as strange?'

I scowl, the pieces refusing to fit together. 'She told the same story to Jake Stroud.'

'Yes, but still not her friends.' Lucy's voice trembles slightly. 'That's what's odd. It's almost like . . .'

'Like what?'

A sharp knock at the door cuts her off. We both freeze, our eyes snapping towards the sound. For a moment, neither of us moves.

'Like what, Lucy?'

Another knock.

'Like she was testing him, you know, to see his reaction. I know. I know that sounds weird. But not to mention it to anyone else — something was going on there. I feel it.'

A louder knock.

'Who the hell is that?' I mutter, setting my glass down. My pulse quickens, the silence of the room now deafening. 'Who the fuck knows with them two. All I know is he's odd. Really sodding odd.'

Lucy doesn't answer. She's staring at the door, her face pale.

CHAPTER 27

Royce

I knock again, sharper this time. The sound echoes in the stillness, and after a moment, the door swings open. William stands there, his face tight, jaw clenched. He looks tired, like he hasn't slept in days, and there's anger simmering just beneath the surface. I can't blame him, not after our last conversation.

'Inspector.' His voice is clipped, barely polite.

'Can I come in?' I ask, keeping my tone steady. His eyes narrow as he weighs the question, his fingers gripping the edge of the door.

'I spoke to your sister earlier,' I add, trying to push the moment forward. 'I said I'd come back to speak with you.'

A beat of silence, and then: 'I guess you'll have to, won't you?' He glances past me, scanning the driveway. 'My brother-in-law not with you?'

'No,' I reply evenly, stepping forward slightly. 'But I'll be speaking with him soon. I wanted to see you first.'

His lips press into a thin line, his posture stiffening. 'Are we doing this again, Inspector? Baiting one against the other? If you've come for another slanging match, then I'll call my lawyer. You remember him, don't you? The one who told me not to speak with you unless it was at the station and in his presence.'

'You won't need him for this.'

His laugh is low and bitter. 'That's easy for you to say—'

'It's about your wife.' My words cut through his protest, and I watch as the colour drains from his face. For a moment, he sways, as if the floor beneath him has shifted. He steadies himself with a hand on the doorframe but doesn't speak.

'May I come in?' I ask again, softer this time.

He hesitates, then steps aside without a word. As I enter, I catch sight of his sister emerging from the lounge. Lucy's eyes dart between us, her expression tight with worry. She smells faintly of lavender, fresh and clean, as though she's just stepped out of the shower. She stands close to her brother, her presence a quiet but steadying force.

'What's this about?' William finally asks, his voice rough, as he closes the door behind me.

I glance at Lucy, who folds her arms protectively across her chest, then back to William.

'It's about your wife,' I repeat, more carefully this time. 'We've received new information.'

William stares at me, his eyes dark and unblinking. He looks like a man teetering on the edge of something — a man who isn't sure whether to lash out or crumble.

'What kind of information?' His words are barely above a whisper.

I glance at Lucy again, her concern etched deeply into her face. She reaches out, lightly touching her brother's arm, but he doesn't react.

'I think we should sit down,' I say finally, my tone gentler than before.

William doesn't move at first, just keeps staring at me with that haunted expression. Then, almost mechanically, he nods and gestures towards the lounge.

Lucy follows, her steps hesitant, her gaze flicking between me and her brother. The air almost crackles with the unspoken fears between us.

As we settle into the living room, I take a deep breath. 'What I'm about to say may be difficult to hear,' I begin, my eyes fixed on William. 'But it's important that you listen carefully.'

His jaw tightens, and I see his hands clench into fists on his lap. Lucy sits beside him, her hand resting lightly on his arm, her worry now unmistakable.

This wasn't how I thought it would go. I was so sure of this one. But now, I can feel it — the ground beneath us shifting, the story unravelling in ways I didn't anticipate.

CHAPTER 28

William

The inspector's words hit me like a hammer. 'Your wife's body has been found.'

I can't move. For a moment, I forget to breathe, my brain refusing to process the sentence. It reverberates in my head, over and over. Found. Body. Cat.

Behind me, I hear Lucy gasp. Her hand tightens on my arm, but I barely feel it. My throat is dry, and the room feels too small, the walls closing in around me.

'Where?' My voice comes out hoarse, unrecognisable.

The inspector hesitates. He doesn't meet my eyes immediately, which only makes the knot in my stomach tighten. Finally, he says, 'Her body was discovered in a car parked on an industrial estate on the outskirts of town. It appears she fought off her attacker — there are clear signs of a struggle. This is officially a murder investigation now, and I trust you understand the gravity of what that entails.'

I sink back into the sofa, the words washing over me, each one heavier than the last. She fought off her attacker. Signs of a struggle. My Cat — alive and fighting. The thought is unbearable.

The inspector continues, his tone measured but grim. 'We're running DNA tests now, to see if we can identify anyone who might have been involved. But I'll be honest with you — this wasn't random.'

His eyes pierce through me, and I feel the weight of his gaze, the unspoken accusation. I swallow hard, but my voice cracks when I speak. 'What do you mean by that?'

He leans forward, his elbows resting on his knees, his tone carefully neutral. 'Given the circumstances . . . it's likely she knew her attacker. We will need to take a DNA swab from you and Jason.'

I flinch, my mind racing. 'You think it was me, don't you?' The words are out before I can stop them, raw and defensive.

The inspector doesn't answer immediately. Instead, he studies me, as though weighing every twitch, every breath. 'I'm not saying that,' he replies, though his tone is anything but reassuring. 'But we have to consider every possibility. I need you to be honest with me, William. About everything. The night Cat disappeared we know you went to Fairhurst Street after you'd been to Turner Green. We need to know what you did there.'

I shake my head, look at my sister. 'It's private, nothing to do with this.'

'Everything has to do with this, William.'

I look at Lucy. 'I'm sorry, Lucy, I have to tell him.'

'Tell him what?'

'I was at the private GP practice with Mum. She found a lump and had a scan. She went to get the results and didn't want to go alone.'

'Oh, God, does Dad know? Is she okay?' She grips my hand and the colour has left her face.

'They've suggested doing a biopsy. She was going to tell him. I think with Cat disappearing she hasn't done it yet.' The inspector looks at me.

'Thank you,' he says. 'And I'm sorry to hear that, truly. You'll appreciate that we will need to corroborate this. It will be quicker if your mum could give the doctor permission to speak with us. We don't need any personal details, we just need to satisfy ourselves that you were there with her as you said.'

I shake my head, anger and disbelief bubbling up inside me. 'You think I'd hurt her? That I'd—' My voice falters, breaking under the weight of it all.

'William . . .' Lucy's voice is soft, hesitant, as though she's afraid I might shatter. She squeezes my arm again, but I can't look at her.

I bury my face in my hands, trying to gather my thoughts, trying to make sense of this nightmare. And then, suddenly, like a flash of lightning, it all makes sense.

'She . . . she told him she was pregnant, didn't she?' I say, my voice barely above a whisper. 'You were right, Lucy. That has to be it.'

The inspector straightens. 'Who did she tell?'

'Cat told Jake, didn't she? You see Lucy said before you arrived that she thought Cat might have left because she was pregnant with Jake's baby. What if she told him and he didn't want it.' I lower my hands and look at him, my chest heaving, struggling with an incredible pain pressing against it that Jake might have harmed Cat. 'Jake. Her lover. He killed her didn't he? Because she was pregnant with his baby, and he didn't want it.' It all makes sense to me now.' The inspector's expression flickers — just for a moment — but it's enough. What's he hiding?

Lucy is sitting up, staring at me. 'You knew? Why didn't you tell me? I just said as much and you said nothing. Will. Why?'

'Okay, because it's nobody's bloody business is it? I didn't want it getting out there. In the press. Mum and Dad. When she came back, I didn't want her to have to deal with all that crap. I loved her. That's why. I won't have her name trashed that way. Okay, Lucy? You happy now?'

'Yeah. Okay. I was just surprised. I thought we were close.'

'We are. But not that close. This is my wife we're trashing.'

'Jake said Cat was upset that she thought he wouldn't want it because it was yours,' the DCI says. 'He said that he was going to bring it up as his own. He said it didn't bother him.'

The words land like a grenade.

I stagger backwards crashing into the wall. 'Mine! She was having my baby? I was a dad? Oh my God! Oh my God! Oh my God!' *She was having my baby?* I can't believe it. Cat is having my baby. After all this time. I can't speak. The shock takes my voice. I never thought this would happen.

'He said she wasn't going to tell you.'

'Lies. Cat wouldn't do that. She might lie about other things, but she wouldn't not tell me I was going to be a father. She knew how desperate I was to have a child of my own. She wouldn't. I'm telling you she wouldn't. He's lying.' My words tumble out, unchecked. 'I bet Jake believed it was his then when he found out he flipped. How did he find out it wasn't his? How could they be so sure?' My voice cracks again, and I have to stop. I can feel Lucy staring at me, wide-eyed and silent.

'The dates. He was away when she got pregnant. She worked it out. It couldn't have been his. He said Cat was distraught.'

'Lies. All lies. She said she wanted to fix things between us before she vanished. I wasn't sure what she meant, I thought she was talking about us. But she was talking about the baby. She must have told Jake she was coming back to me and he lost it.' The words feel like glass in my throat. 'She wanted to come back to me didn't she?' I ask, desperate for him to tell me I'm right. 'I know that now. I see it clearly now. I read it all wrong. But she was going to come back to me. That's why I bought the wine that evening. I told you that we were going to celebrate having another go, but she was already pregnant, and I didn't know. She must have been in a state knowing she was having my baby and having an affair and not knowing how to tell me. She must have thought I wouldn't want her back, that I'd believe it wasn't mine. Oh, God, she must have been so worried about what to do.'

The inspector leans back slightly, his expression unreadable. 'When did she tell him d'you think?' he asks.

'I — I don't know. A week before she disappeared. Maybe two? That's when she really was on edge. She was short tempered with me. Edgy all the time now I think back. But caring and loving towards me too. I was getting mixed messages. We hadn't been that way for a while.' I shake my head, frustrated at my own inability to think clearly. 'I don't know. Maybe he thought he'd be okay with it not being his then changed his mind. Got angry with her because she wouldn't get rid of it or that she wanted to come back to me. Realised she was still sleeping with me and that angered him. Maybe he thought we weren't anymore. I don't know. I don't know anything about him.'

'Did you know she was having an affair before you read the emails?' the inspector asks.

'Not for sure, I thought it was a possibility. By the way she was acting. You know, the way we'd grown apart. I thought she'd lied and stopped the IVF. I didn't say anything. I was too afraid of losing her. But part of me still believed she wouldn't do that. All I had were suspicions, but I put them down to my paranoia.'

'But you could have told me,' Lucy says gently, still upset she was kept out of the loop. 'You know I wouldn't judge. You could have told me when you first suspected.'

'I didn't want to besmirch her by telling you,' I snap, more sharply than I intend. 'I thought—' I stop, swallowing hard. 'I thought if she was, that it was just a phase, and she'd stop. Then

I read the emails, and it confirmed it all. I thought I was making it up in my head because of us drifting. I didn't think it was real. I loved her. I would have forgiven her anything.'

The inspector's gaze is heavy, unrelenting. 'We'll confirm it during the autopsy. We might be able to confirm whose baby it was. That could be significant.'

I stare at him, my mind reeling. 'Significant how?'

'Motives, relationships, the people in her life . . .' He trails off, but I don't miss the way his eyes flick towards me.

Something inside me surges angrily. 'You're still looking at me,' I say, my voice shaking with anger and fear. 'You think I did this because of the baby? Because of her affair? Because I thought it was his? You're wrong. I didn't hurt her. I couldn't—'

'Then help me understand,' the inspector cuts in, his tone firm. 'Help me understand the dynamics between you, your wife, and Jake Stroud. If what you're saying is true, it changes things. But I need the whole picture, William. No more secrets.'

Secrets. The word lingers in the air like a taunt.

I glance at Lucy, who's staring at me with a mix of concern and something else — doubt? Fear? I can't tell anymore.

'There's nothing else,' I say quietly, but even I don't believe it.

The inspector watches me for a moment longer, then nods. 'We'll be in touch once the DNA results come back.'

'Inspector? Deep down I know there was something else going on with her. But honestly, I have no clue what it was. Maybe it had something to do with that ten grand she gave the women's refuge.'

'We're looking into it, I'll be in touch.'

He stands, and Lucy follows him to the door. I stay on the sofa, my head in my hands, my thoughts spiralling.

Cat is dead. She was pregnant. The baby was mine. And now . . . now, it feels like something inside me has truly died.

CHAPTER 29

Royce

The office is deathly quiet, the kind of silence that makes your ears ring. I sit back in my chair, staring at the faint glow of my laptop screen. The trail has gone cold again, and my jaw aches from hours of clenching my teeth.

Your credit card flagged another transaction today — fuel, this time, at a station off the A456 near Birmingham. Before that, it was Wolverhampton. Before that, Stourbridge. At first, I thought it was a trail, a neat little breadcrumb path leading me straight to you.

But no. You're playing with me. You're moving too quickly.

I can see it now, the pattern unravelling into chaos. Every charge, every stop, is nothing more than a decoy. You are trying to keep me running in circles, wasting my time, laughing at me from somewhere far, far away.

But you underestimated me.

Helen knocks on my door. 'Can I come in, boss? I've got more information about that number plate in St Helens.'

I beckon her in. 'Shut the door. What you got? Show me.'

'Well, here's the thing — the number plate's tied to a car supposedly bought by a Jill Hart. And here's where it gets interesting:

Jill claims her driving licence was nicked. She only realised it was gone when a V5 landed in the post, saying she's the registered keeper of the vehicle we're after. But here's the kicker — she isn't. Says she's never bought a car in her life. Went straight to the police when she got the paperwork. Turns out the car was bought cash in hand at a second-hand forecourt in Clapham. Seven grand. The salesman reckons a Jill Hart bought it, but he's got no clue what she looked like. Can't remember, he says.'

* * *

Seven grand! Shock and rage surge through me.

'And no there's no CCTV, well nothing that can help us,' Helen says. Typical. 'Their camera wasn't working that day, I've already checked.' Of course it wasn't. Wasn't that convenient.

'He can't remember a thing about a woman who pays him seven grand in cash?' I stress. Probably didn't care enough to pay attention to her. You must have stood out to him. Not many cash buyers these days unless they're dodgy. Great, so he's no help. 'Have you spoken to this Jill Hart?'

'We have and guess what? She got another V5 in the post for *another* vehicle bought in her name, this time in Edinburgh. What's this got to do with the missing wife?'

'I don't know yet. Thanks, Helen. Just keep this between us for now, will you?'

'Okay, yeah, but what if Camilla asks me what we're talking about?'

'Tell her to mind her own business.'

'Right . . .' she says, her tone edged with suspicion, as if unsure where this is going. Her eyes flicker with a shadow of unease. 'And — wait — the Edinburgh police said they were emailing you about . . . Mrs Johnson-Smyth. A sighting. Up there. Isn't the wife dead?'

As if everything was aligning beautifully, the email from Edinburgh police hits my inbox. A witness reported seeing Cat Johnson-Smyth up there. The irony is almost too much: a woman claiming to have seen Cat — the very woman whose death I've spent the last few days unravelling and whose body we've just found and who has been dead for a few days. But it's not Cat up in Edinburgh. It's Jill Hart.

My wife.

* * *

They went to follow up, of course, but the would-be Catherine Johnson-Smyth vanished before they could get to her, the email says. Elusive, as always, aren't you, my darling.

You can't outrun your mistakes. I wonder if you know I've found you yet or even if you suspect I might have. If you have any suspicions the police have been called, you'll be long gone. But I'll have a trail now.

The follow-up report is what does it: a partial plate, caught on a traffic camera outside the city of possibly the last vehicle bought by Jill Hart. I spend the next two hours running it through every system I have access to, and when the answer finally flashes on my screen, my pulse quickens. *You. I knew it.*

You were at a guest house. A little place, just outside Edinburgh it says in the report. I google it. Small. The kind of place where secrets settle, and no one asks questions, I bet. But somebody clearly has.

I sign out of my desktop and grab my coat, my movements sharp and efficient. My heart is pounding as I head for the door, a steady rhythm that drowns out everything else. You think you can outsmart me, but you ought to know better. You understand who you're dealing with and how good I am at my job. Camilla calls out to me with a question, but I ignore her, keep walking.

Days. I've spent days tracking you down, playing the dutiful inspector, pulling every string I could without raising suspicion. No one questions my requests. Why would they? I'm Inspector Royce Benedick. I solve cases. I get results.

They don't need to know that this case is personal. It neatly spun into the Johnson-Smyth misper. Didn't it just.

Then I uncovered what the ever-so-magnanimous Cat Johnson-Smyth has really been up to — what she's been hiding beneath that perfect, polished exterior. It's almost impressive, the lengths you've gone to. But I've found out, haven't I. Like I wouldn't. Did you think I wouldn't? And now, standing here with the truth burning in my chest, I can't decide whether to laugh that this case fell into my lap. Six degrees of separation, isn't that what they say? By God, how true that is. It's not just what you've done — it's *who* you've done it to, and the twisted, reckless audacity of it all. This discovery changes everything. Or, maybe, it changes nothing.

I slide into my car and start the engine. The rumble is a comfort, grounding me as I pull out onto the darkened street. The road stretches ahead, a ribbon of black under the headlights, but I don't need to see it. I know where I'm going.

My grip on the wheel tightens as I drive. Anger simmers just beneath the surface that you've put me in this situation, a familiar heat that I've learned to control over the years. But now, with every mile, it rises, spilling over.

You left me. After everything I've done for you, after everything I gave you, you ran. You played the victim, turned me into the villain, and ran.

Ungrateful.

I clench my jaw, my teeth grinding together. You don't understand that I'm the only one who can help you.

I arrive at Heathrow to catch the next flight to Edinburgh.

* * *

The cold air bites at my face when I step out of the rental car, parking a few streets away from the guest house.

The temperature is biting, a cruel contrast to the milder chill of London. Here, the air cuts sharper, slicing through layers as though they aren't even there. My coat, thin and woefully inadequate, does little to fend off the creeping cold that tears at my skin.

I walk the rest of the way, my footsteps silent, my eyes scanning the windows of the guest house when I get to it.

A dim light glows in the upstairs rooms, casting long, distorted shadows that flicker like ghosts behind the thin curtains. I know you're not here — I can sense your presence like a hollow ache. This place holds the answers I need. You're close. I can feel it, like a presence lingering just out of sight, a whisper at the edge of my thoughts.

You're not far away.

I stand across the street, shrouded in the shadows, watching. The house stares back at me, its lit windows like eyes, daring me to come closer. My breath fogs in the freezing air, but I barely notice. What have you been thinking? What's been running through your mind as you tried to slip away from what we had. Do you think you're safe? Do you think this is over?

No more running.

No more hiding.

I'll make sure of it.

The urge to call in the local police flickers in my mind, but I push it aside. No. This isn't about the law. This is about you and me. And what you've done.

Crossing the street, I stop at the door. For a moment, I hesitate, my hand hovering over the knocker. My heart is racing, my breath coming in short, sharp bursts.

I knock.

Nothing.

I knock again, harder this time.

The door creaks open, and an attractive middle-aged woman is standing on the other side. Well turned out with long acrylic nails in fire engine red. A welcoming smile spread across her face. It's late; she's probably wondering who's knocking on her door at this hour.

Her face goes pale the moment she sees me, her eyes wide, her lips part in shock like she knows instantly I'm the law.

For a moment, we just stand there, staring at each other, and I know this woman knows my wife. I can feel it.

'Hello,' I say, my voice low and smooth. 'I'm looking for someone I believe has been staying with you or may still be here.' I flash my ID.

She moves to slam the door, but I'm faster, jamming my foot against it. Her strength is laughable compared to mine. I push the door open, stepping inside, closing it behind me with a quiet finality.

'Now why would you do that to the police?' I murmur, my voice dripping with venom at what you might have said to her about me.

CHAPTER 30

Jill

I grip the steering wheel tighter, my knuckles white against the dark leather. The road stretches out in front of me, empty and desolate, but my mind is anything but calm. Heat claws up my throat, and my skin prickles with unease, all I hear is the hum of the tyres against the asphalt. I have to keep driving. I can't afford to stop. Not now. Not when the fear that has been tormenting me for days has finally caught up with me. I know Martha calling the police about Cat's picture in the newspaper will get back to you. Have you found out she was helping me?

When I realised Martha *had* called the police it sent a fresh wave of panic crashing over me, and I had to swallow down the fear to keep myself calm and get myself out of there as quickly as possible. I can't let you find me. Not now. Not ever. No one will ever believe me against you. You, taking on the role of the police — honourable and admirable, as always. The inspector who everyone respects and admires. No one would.

My eyes dart to the rear-view mirror, nervous and searching, but there's no trace of you. Not yet. You're not a fool, though. You'll have figured it out by now. You'll know what Cat was doing, how she got involved, how much she tried to help. I pray I'm wrong. God, I hope I'm wrong.

St Andrews is the one place you'd never think to look. The one place you have no reason to check. Because you won't think it's a place I'd want to return to. The place you took me to when we first met, where we laughed and loved and where the truth was revealed. I don't even know how I lasted as long as I did. I never saw myself as that kind of woman. Never thought I'd end up here. And yet, somehow, here I am. Even the idea of that safe haven makes my skin crawl. Will it really be safe? Will anywhere? I can't shake the feeling that maybe the danger isn't something I can outrun.

The harsh memories of how I ended up here are crashing over me once again. The image of Cat's face flickers through my mind, like a ghost rising from the depths of my thoughts and then that picture of her in the newspaper saying she'd vanished. I never expected to meet someone like Cat. A woman so ordinary, so familiar, with a smile that made me feel instantly at ease. But Cat wasn't like everyone else. She had this way about her, this kindness that felt almost invasive, like she could see straight through you. She wanted to understand women like me. Women who'd been through it all. Women who'd lost themselves somewhere along the way, who carried the weight of bruises no one else could see.

It was Cat who introduced me to Simone, the woman who would lay the breadcrumbs to throw you into a tailspin of confusion. Cat volunteered at the National Domestic Abuse Helpline, her voice calm and steady through the phone, guiding desperate women like me towards a semblance of hope. I reached out when I finally understood I couldn't do this alone anymore. I needed help. I wasn't truthful though. But she was there, willing to give me help, no questions asked. But she didn't stop there; she went further than she should have, further than I ever expected. And now, I can't stop thinking about how it all went so wrong that day in the industrial estate where we'd had our last meet up.

She had a way of making it all sound so easy, so seamless, as if it was just a game of chess where she always stayed ten moves ahead. She told me how to send you on a wild goose chase, how to make it look like I was spending money recklessly, leading you nowhere. She made it seem foolproof, and for a while, I actually believed it could work. When I saw the article about her disappearance, though, my stomach dropped. I knew you'd figure it out. You'd know I couldn't have done this alone once you found out where she volunteered. It wouldn't be long before you put the pieces together.

I can still hear Cat's voice, calm and steady, as though she had everything under control. *Trust me*, she kept saying. *I'll make sure he never finds you.* I wanted to tell her everything — to confess — but something held me back. Fear, maybe, or guilt. It felt like if I admitted the truth, everything would unravel. But she was so kind I thought I could trust her. The moment I told her the *real* truth, everything fell apart.

The day before I ran, there was something different about you that day, something sharper, more certain. I could sense it. It felt like you'd discovered what I'd been up to. I was certain of it. I got scared. I thought you knew who I'd been talking to. That's why I had to leave so quickly. That's why it all went wrong with Cat. I was panicked. In a rush. Terrified. I had to confess to her to get it off my chest. I just had to.

And now, I can't stop thinking about how it all went so wrong. How you got inside my head. How I misjudged Cat.

My voice trembled when we spoke that last night, Royce. I was sure you could hear it. Terrified that you'd found out the truth about what I was planning, but were being evasive, your words veiled in something I couldn't quite place. I had a twisted sense of anticipation that you could read my thoughts. We were supposed to go down to Cornwall to see Sid and Mel. But I didn't dare; I was so sure you'd found out what I was up to — I didn't dare put my plan off any longer. I was sorry, because I loved spending time with their kids. I knew what you were thinking. You didn't have to say it. And I get on so well with Mel. A stab of guilt pierces that she'll have been trying to get in touch with me. You looked at me like you were holding on to a secret, my secret, that you burned to share but couldn't — wouldn't — not yet. I didn't want to wait around. You shouted at me and I hit you, caught you above the right eye with my ring. There was so much blood from such a small gash. But you were calm and dealt with it. That made me angry. And scared. Why didn't you fight back? Yell at me? I was so certain that you had truly discovered my plans.

Cat's voice that last day I saw her . . . was sharp and brittle like she had something on her mind that was really bothering her. She seemed terrified. She didn't say much, just that she was scared about something she had to tell her husband. Then when I told her what I'd been hiding she really flipped. I wasn't expecting it. It just came out of nowhere. Her anger towards me for lying to her.

My breath catches in my throat, the memories playing in my mind like a sickening film reel. I can still see the look in Cat's eyes through the glass that told me everything was about to implode. That she didn't trust me anymore and that hurt. It really hurt. I thought she was going to pull out and not help me. Call Simone off. I thought I was going to be on my own.

I shift in my seat, my fingers trembling as they brush the dial of the radio. The static buzzes for a moment before an old song plays, a lullaby sung by Judy Garland of all things that should be comforting, but it only heightens my sense of unease. The silence of the road presses in on me, oppressive, suffocating. Just how I felt that last day with Cat. I shouldn't have told her. I just should have kept it to myself. I know that now.

The fog of doubt settles back in, but I can't afford to doubt myself now. I have to keep going. There is no turning back. I can't change what happened. The police will be looking for me, but they'll have no idea where to start. Or will they? No, perhaps not. You won't want them involved in this. You'll brush it off, this alleged sighting, because you know the tangled web we've weaved. I will disappear into the fog of St Andrews, and for once, I will be free. I won't let you find me.

At least, that's what I tell myself. I don't know how long I can keep running before the weight that you'll never give up looking for me crushes me. But in the silence of the car, as the miles between me and you grow, I allow myself one fleeting thought of hope.

Maybe, just maybe, there is still a chance I can get away.

And then . . . I hear the news over the radio: '*The police have revealed that the body of Catherine Johnson-Smyth, who has been missing for a number of days, has been found in an abandoned car on an industrial estate.*'

CHAPTER 31

Cat

From the outside, my life looked perfect. I was married to William, a wealthy man, and lived a life of privilege and luxury. But beneath the polished veneer, I felt like a ghost in my own home — silent, unseen and slowly disappearing. The grandeur suffocated me. Every opulent dinner, weekend party or elegant gathering left me feeling more hollow. I told myself I should feel lucky, grateful even, but a quiet loneliness perturbed me, an emptiness too shameful to admit.

Our marriage wasn't without its complexities. We had been trying for a baby and were going through IVF, a process fraught with pressure and expectation. But in a moment of weakness, I had an affair. I thought I'd fallen in love, but when I found out I was pregnant, I assumed the child wasn't William's. The guilt was unbearable, a persistent shadow that followed me through my days. Every glance from William, every tender smile, felt like a silent accusation. I wanted to tell him, to confess and free myself from the smothering shame, but the fear of shattering our lives that way when he'd dreamed of having a child, and his trust in me, kept me silent.

When the pregnancy test turned positive, my gut twisted in a sick mix of relief and dread. This lie, I realised, would become the foundation of our future if I stayed with him. And yet, when I checked the dates, it turned out the baby was William's. The relief was overwhelming, but the scars of my secret affair remained, lingering in the quiet spaces of our marriage. I broke it off with Jake after the dates didn't align with how far gone I was. He begged me to stay with him, that he'd bring it up as his own. But he'd always loved me more than I'd loved him, and anyway, I wouldn't do that to William. We fought. He got angry. Refused to let me go. Threatened to tell William about us.

Amid this turmoil, I found solace in a secret of a different kind. Without William's knowledge, I had begun working at the National Domestic Abuse Helpline changing my work hours at the florist to part-time and asking Rita to not mention it if William or Jason ever asked. I donated a large sum of money. It was my way of reclaiming a sense of purpose, of doing something meaningful in a life that felt increasingly hollow. But I knew William wouldn't understand — nor would his family. To them, it would seem beneath me, an unnecessary risk for a woman of my status.

Even more troubling was my fear of my brother, Jason. Jason's temper and violent tendencies had left a lasting impact on me. His inability to control his fists had ruined every relationship he'd ever had, and I knew he'd see my work at the helpline as a betrayal. I wanted to understand men like Jason — to help if not him, then the women who suffered at the hands of men like him.

When Jason eventually found out, my worst fears were realised. His anger terrified me, and to protect myself, I lied. I told him I was seeking help because William was hurting me. The words felt like poison, a betrayal of my husband that broke my heart. But it was the only way to stop Jason from harming me or confronting William. It got worse when he found out about my friendship with Jake and told him those same lies. I never dared tell him what Jake was to me. The waters were getting dirtier, and

I didn't know how to correct it. Time would sort it out, I thought. Little did I know how little time I had left.

My work at the helpline wasn't without its dangers. One of the women I was helping, Natalie Benedick, was in an especially dire situation. Natalie's husband, Royce, was a detective inspector. His badge gave him power and protection, making him untouchable and always one step ahead. *If I run*, Natalie confided to me one night, her voice barely audible, *who would believe me? He knows every move I'll make before I even think it.*

Despite the danger, I helped Natalie carefully plan her escape. But Royce had grown suspicious, she said and was watching her. He began monitoring Natalie's phone calls and movements, his presence looming like a dark cloud, she told me. One night, Natalie told me about a chilling comment Royce had made: *People should know better than to stick their noses where they don't belong.* I tried to reassure Natalie, brushing it off as paranoia. But she believed he knew about our meetings. After that I felt as though I was being watched and followed. I told myself it was Natalie's paranoia creeping into me.

Days later, the night before I vanished, William and I were planning a celebration the next night to patch things up — I was going to tell him about the baby. Only I got a call the next morning from Natalie telling me she was leaving, that she suspected Royce knew she was going to run.

My world unravelled that morning when Natalie showed up at my front door half an hour after her call.

CHAPTER 32

Royce

The door creaks softly as I push it shut behind me, sealing out the howl of the Scottish wind. My boots thud against the wooden floor as I step inside. Amanda's head snaps up, her face pale. She doesn't speak, but I catch the way her eyes dart towards the staircase and that she knows exactly who I am.

I smile, a cold twist of my lips that I know doesn't reach my eyes. 'Now then,' I say, my voice low and deliberate. 'I think we ought to have a quiet word about one of your guests, don't you?'

Amanda blanches, then moves, slow and careful, towards the desk at the far end of the room. She puts it between us, like a shield, her hands gripping the edges. *So you've told her your story about us, how could you.*

'Your local police have been in touch,' I continue, stepping closer, my tone casual, almost conversational. 'They passed on some information about a person of interest we're searching for. Maybe you've heard about it. Catherine Johnson-Smyth? It's been all over the papers. The news.'

Amanda stiffens but says nothing. Her knuckles whiten where they grip the desk. I know she knows what I'm talking about.

'We received a tip,' I say, letting the words suspend between us as I take another step. 'From someone — Martha Barrie — who thinks our missing person was staying here or someone who knew her. In this guest house. Under a different name. Jill, wasn't it?'

Amanda's face hardens, her voice steady but strained. 'I heard today that Mrs Catherine Johnson-Smyth's body was found in London. So, it must have been a mistaken identification. Martha got it wrong.'

I pause, narrowing my eyes, the corner of my mouth twitching upward. 'Indeed. But that doesn't explain the woman who this Martha thought suspicious, does it? I'd still like to know about this . . . Jill. If you don't mind.'

'But I do mind,' Amanda snaps, her voice sharp now. She straightens, her false bravado giving her some height. 'You'll need a warrant for that. Do you have one?'

Her sudden defiance is like a slap to the face. My jaw tightens as a hot surge rises in my chest, seeping into my voice. 'I could get one,' I say slowly, each word measured, heavy with menace. 'But wouldn't it be easier all around if you just handed over the information now? You'd be helping the police.'

Amanda's expression doesn't waver. 'Without a warrant, you won't get anything from me.'

The air between us feels electric, taut as a wire about to snap. My fists clench at my sides, and I step closer, looming over the desk. Amanda doesn't flinch, but I can see the tremor in her hands. She's holding her ground, but she's terrified, and I savour it.

I lean forward, planting my hands flat on the desk. My fingers spread, slow and deliberate, until the wood creaks beneath the pressure. Amanda stiffens, her eyes glancing to mine, and I see it there. That flash of panic she's so desperate to hide.

'I'll tell you what I think, Amanda,' I say, my voice dropping to a near whisper, each word dripping with venom. 'I think you're hiding something. And I think you know exactly where Jill is.'

'I told you,' she says, her voice wavering now. 'Without a warrant—'

'Don't,' I snap, cutting her off. 'Don't insult me by repeating that rubbish. You know as well as I do that a warrant is just paperwork. Red tape. It's nothing compared to the trouble you're inviting by lying to me.'

She shrinks back slightly, but she's still trying to put on that brave face. It's almost admirable. Almost.

'You're protecting her,' I continue, my tone soft but lethal. 'And I get it. You think you're doing the right thing. You think you're helping a poor, scared woman who's been wronged. But let me make one thing crystal clear, Amanda. You have no idea who you're dealing with.'

I straighten up, dragging the moment out, letting the silence between us swell until it's almost unbearable. My gaze locks on hers, and I let the mask slip just a little. Enough for her to see the raw emotions beneath.

'Do you know what she's done?' I ask, my voice low and almost tender, as if I'm sharing a secret. 'The lies she's told? The chaos she's caused? Jill isn't some helpless victim. She's a manipulative, conniving little liar who's dragged you into something you can't possibly understand.'

Amanda doesn't respond, but I see the crack in her armour widening. Her breathing is shallow, her grip on the desk tightening as if it's the only thing keeping her upright. Good. Let her feel the weight of it.

'You don't want to be on the wrong side of this,' I say, stepping around the desk now, closing the space between us. She backs up instinctively, her eyes darting towards the door. 'And you don't want to make an enemy of me. I'm a patient man, Amanda, but my patience has limits.'

I'm close enough to see the pulse hammering in her neck, the faint sheen of sweat on her brow. She's out of moves, cornered like a rabbit staring down the fox. The temptation to press further, to push until she breaks, is almost overwhelming. But I have to be careful. I must tread that fine line between intimidation and outright force.

'Let me make it easy for you,' I say finally, pulling back just slightly, giving her room to breathe. 'Tell me where she is, and this ends here. No more questions. No more visits. You get to go back to your quiet little life, and I get what I came for. Simple.'

She hesitates, her lips parting as if to speak, but then she clamps them shut. I can see the battle raging in her head, the desperate calculations as she weighs her options. She's close, so close, but she's still clinging to that last shred of defiance.

I step even closer, my voice dropping to a whisper. 'You're not just protecting her anymore, Amanda. You're obstructing me. And that? That's a crime. You don't want to go down for her, do you? Because I promise you, you will.'

Her eyes widen, and for a moment, I think I've got her. But then she shakes her head, her jaw tightening as she steels herself again. 'I won't tell you anything,' she says, her voice firmer now, though I can still hear the tremor beneath. 'Not without a warrant.'

The rage flares hot and fast, but I tamp it down, forcing a smile. 'All right,' I say, stepping back at last, giving her just enough space to think she's won. 'Have it your way. For now. But think about whose side you really want to be on. There are always two sides to every story, you know that, right?'

But as I turn towards the door, my mind is already racing.

The storm outside is nothing compared to the one churning in my chest as I step back into the night.

Amanda slumps against the desk, her breath coming in shallow gasps. Her heart hammers in her chest, her hand clamped tightly over her mouth to silence the sound of her breathing. She knows that was no idle threat. She picks up her phone and sends a text message.

CHAPTER 33

Jill

St Andrews on the Fife coast looks as serene as it did the first time I saw it. A postcard-perfect town with cobbled streets and old stone buildings. But as I pull into a narrow parking spot, its charm barely registers. My hands grip the steering wheel tightly, my knuckles white. I still can't believe what I've just heard on the radio. I glance at the map on my phone, searching for the guest house I booked. My nerves a mess. It's right in the centre of town, on a busy street. Perfect. Noise, people, witnesses — it's exactly what I need. It's taken me just under two hours, better than I'd anticipated.

My phone pings, and the sound cuts through the tense quiet like a gunshot. The notification is from an unknown number. I freeze. Could it be you?

My finger hovers over the screen, trembling. *Don't open it*, I think. But the curiosity and the fear wins. I tap the message.

> *Rest assured your number has now been deleted. You should know someone was here looking for you. If you remember you gave me your number when you registered. I thought I ought to let you know. I didn't tell him anything. He wasn't best pleased. I hope you're far away, lass. Good luck. Amanda. X*

The words blur as tears sting my eyes. I feel bad that I never said goodbye to her, but she'll know now why I had to leave in such a hurry. I can barely breathe. Amanda didn't deserve this — none of this. She probably just wanted to help, but now, because of me, he's been to her door.

A ragged sob escapes, but I clamp my hand over my mouth, swallowing the sound. My breath hitches, and I cough violently, grabbing my water bottle and taking small, careful sips until the choking subsides. But the panic doesn't.

He's here. Already. It didn't take him long.

I press a hand to the front of my neck, the pressure grounding me, or maybe it's a desperate attempt to keep myself from falling apart. Images of Cat flash in my mind, unbidden and brutal. Her laugh, her wide, trusting eyes, the way her voice used to brighten the day.

Then the news on the radio, the cold, detached report of her death.

My throat tightens further. *Do you know who killed her?* I want to ask you.

Cat wasn't strong in that way. She wasn't built for the kind of cruelty in this world. The thought is unbearable, but the answer is clear.

My jaw hardens, and my grip on the bottle tightens. You may have found me, but I'm not going back. Ever. If you come close, I'll do whatever it takes to stop you.

I wipe my face quickly, stuffing the phone and water bottle into my bag. The guest house is just down the street. I need to get inside, where it's safe. At least for tonight. As I leave my car I glance behind me. I'll need to get rid of it because he'll know by now my new identity as Jill Hart. A few flakes of snow begin to cover the windscreen, I don't think it'll amount to much.

I clutch my bag, and the ones stuffed with food and drink. Heading towards the guest house, my eyes dart around, scanning my surroundings, every sense on high alert. A few people glance my way, their eyes brushing past me before turning elsewhere. Keeping my head down, I press forward, willing myself to blend in. Please, I think, don't let them ask for ID here.

The guest house comes into view, a Victorian semi with a tarmac driveway and half a dozen parking spaces all in use. It's not exactly inviting. I quickly switch off my phone, silently berating myself for not doing it earlier. But I needed the maps, didn't I? I steal another glance at the building. It doesn't have the polished charm of Caledonian Nights. It feels a little worn, a little tired. Still, I remind myself, I'm in no position to be picky. This place costs more than I'm used to paying, and I don't even know how long I'll stay. Three nights. That's all I've booked for. After that, I'll have to move on again. I rub my hand across the money belt subconsciously.

The entrance is clean, with a sharp, biting scent of disinfectant that oddly makes me smile. The reception desk is unimpressive, certainly no match for Amanda's, and the woman behind it looks equally weary. Her smile is thin and tired, the kind of smile that feels rehearsed, as though reserved strictly for guests. I wonder fleetingly what her real face looks like when it isn't hidden behind that mask.

She barely glances up as I approach. Her face is deeply lined, free of make-up, and framed by a mug of tea and two digestives perched precariously on the edge of her desk. The mug catches my eye. There's writing on the side: *The Office Karen*. I can't help but wonder if she even knows what that means. Somehow, I doubt it's hers. Just a random mug someone left behind. Still, the thought lingers — who *is* the Karen here? And are they about to make my life harder?

'You Rose?' she asks, her accent thick, her voice flat and sharp, like she's already tired of me. She clearly hasn't been to the university of customer care.

I nod, swallowing hard as she finally looks up. The name wasn't exactly a masterpiece of creativity. It was the first thing that came to mind when I called while I was stuck in traffic. A poster on a wall flashed by advertising fabric softener scented with roses. Now I'm Rose Lenor. The blush creeps up my neck, but when she repeats the name, it doesn't sound quite as ridiculous out loud.

'Three nights, 'eah?'

'Yes,' I reply quickly. 'Three. You said you had availability.' My chest tightens as the words leave my mouth.

'I do. Didn't I say I do? You said cash, too.' She lets out a sigh, as though I'm exhausting her already. 'Only thing I've got is the ground-floor double. You're single, so it'll cost you more.'

I bite back my annoyance. *Miserable cow.* 'You didn't mention that on the phone.'

'Probably didn't realise it then.' She shrugs, clearly not giving a damn.

She didn't *realise* the only room she had was a double? Ground floor, too. God knows what kind of security that has if you do turn up. But maybe it's better this way, easier for me to get out quick if I need to. 'How much more?'

'Double,' she says curtly, her tone leaving no room for negotiation. 'You said cash, right?' she asks again.

My first instinct is to turn around, walk out, and tell her exactly where to shove her room. But I can't. I'm here now, and I need a place to lie low. 'Fine. That's fine. But isn't that a bit expensive? And yes, it's cash.' £450 in cash.

I need to start earning, just enough to keep me afloat — cash in hand work, nothing that leaves a trail. I never did take what Amanda owed me. My hand inside my pocket wraps around the pendant. I don't feel too bad about taking it, after all, she got me to do all that work for free.

'If ye dinnae want to stay, ye dinnae have to.' Her eyes narrow slightly as she looks me up and down, then slides a stack of leaflets towards me. The Wi-Fi code is printed at the top, slapped onto a list of 'Do's and Don'ts'.

By now, I'm sure you know about the car. If you've flagged it, if it's being watched, then staying here isn't just reckless, it's suicidal. I'll have to move on. I don't mention that in case she throws me out.

I take the leaflets, mumbling a quick thanks, already planning my next move. I need to switch my SIM card. Good thing I packed an extra one for emergencies. There's no way I can risk keeping my number, not if Amanda accidentally hands it out or he forces it from her.

The car is a problem. I glance out at the fading light. It's not something I can deal with tonight, but first thing tomorrow, it has to go. The snow is still falling. I've probably been caught on half a dozen ANPR cameras on the way here, and it's only a matter of time before someone gives you the nod.

I clutch the leaflets tightly, steadying my breath. One step at a time. For now, I just have to make it through the night.

Further north. That's my only option. Somewhere quieter, harder to track. But how? By train? Coach? Both feel like a trap waiting to spring. Cameras are everywhere. On platforms, in stations, even on the roads leading there. Every step I take now feels like it's lit up, exposing me like a firefly for you to find your way to me.

I press my palms into my temples, forcing my thoughts to slow. I need a plan. A way to slip through the cracks, to vanish completely, if only for a little while. But the harder I think, the more the walls seem to close in. I wish I could call you, Cat, and ask you. Just to hear your voice would give me strength. Every move feels dangerous. Every option, flawed. Thoughts of Cat make me quiver with dread.

I can't stay here. Not with the car here too — that's too dangerous. Too risky. The woman hands me the key and I make my way to my room. I probably won't get my money back if I leave early.

CHAPTER 34

Jason

When the detective inspector leaves, I reach for the scotch and a glass. One is never enough. Six later, and it still isn't enough to numb the pain that they've found Cat's body. The burn doesn't touch the edges, doesn't blur the memories, doesn't soften the jagged ache. They've found you. I never thought they would. Not after all this time. What surprised me more was what he didn't say. Nothing about your secret work with the National Domestic Abuse Centre. He has to know by now, surely. Did he tell William? Christ. I hope not. He never wanted her working as a lawyer; I can't imagine his reaction to her playing saviour for battered strangers. Not that what he thinks now makes any difference.

I didn't mention it to the police either. What would've been the point? As far as they're concerned I'll say I never knew. It wasn't relevant — at least, I didn't think it was. It could have linked your disappearance to me. I didn't want that. Too many questions. If I brought it up, they'd start asking questions, digging through your files, prying into lives you were trying to protect. And knowing you I bet you had a file on me. You'd have hated that, your cases turned into evidence, your clients dragged through the muck. You trusted me to keep it private. I couldn't betray that.

And then there is William. If the police started asking him about your work at the centre . . . well, I didn't want to stir up anything there either. That was before they found your body. Now it would seem weird to say anything. William might've snapped over it. Probably would have. Finding out you were working there behind his back. Or worse, he might've known all along. I can't be sure he didn't. I doubt it though. He'd have really put his foot down about that. I'm sure of it. Wasn't that why you wanted to keep it secret? And what if he did and if you'd told him about my problem as you liked to call it? Was that why he was the way he was with me after you disappeared — tolerant even after everything I threw at him. I don't know. I can't be sure. I'm hardly going to ask him. Probably his lawyers told him not to agitate the situation.

It was wrong of you, getting involved with people like that and then coming to *me* with your little crusade. Trying to *fix me*. God, I hated that phrase. *Fix me*. Like I was some broken thing in need of repair. You actually suggested counselling once. That was never going to happen.

But what I couldn't understand — what you never explained — was why you told *me* about William. If he was hurting you, why come to me? Why not just leave him? That's what you preached to your clients, wasn't it? Pack your bags. Get out. You told me you helped men too — abused by their wives or girlfriends. Men. Beaten by women. It was laughable. I actually laughed when you said it, right in your face. Who wouldn't? Men letting women hit them? Losers, that's what they are. You tried to get me to see it. To understand it. I laugh, no way. I was never going to agree with you about that.

You didn't take it well. For the first time, you got properly angry with me. Telling me I didn't understand, that I was a chauvinist, and you stopped taking my calls. At first, I thought maybe one of those pathetic men you were helping had done something to you. Or William — maybe *he* got carried away. He was evading me too, the twat. Telling me not to bother you. What did you tell him? I thought the worst for you. It's easily done. I mean, sometimes women push too hard. They step out of line. If William found out you were working at the abuse centre, that might've been it for him. The trigger.

Posh sod. He always thought he was better than me, looking down his nose every time I was around. I never asked you if you'd told him about me, but maybe that's why he could never stomach me. I think you did.

Or maybe . . . maybe he knew what I was capable of and never said anything.

I drain the last of the scotch, then pour another. What's one more, anyway? It's not like anyone's watching. Not now.

The thing is, I wasn't entirely honest about where I was the day you disappeared. Not to William. Not to the police. It wasn't a big lie, really. Just . . . a small adjustment to my truth. I told them I was home all day, nursing a hangover after watching the football the night before. They didn't question it much. Why would they? They checked what match was showing and the finish time, that sort of thing. I'm not exactly the responsible type. So, the fact I was vague tied in with my personality. For once it worked for me. I'm sure William told them that. And I was upset, worried about you so that made my vagueness credible.

But the truth is, I wasn't home. Not all day.

I was at the park, in the woods. Holland Park, to be exact. It's where I used to go when we were younger — when things got too much, when you were being too loud, too perfect, too *Cat*. That day, I just needed to clear my head. You finally answered my call, and we had a fight about the other night and what you'd said to me. I wasn't buying it, and you weren't backing down. You started preaching at me again, going on about how I needed to change, to grow up, to *fix myself*. You called me a coward. Said I never took control of my life and blamed everyone else. I said things too. Things I regret now. It all got really heated between us. But we decided to meet at the park — I wanted to see you and try to explain. Then we took a drive.

I came back to the park later. Stayed at the park for hours, pacing the paths, smoking, watching people walk their dogs in anoraks, hoods up, couples passing hand in hand, their faces blurred. I kept to the quieter parts of the gardens, the places where no one notices you, where you can think without interruption. The weather wasn't great. I lost track of time.

By the time I got home, it was late, and you weren't answering your phone. You never answered me again after that.

I never told anyone about the park. Why would I? They'd only look at me as being the last person who saw you alive other than William.

CHAPTER 35

William

I can't believe Cat is gone. Dead. And for days now, while I was searching and hoping. The inspector said you probably died the day you went missing, but they'll know more after the autopsy. The thought of that — of them opening you up — makes me want to scream, to tear out my hair. You. My Cat.

'Drink this,' Lucy says softly, pressing a crystal tumbler of brandy into my trembling hands. 'For the shock. Just drink it.'

I take a long gulp, hoping for numbness, for something to dull the agony clawing at my chest. But all it does is burn on the way down, leaving the ache untouched.

'I'm so sorry, William,' Lucy murmurs, sitting beside me. Her voice trembles, barely above a whisper. 'It's just . . . so sad. All of it.'

Sad? No one can even begin to understand how sad. How devastating. How broken I feel. You were pregnant — *our baby*, Cat. After all this time trying. After all the hope and heartbreak.

'She was pregnant, Lucy,' I choke out, staring at the tumbler in my hands like it holds the answers. 'We finally did it. We were going to have a baby.'

Lucy squeezes my hand, her touch gentle but unable to reach the chasm of grief inside me. She doesn't say anything. What could she say? There *are* no words for this.

'Do you believe me?' My voice cracks, raw and desperate. 'I mean . . . that she wouldn't lie to me. She would have told me it was mine, right? She wouldn't have left me after she knew. Would she?'

Lucy's hesitation is almost imperceptible, but I feel it like a knife twisting in my chest.

'No,' she says finally, her voice shaky. 'I don't think so. Not Cat.'

'Then why?' My voice rises, unsteady and jagged. 'Why did she have that damned affair? Why, Lucy? She loved me. I *know* she loved me. Even after everything. Despite what she did.'

'I don't know,' Lucy whispers, her eyes glistening with unshed tears. 'The hormones . . . maybe they messed with her. Maybe she wasn't thinking straight. Maybe she was just so desperate to get pregnant she . . . she lost her way. I don't know, William. I wish I did.' She squeezes my hand.

I press the knuckles of my free hand hard against my forehead, as if I can knock the questions out of my skull, but they're relentless. They echo, unanswered, in the emptiness Cat has left behind.

Anger rises in me like a storm, sudden and uncontrollable. I slam the tumbler down on the table, the sharp crack of glass on wood startling Lucy. 'She *lost her way*?' I spit, my voice trembling with rage. 'What the hell does that even mean? She was *mine*, Lucy. My wife. We were supposed to be building a life together! We were finally going to have the family we dreamed of, and she — she *threw it all away* for what? For *him*? Because I couldn't give her a baby?' My fists clench, nails digging into my palms as the words tumble out, each one sharper than the last. 'Did she really love him? Did she laugh with him the way she laughed with me? Did she *think of me at all* when she—' I can't finish. The words choke me, too painful to say aloud. The room feels too small, too suffocating, and all I can hear is the pounding of blood in my ears. 'Why wasn't I enough? She said about adopting, when we thought

231

the IVF just wasn't going to work for us, but we never spoke of breaking up. I know I was stubborn about it, but I came round to the idea, but it was too late then,' I shout, my voice breaking as I turn to Lucy, desperate for answers she doesn't have. 'Why the hell wasn't I enough for her?'

The anger burns itself out as quickly as it came, leaving me slumped in my seat, hollowed out and exhausted. I rake a hand through my hair, my voice quieter now but still laced with frustration. 'The last few months . . . she was different. I should have seen it, Lucy. She'd take calls and leave the room, whispering like she didn't want me to hear. When I found the emails, and thought back on it all, I assumed the secrecy was about meeting *him*. She'd nip out to run errands that couldn't wait, even late at night. And her mood . . .' I trail off, trying to find the words. 'She wasn't herself. It was like she was afraid, but not of me. Of something or someone else. What if there was something else going on?'

Lucy watches me. 'Why didn't you tell the police any of this?' she asks gently.

'I don't know,' I admit, shaking my head. 'I forgot, I guess. With her missing, I . . . I couldn't think straight. All I could focus on was finding her. But now . . .' My voice drops, barely above a whisper. 'What if something was going on with her? Something I didn't know about?'

The thought sends a chill down my spine, and then it hits me — like a puzzle piece snapping into place. 'Rita,' I mutter, more to myself than to Lucy.

'What about Rita?'

'She told me Cat asked to leave work for an appointment,' I say, my mind racing now. 'But no one knows anything about it. She didn't tell anyone what it was for. She didn't even tell *me*. Jake doesn't even know so it wasn't to meet him.' My heart pounds as I look at Lucy, a terrible new fear creeping into my voice. 'What if it wasn't just an appointment? What if it was something . . . something bigger? What if that's why all this happened? She . . . now I think of it — Lucy, Cat was up to something she didn't want me or anyone to know about. Oh my God,' I whisper, my chest tightening as the memory slams into me like a train. 'She . . . she knew about the CCTV cameras being out of order around here.' My voice trembles, the weight of it sinking in. 'I'm just remembering it now. How the hell did I forget that?' My hands grip the edge of the sofa as the realisation takes hold. 'It was on some community Facebook page she followed — about the neighbourhood. I saw her reading it, Lucy. She told me! She *knew* that day they weren't working.'

The room feels colder, darker, as the words settle between us. My mind reels, the pieces shifting uneasily into place. How could I have been so blind? So careless? The stress, the panic of her going missing — it had buried everything, every detail that might've mattered. But now it feels glaringly obvious, like a warning sign I'd walked right past. A sickening wave of guilt and dread washing over me.

'She *knew*, Lucy,' I repeat, my voice barely above a whisper, as though saying it louder would make it worse. 'What was she doing? Why would she need to know that?' My breath catches, the implications swirling like a storm in my mind. 'What if . . . what if this wasn't random? What if she planned something, and I've been too blind to see it?'

'You need to tell the police this . . . what about Jason!' Lucy says, her voice sharpening as she sits forward. 'D'you think he knows what she was up to? He was always so close to her, William. Too close, if you ask me.'

The name swings in the air like a blade. Jason. He had always been *odd*, hadn't he? Always hovering around Cat, like her shadow. He didn't like me much — never had. Even after we got married, he acted like I'd stolen her away from him, like I had no right to be part of her life. And then there was the way he'd look at her sometimes, with this fierce, almost possessive intensity that made my skin crawl. 'He *must* have known something,' I mutter. 'If anyone knew what was going on with her, it'd be him.'

Lucy's eyes narrow, her voice dropping to a conspiratorial whisper. 'Do you remember how he acted at the wedding? The way he clung to her like he couldn't bear to let her go? And now, with all this . . . he hasn't exactly been falling over himself to help, has he? Just blaming you. Like he wants the police to *look* at you as the suspect. And didn't he say you hit her? Nobody else said that, only him.' And *Jake*.

I swallow hard, my mind churning. 'Jason came to the house after Cat went missing. Almost immediately. I hadn't even thought of her as missing, not properly, anyway. It was him who made me think that way. He went to the police before me. When I tried to reach out, he was evasive, curt, like I was bothering him. Accusing me of being responsible.' And now, the memory of his cold, distant tone feels like a warning I should've heeded. 'What if . . .' I hesitate, my voice cracking. 'What if Jason *knew* something? What if he's hiding something?

'She knew the cameras were down,' I say, my voice barely steady. 'She planned it, Lucy. She didn't want anyone to see her. She was meeting someone — someone she didn't want me or anyone else to know about.'

Lucy's eyes widen, her face pale in the dim light. 'But who? Who could it have been?'

'I don't know,' I admit, running a hand over my face, the frustration and fear bubbling under my skin. 'But it wasn't random. She was scared, Lucy. I can see it now — those last few weeks, the calls, the secrecy. I knew something was wrong. Maybe she thought she could handle it, but . . .' My voice cracks, and I force the words out. 'But what if she couldn't? What if that's why she's dead?'

Lucy leans in, her voice dropping to a hushed urgency. 'What if whoever she was meeting . . . killed her? What if they're the reason she's gone, William?'

I catch her eye in the dim half-light, and for a moment, silence swallows all sound. A cold tremor ripples through my chest and outpaces my scattering thoughts. The space between us feels charged. My voice quivers as I murmur, 'If that's true, then somewhere out there, someone holds the pieces of her untold story.'

Lucy's hand tightens on mine, her voice trembling. 'Then we need to figure out who. Because if Cat didn't want anyone to know . . . there must've been a damned good reason.'

A chill runs through me, the kind that doesn't go away. I stand abruptly, my pulse thundering in my neck. 'I need to go back through her things,' I say, more to myself than to Lucy. 'There's got to be something. A clue. A name. Anything.'

'William, wait,' Lucy says, standing with me. 'Think about it — if she was meeting someone that she didn't want anyone to know about, and now she's dead . . . then whoever she met — whoever *did this* — they're still out there.'

I stare at her, her words sinking in.

'They could be anyone,' she whispers, her eyes darting to the window as though expecting to see a shadow moving outside. 'What if it's someone we know? Someone who's been right here with us, pretending they don't know a thing?'

The thought chills me to the bone: someone walking among us, hiding in plain sight. My stomach knots as Jason's cold, distant face rises unbidden in my mind — and for the first time, I wonder if the person who killed my wife has been right here all along.

CHAPTER 36

Jason

I stare out the window of my flat, my fingers drumming nervously against the worn wood of the sill. The words play on repeat in my head: *I wasn't entirely honest.* The thought of it claws at my insides, growing louder with every passing minute.

The truth isn't damning on its own, but it isn't good either. What if someone saw me at the park? What if William knew we'd met up? I can't shake the way William's eyes burned into me during the questioning — sharp, calculating, like he already suspected I was hiding something. So why not say anything to the police? Because he was hiding something that might come to light if he did mention it?

It wasn't the first time I felt William's suspicion, either. He's never liked me much. He was the one who always said I was a bad influence on Cat, pulling her into my chaos. Maybe he wasn't wrong. But I loved Cat in my own way, even if we didn't always get along. Even if our fights sometimes got out of hand.

And that night — *that* fight — it was worse than I want to admit. The way your voice had cracked, how your face flushed with anger as you shouted at me in the car. I can still see your knuckles white against the seatbelt. I had never seen you so angry before. You called me selfish. A leech. I called you a sanctimonious hypocrite. I hadn't meant it, not really. But it was one of those arguments that didn't have a resolution. There was no fixing it.

I clench my jaw. It wasn't my fault, was it? That you're dead, I mean. You stormed off after the fight, gone God knows where. Back to William? Maybe you went home venting about me, telling William everything I'd said, everything we'd argued about. I called the house, and he told me where to go, slamming the phone down on me. I still don't know for sure if you were there. He never answered me when I asked. Maybe I was just another screw-up you could add to the long list of people you needed to save, now that you were in your new *saving mode* since starting at the Domestic Abuse Centre. And don't get me started on that place. You were so insistent that you had to get involved, to do something. To save them all. You'd even befriended that bloody woman, a decision I had flat-out told you was a mistake. I mean you didn't know anything about her. And then donated ten grand!

'You're playing with fire, Cat,' I warned you, but you didn't listen. You were stubborn like that. Always the martyr. Always thinking you could fix the world. I could see how it might've played out: William finding out about the woman, about you meddling where you shouldn't have. He was controlling, after all. And that black eye. You told me that yourself, though you'd brushed it off quickly, as if you shouldn't have said it. But I remembered.

It all makes sense, doesn't it? William must have snapped. It wasn't *my* fault. I wasn't the one who killed you. But why do I keep feeling like I have to keep looking over my shoulder?

The knock at the door startles me, a sharp rap that sends a shiver down my spine. I stand there for a moment, frozen, my mind racing. Wondering if they've found out about you and me that night. When I finally open it, a woman stands on the other side. I know instantly by the way she's standing tall that she's with the police. In fact, I think I recognise her — yeah, she was at the house that day we called them when you went missing.

'Jason Riley?' the officer asks. 'I'm DS Camilla Santos and this is DC Glennon.' I've seen her before with the DI, I'm certain of it.

I nod, my throat suddenly dry. 'Yeah, that's me.'

'We'd like to ask you a few more questions about the night before your sister, Cat, disappeared. Do you have a moment?'

My heart thuds in my chest, but I force a casual shrug. 'Sure. But like I told you before, I don't know anything else.'

DS Santos tilts her head, her eyes narrowing just slightly. 'This won't take long. We just need to clarify a few details about your whereabouts that night.'

My stomach drops. They know. Or they suspected. Either way, it's suddenly hard to breathe.

I step aside to let the officers in, my pulse pounding like a war drum in my ears. The room feels smaller with the woman standing there, notebook held like a weapon, eyes scanning the flat with practised precision. I struggle to swallow the lump in my throat. I can almost hear your voice in my head, mocking my attempt at composure. *You were never any good at hiding things*, you would have said, your tone half-joking, half-exasperated.

The officer clears her throat. The other one stands behind her. 'You mentioned before that you went straight home after work that evening, and didn't go out again. You watched the match on TV,' she says, her voice calm but edged with something sharper. I know they've checked all these details before. 'But we've received some new information that suggests otherwise. Care to explain?'

My vision blurs for a moment. New information? Who could have said anything? Nobody saw me. Well, nobody that could name me. Had someone seen me? They must have. Or is this some kind of game. The park flashes in my mind again — your tense face, your words like daggers, the way you stormed off and got into the car. That could be perceived the wrong way. The DS's gaze pierces through me. 'I—' I stammer, my voice cracking under the weight of the silence. 'I already told you everything I remember.' I don't want to answer that question.

DS Santos raises an eyebrow, unconvinced. She flips through the pages in her notebook, the sound like nails scraping against my nerves. Then, she pauses, tapping a finger against one of the sheets. 'Funny,' she says, almost casually, 'because we've got a witness who says they saw you arguing with Cat that evening. Near the park. And another who saw you leaving her house the morning she disappeared, and you both then walking down the street. Right before she disappeared.'

My chest tightens, my world tipping sideways. My grip on the doorframe falters, my knees threatening to buckle. She's watching me too closely now, her calm demeanour slipping into something more predatory. My mind screams for me to say something, anything in my defence. But all I can hear are the echoes of William's last words the night before when I called her and we had another argument, and he snatched the phone from her: *You'll regret this*. And for the first time, I wonder if he's framing me.

CHAPTER 37

Royce

Camilla speaks in a rush, but the phone reception is so terrible I catch only fragments of her words. When I try calling her back, the line crackles so loudly it's like she's trapped inside a crisp packet. Frustrated, I send her a text, asking her to email or message me the details instead.

When her reply comes through, I sit back and read it twice. Well, well. A witness places Jason with Cat both the morning she vanished *and* the night before. Curious, isn't it? Convenient, even. It's a detail Jason conveniently *forgot* to mention during our chats.

And yet . . . I can't shake the feeling that this is all a bit *too* neat. Almost as if it's been gift-wrapped and handed to me. Falling into my lap like this. It's perfect — so perfect that it could almost seem like *I* had orchestrated it. Almost.

Helen's email pings as I sit in the car, its subject line as stark as a beacon: *ANPR hit* — Natalie's car's been spotted. The message is short, clinical: the number plate registered to Jill Hart logged heading towards St Andrews.

The air in the car is freezing, but I barely notice as my pulse kicks up. I turn on the engine then crank up the heater as I connect my phone to CarPlay. My fingers hover for a second before

I tap St Andrews into Google Maps. Fifty miles. An hour and a half, give or take. It's starting to snow. If I'm lucky I can get there before it gets too bad.

I sit there a moment longer, gripping the wheel, staring at the map as it calculates various routes. My breath fogs the windshield, blurring the screen like a veil. I wait for it to clear, turning the fan on max then selecting a route. The road ahead feels more than just physical — something I need to chase down, something I need to end.

She's there. I can feel it, like a pull in my gut. All this time, she's been slipping away, a phantom on the edges of my vision. Not anymore. I reply to the emails before pulling out onto the empty road.

The faint glow of the GPS guides me further north. Each mile feels heavier than the last, the silence in the car pressing in, coiling tighter. I don't even know what I'll find when I get there. Not exactly.

But I do know this: I'm not leaving without you.

Whether you want me to or not.

When I arrive in St Andrews, the town is cloaked in an eddying snowstorm, the icy Nordic wind shrieking through the streets. It's not looking like it will stick — we're too near the coast. Flurries of snow whip against my windscreen, obscuring my view as though nature itself is waging a blizzardy assault. Anticipating the challenge ahead, I pull over and search online for a place to stay. Luck is on my side — off-season means vacancies. I quickly secure a room for the night and drop a pin on the map, the directions promising a brisk ten-minute walk. The place has on-site parking, but all the spaces are taken.

I step into the B&B, the icy air clinging to me as I pause in the doorway. The place feels . . . indifferent, not cared for. Not what I expected. Not like the first time we came to this town.

The wallpaper peels at the corners in places, the lamp by the door buzzes faintly, and the slight smell of mildew and disinfectant curls in my nostrils. A place like this doesn't try to make friends. No wonder it has vacancies. Though I wonder who's using the car park.

Behind the counter sits a woman who looks about as welcoming as a thundercloud.

'Aye, ye just rang fer a room, did ye?' she asks, her tone clipped in a heavy Scottish accent, her fingers already hovering over the keyboard.

'That's right. DCI Benedick,' I reply, hoping my title will force a better attitude. It doesn't. Glancing at the chipped mug on the desk, I read *The Office Karen*. I glance back at her, trying to decide if it fits. Maybe it does.

She types on the keyboard with the efficiency of someone who's done this a thousand times and stopped caring after the first hundred. 'I've only got a double left. D'ye want it?'

She doesn't need to ask. She knows I'm stuck here, knows I don't have the luxury of options. 'You didn't mention it was a double.'

'Ye didnae ask,' she says flatly, her small beady eyes on the screen. 'Ye asked if I had a vacancy, an' I do. Do ye want it or no?'

She glances out the window as the snow, now turned to rain, lashes violently outside, the storm thickening by the second. She probably does this trick all the time. It's a silent reminder that I have no other options. She knows it, too. 'Then I guess I do,' I say, keeping my voice level. 'How much for the double?'

'Aye, twice what a single costs,' she says, her lips curling into the faintest smirk. 'Take it or leave it.' I fish my credit card out of my pocket, and she slides the Bluetooth card machine across the desk. I tap my card like I'm buying a ticket to hell.

Her face is still set in that expression of permanent annoyance. For a moment, neither of us speaks. The only sounds are the storm outside and the faint hum of the ancient radiator rattling in the corner.

Then, as I pick up my bag, she leans back slightly, her gaze drifting to the window again.

'Seems tae me,' she says slowly, her voice almost thoughtful, her thick accent making it difficult to understand her, 'the weather's blowin' in an ill wind tonight.'

The words, heavy and sharp, cut through the already suffocating silence. I don't answer. I can't. The way she says it, offhand yet deliberate, feels like it's meant for someone else. Or maybe it's meant for me.

I walk towards the stairs and glance at the only room on the ground floor.

The air thickens as I walk past, creaking wooden boards beneath my boots moaning like restless spirits. My room is at the end of the hall on the first floor, but I stop here and look at the door. I don't know why. I can't explain it. My eyes drift there. Something holds me, an invisible thread wrapped tight around my ribs, tugging me closer.

It feels colder now, like the chill has seeped in from the outside. For a moment, I swear I hear it — a faint sound from the other side. Not a voice, not exactly, but something . . . soft, rhythmic, almost like breathing. My hand drifts towards the knob before I realise what I'm doing, fingers hovering just inches away. The air feels charged, electric, like the moment before a storm cracks open the sky. I pull my hand away. I'm imagining it. What are the chances.

Someone's behind that door. Watching. Waiting.

No. I'm tired. Stressed. It's been a long day.

The floor groans again, but this time it's not under my feet. But behind the door. I take a step away, but I can't bring myself to turn. My room is on the next floor. I should go.

But I can't shake the feeling that you're here, behind that door.

I shoulder my bag and head towards the stairs and the well-worn carpet, replaying the woman's words: *Seems tae me, the weather's blowin' in an ill wind tonight.* Somehow, this woman — this unpleasant, cold, ordinary woman — has managed to pull that storm right into this building with her. Somewhere in this building, someone else checked in earlier. Someone I'm looking for. I can feel it in my bones. I glance at the room on the ground floor once again as I start up the stairs.

The stairs creak under my weight as I ascend, the sound swallowed by the eerie quiet of the Victorian building. The storm's howl presses against the walls, a low, mournful wail that seeps into the bones of the place. At the top of the landing, the faint smell of damp wood mingles with something sharper, metallic — like rust, or blood long dried. I stop for a moment, straining to hear beyond the groaning storm, and catch the faintest sound from somewhere downstairs. A door closing? Footsteps retreating?

I tell myself it's nothing, just the old building settling in the storm, but my gut knots anyway. My hand tightens around the strap of my bag as I glance back down the staircase. The front desk is empty now, but I can still feel her words trailing after me, curling like smoke around my thoughts. *An ill wind tonight.* I lean over the banister rail to look at the room on the ground floor. Nothing.

The corridor ahead stretches long and dim, the energy-saving low watt bulb casting shadows that seem to shift when I'm not looking directly at them. I know she didn't mean anything by it — just a throwaway comment about the weather — but the weight of her words lingers, burrowing under my skin. Somewhere in this place is my wife. I know it.

CHAPTER 38

Jill

I sit up suddenly. I've not been able to rest. There's a restlessness in me that has my mind working overtime. I sit on the edge of the bed, my fingers gripping the thin duvet so tightly that my knuckles ache. The storm outside thrashes against the window, rattling the glass like it's trying to claw its way in. I tell myself it's just the wind, but it sounds wrong somehow — like a voice screaming through the night, low and guttural, rising and falling in patterns that churn my stomach. *Get out. Get out. Get out.* I pull the duvet tighter around my shoulders and glance at the door. The lock looks flimsy. Too flimsy.

A sudden shift in the air makes me freeze. Something has startled me. The radiator ticks and clanks softly under the window, but beyond it, there's something else. A sound so faint I almost convince myself it isn't real: a soft creak of wood, like a weight shifting somewhere beyond my door. But it is real. My pulse quickens. I force myself to stay still, listening, straining against the oppressive silence that's suddenly descended. The storm feels further away now, like the building itself is swallowing it whole, leaving only the sound of my breathing. Loud and deafening inside my head.

The temperature feels like it drops, goosebumps rise on my arms, but I think that's from fear. My breath coming in shallow bursts. There's a sensation — a prickling at the back of my neck, as if someone's watching me. But that's impossible. The room is empty. Isn't it? My eyes dart to the shadows pooling in the furthest corners, deeper and darker than they should be. For a moment, I swear one of them shifts. Moves. I'm frightening myself and shut my eyes tight for a moment. When I open them, they're gone.

A chill races down my spine at a creak behind the door, and I bolt upright, my heart slamming against my ribs. Someone's there. On the other side. I cross the room in three quick strides, grab the chair from the corner and wedge it under the doorknob. My fingers tremble as I step back, my eyes locked on the door. On the knob. I know he's here. I can feel him — somewhere in this building, closing in. Outside my door. But that's insane. How could he know I'm here? In this guest house?

My throat tightens as I swallow hard. I lean in closer to the door. Press my ear to the wood. The floor beneath my feet creaks and groans. I hold my breath. Step back. Eyes wide on the knob. I'm waiting for it to turn. I step back some more. Instinct telling me he might kick in the door.

Running from him wasn't my worst mistake. Being found — is.

When I think whoever was there has gone, I open the door, step out. Nobody's here. I walk towards the stairs; the floorboards creak. I stop. Look up. A shadow moves along the landing. Carefully, quietly, I step back and lock the door.

And breathe.

CHAPTER 39

William

I sit across from DS Camilla Santos, the harsh fluorescent light overhead amplifying every flaw in the drab interview room. I remember the last couple of times I was here. My hands rest on the table, trembling slightly, though I try to keep them still. She watches me, her eyes sharp, unreadable, like she's peeling back layers I don't even know I have. Somewhere out of sight, I imagine DI Benedick, his scepticism weighing on me even in his absence. I can feel it, like a noose tightening.

I take a deep breath, my chest heavy with the effort. 'Jason,' I begin, my voice breaking on his name. 'He came to the house the day after Cat disappeared. Practically barged in. At the time, I didn't think much of it, but now . . . now it feels wrong. Almost too soon, you know? I hadn't even let myself think of her as missing, not properly, but he . . .' I trail off, swallowing the lump in my throat. 'He was the one who planted that seed. Made it real before I was ready. Like he wanted me to think that way.'

DS Santos doesn't respond, just jots something down in her notepad. The scratch of the pen sets my teeth on edge. I press on. 'He went to the police before I even had the chance. That struck me as strange. I mean, why would he do that? Why wouldn't he talk to me first? When I reached out to him, he was . . . evasive. Cold. Like I was bothering him. And then he — he accused me.' My voice cracks, the memory of Jason's distant, cutting tone slicing through me again and again. 'He said it outright, like he'd already decided I'd killed my wife when she hadn't even been found yet. We, well at least, I didn't know she was dead. But he said I'd killed her. Don't you see? I never thought of it that way. He knew she was already dead.'

'Did you two argue?' Santos asks, her tone calm but probing. 'You weren't getting on when we first interviewed you. Has something happened since?'

I hesitate, the room closing in. 'No. Not really. Apart from him accusing me all the time. But that day, he wouldn't let it go. He just . . . shut me down when I tried to say that I didn't think she was missing at that point. He brushed me off like I was lying, insisting something had happened to her, but I wasn't worried so much at that moment in time. And now, I can't help but wonder if there was more to it. What if he was hiding something? What if Jason knew something about Cat that he didn't want me to find out? And he was trying to protect himself?'

Her pen stops moving. She glances up, her gaze steady and unrelenting. 'What exactly are you suggesting, William?'

I exhale sharply, dragging a hand down my face. 'I don't know. But Cat . . . she knew the cameras were down that night. She planned something that day, I'm sure of it now. I remember her telling me she'd read it on the local neighbourhood watch Facebook page. She didn't want anyone to see her that day she left. That much I'm sure of. She was meeting someone. Someone she didn't want me or anyone else to know about. And now she's—' I can't say the word. It lodges in my throat like a shard of glass. 'Now she's dead.'

'What makes you think she was meeting someone?'

'I can remember now more clearly. She acted oddly and kept looking out of the window that morning before I headed to work, as if she was waiting for someone to turn up. I didn't notice it at the time, and I forgot all about it until I was talking to my sister about that day.'

Santos leans back in her chair, her expression carefully neutral, her dark hair pulled in a high ponytail that swings back and forth when she moves her head. 'And you think Jason was the person she was meeting?'

'I don't know,' I admit, the frustration bubbling up again. 'But something wasn't right those last few weeks. I did hear her arguing with him on the phone. When I questioned her, she wouldn't talk about it. Said she'd sort it. She was on edge. Scared, even. Taking calls in secret. Acting like she was carrying this huge weight she couldn't share. She'd never been that way before. I thought, at first, she was probably talking to Jake, but not anymore. I'm telling you — she was protecting someone, and I think it was him. I should've seen it. I should've asked more questions, but I didn't.' I drop my head. 'I just — I thought it was stress related from the IVF or . . . or something else, you know. It was all that was on my mind. I thought it was the same for her. Now I know more it must have been the pregnancy. And how to end it with Jake. And maybe how to tell me about Jake. I didn't think she was in danger. But Jason if he found out she hadn't told him everything would have been mad.' My voice drops to a whisper.

'Don't you think it could have been Jake she was afraid of?'

'No, maybe. No. It was the calls with Jason that I know pissed her off.'

'How d'you know it wasn't Jake?'

I sigh heavily. 'She had a way of talking to her brother. You know, pissed off. Like he annoyed the hell out of her. I doubt she'd talk to Jake that way. I've never heard her talk to anyone like she talked to Jason.'

'But you can't be sure it was him, and if you could be, you can't be sure it was anything dangerous. You could be manifesting all this because you want to have someone to blame.'

'I mean, why would I? But what if she was? You know Jason was way too close to her. It wasn't natural, it wasn't brother and sister closeness, not for him anyway.' I see the look she gives me. 'Christ, no, don't go there. There was nothing like that. But he was weird with her. He said he knew about Jake being just a friend but not that she was having an affair with him. That really knocked him for six when it all came out. And then finding out about the baby. Maybe he lost it with her when he found out that she hadn't told him? You have to understand that Jason was *really* weird about Cat.'

'And why would he lose it with her if he found out? And what if it wasn't Jason on those calls but someone else?' Santos counters, her voice cool, deliberate. 'What if it was someone else entirely? Someone you haven't even thought of?'

The question hangs between us, heavy and oppressive. I try to hold her gaze, but I can't. My mind races, images and fragments of memory colliding in a chaotic swirl. Jason's face rises uninvited, his cold, distant eyes boring into me. The way he looked at me that day — not with concern, but with something darker. Something I didn't recognise at the time.

I look back at Santos, my pulse hammering in my neck. 'Who else could it be? Someone out there knows exactly what happened to her. And I think it's Jason. Someone's hiding the truth. He knows more than he's saying.' My voice drops, trembling with an edge of desperation. 'And what if they've been right here all along? What if they've been pretending to care, to grieve, while all the time they're the reason she's . . . He said to everyone after she went missing that I used to hit her, and you know now that's a lie. She had no bruises on her apart from the ones on her wrist and you said they were relatively new, maybe even acquired at the time of her death. Someone grabbing her, hard.' I stop myself before the word escapes, my chest tightening painfully. Santos doesn't look away, her pen hovering over her notebook again, scrawling something I can't read.

'If you're asking me to follow this lead, you'd better be ready to answer more questions of your own. Like you've suddenly remembered all this. And also, to what we might discover about your wife when we dig deeper. For your information we questioned Jason only a few hours ago. Someone did see Jason on the day of your wife's disappearance. They were seen leaving the house together, and the night before in the park, arguing.'

And for the first time, I'm not sure if I can take any more of your secrets, Cat. What more am I going to discover?

CHAPTER 40

Natalie

I'm not ready for him to find me yet. Not like this. Not here. My chest heaves with every breath, each one louder than the last, and I force myself to steady it. Slow it. I can't let him hear me. The storm outside howls again, a brief reprieve from the crushing silence in the room, but it only serves to heighten the dread knotting my stomach.

I glance around, searching for an escape. The window? No, it's a sash and only opens so far. It opens onto the courtyard. I check the frame to see a small block of wood on either side of the sash to stop it opening too far. Security, I guess. I glance at the small bathroom window. Useless. I'm cornered, and I know it. A cornered animal has nothing to lose, and that's what I have to remind myself. *Stay sharp. Stay focused.*

The faintest click from outside my door jolts me — like a foot pressing against a loose floorboard. My heart thunders. Whoever is there they're moving away. Pacing. Waiting. I have such a strong sense it's him. Why doesn't he just break it down? Why doesn't he just come for me? The suspense is worse than the chase, worse than the fight. He's toying with me. Punishing me the way he always does.

I grit my teeth, fury bubbling up to fight the fear. *No. Not this time. This time, I'll end it.*

I move to the dresser, yanking open the drawers, desperate for something sharp, something heavy. My fingers close around a small lamp, its cord tangling as I pull it free. It's not much, but it'll have to do. I hold it tightly, my knuckles white as I step back towards the centre of the room.

I stare at the doorknob almost willing it to move. A breath catches in my throat. He's testing me. Slowly. Methodically scaring me. Building up the fear inside me. Letting me know that he's found me. My pulse pounds in my ears, my grip on the lamp tightening. My mind races with images of his face, the things he's said. His lies. My lies. He's always been so good at turning the story around, hasn't he? Making himself the victim. Convincing everyone he's just trying to help me.

But I know the truth. I *know* what he really is. And I won't let him win this time.

The chair under the doorknob shifts slightly, or does it? A low sob escapes me before I can stop it. I can hear what he's going to say to try and trick me.

'Natalie,' he says, and I can hear the strain in his voice just like always. 'Please. Let me in. I just want to talk.'

I shake my head even though I can't see him. Even though it's not actually happening. *Liar.*

'Natalie,' he says again, his tone softening. 'I'm worried about you. You're not thinking clearly. Just let me in, and we'll figure this out. Together.'

Together. That word twists in my stomach like a blade. He always says that. Like we're some kind of team. Like he hasn't spent years tearing me down, piece by piece, until I'm nothing but a hollow shell.

'I'm not going anywhere,' he says firmly, and I know he means it. 'You can't run from this. You can't run from me.'

Sadie Ryan

A surge of anger overtakes me, hot and blinding. I won't let him control me anymore. I won't let him twist the truth. I won't let him win.

Leave me alone! I scream in my head, my voice cracking. I stare at the door fearful I've inadvertently said it aloud.

'Natalie, please.' His voice falters, and for a moment, there's a note of raw desperation that catches me off guard. 'I'm begging you. Don't do this. Don't hurt yourself. Please.'

Hurt myself? The words throw me. Confuse me. Twist in my mind like poison. I grip the lamp tighter, my mind racing.

He doesn't know. He doesn't understand. None of them do. Not Royce, not Cat. Sweet, naive Cat, with her brochures and her pitying looks and her endless questions. *Are you safe, Jill? Do you have someone you can talk to? Do you want me to call someone?*

I told her to stop. I told her to leave it alone. But she didn't listen. She *wouldn't* listen.

The memory flashes before my eyes: Cat's startled expression, her wide, terrified eyes as I shoved her. The way her head hit the edge of the car door with a sickening crack. The way her body crumpled, lifeless, to the floor.

My hands tremble as the weight of it crashes over me. *I didn't mean to. I didn't mean to.*

But that's not entirely true, is it?

The doorknob rattles again, and I snap back to the present, my heart racing. Royce's voice is louder now, more frantic.

'Natalie, I love you. I just want to help you. Please, let me help you.'

I let out a bitter laugh, the sound foreign in my own ears. Help me? He doesn't even know what I am.

What I've done.

What I'm capable of.

And then it's all quiet outside the door.

The silence presses in, heavier than the storm howling outside. I hold my breath, straining to catch any sound, any sign of movement. Is he still there? Waiting, watching, just as he always does? Or has he given up — for now? Maybe it wasn't him? Maybe I'm just manifesting my fear.

The quiet is unbearable, like the calm before the final blow. I edge towards the window, my movements slow and deliberate. Rain lashes against the frosted glass, the wind rattling the thin panes. The rainstorm is raging out there, the snow gone, but it's nothing compared to the tempest inside me.

The latch on the window is stiff from the cold. I take the knife I use for cutting up fruit from my bag. My fingers fumble with the knife, jerking out the small bits of wood inside the frame. I wrench it upward, the movement jerky and loud, and I freeze, listening again. Nothing. The bits of wood pop out. I push the window up as far as it will go and the howling, freezing wind takes my breath away.

I quickly get dressed thinking I should have done this first. The squeeze through the window shouldn't be too bad, just awkward. I'm on the ground floor but it's still a bit of a distance. I toss out my coat to make it easier to climb out, together with my bags. The biting cold slices through my jumper like a blade. The wind blows in my eyes, my face, my hair. My breath clouds the air in front of me, and for a brief moment, I hesitate. What if he's waiting out there? What if this is exactly what he wants me to do? Am I being predictable? I told myself I had to do the opposite. I don't think I have a choice right now.

But there's no time to second-guess. I grit my teeth and go for it, jumping to the ground outside. The concrete is unforgiving, and pain shoots through my ankle as I slip and tumble to the ground. I bite back a cry, forcing myself to roll and not injure myself any more. I'm wet through. The blizzard has stopped; in its place is cold rain. I'm freezing already. My jumper icy against my skin. I get to my feet. There's no time for weakness. Not now. Quickly I throw on my thick coat. Pull the woolly hat from the pocket, jamming it on. Distant voices grow louder. A door opens ahead spilling out students from a pub, drunk and revelling in the night. Shit. I don't need this right now.

The guest house looms behind me, its windows dark and menacing. I throw my rucksack on my back and grab the shopping bags. I can almost feel his eyes on me, even if he's not there. My neck prickles and I begin to shiver violently from the cold. I need to get to my car and change my jumper otherwise I'll get hypothermia. He always has a way of making me feel watched, hunted. The cold air burns my lungs as I force myself to move. I move carefully with a slight limp. Dammit, I could do without this, too. There isn't much pain, but I'm certain that's because the cold is numbing any sensations. My car is parked just around the corner, hidden in the shadows of the narrow street. If I can just get to it, I can—

A light flickers on in one of the upstairs windows catching my eye. My heart leaps into my throat. Did he hear me? Is he coming? I push forward, slipping and stumbling on the wet pavement, my breath coming in ragged gasps. Tiny sharp stabs in my ankle. I know it's him. I sense it.

The car is where I left it. I yank open the door and collapse inside, my fingers numb as they fumble with the keys. They jingle, cold and foreign, as I shove them into the ignition and twist.

Nothing.

'No,' I whisper, my voice trembling. I try again. The engine whines, then falls silent. I try again. It starts, then a blinking orange light fills me with panic. 'No, no, no!'

I slam my fist against the steering wheel, frustration boiling over. How could I have been so careless? The fuel gauge glares back at me, the needle nearly buried deep in the red. I knew I was running low. I knew and still I forgot. I can't go anywhere in this weather with hardly any petrol.

The wind rocks the car as it buffets, the storm's fury growing. I'm trapped, stranded, with nowhere to go. My chest heaves, anxiety tearing at my throat. I can't stay here. He'll find me. He always does.

Think, Natalie. Think.

The streets are deserted, apart from the drunks rolling about. Shadows stretch long and menacing under the dim streetlights. I could run, but where to? The beach? The thought of hiding in the dark, alone and exposed, sends a shiver down my spine. I check my phone and gasp. *You have to be kidding! Battery low — 12 per cent left.*

And then, as if to mock me, a figure appears at the end of the street. Tall, broad-shouldered, moving with that familiar, deliberate stride. My blood runs cold. I slide down the seat practically into the footwell.

It's him. *I knew it!*

I duck down lower, pressing myself between the steering wheel and the seat, my breath coming in shallow bursts. He can't see me. Not yet. Not like this. I realise I'm jammed now.

But I know it's only a matter of time. He's always been patient, always been relentless. And now, as the storm rages on and the cold seeps into my bones, I realise the truth: there's no escaping him. Not tonight. Not ever.

Unless I end this. For good.

My hand tightens around the keys. One way or another, this ends now.

I crouch low in the car, my breath fogging the windshield as I try to steady myself. Royce is getting closer. I lift my head. I know that stride — calculated, unyielding. He's found me. I knew he would, but I thought I'd have more time.

The engine's dead. The tank empty. I can't run. I'm jammed in. Trapped.

Through the rain-soaked window, I see him come closer. He stops at the edge of the street, his breath clouding in the frigid air. He's not charging towards me. He's just standing there, watching. Waiting.

The sight of him sends a surge of anger through me, hot and blinding. How dare he come here, acting like the saviour. Like he's the victim. My chest heaves, and I shove the car door open, and step out ungracefully.

'Stay back!' I shout, my voice raw and cracking. I clutch the car door for balance, my legs unsteady.

He doesn't flinch. He doesn't even look surprised. He just takes a step closer, his hands visible, his expression calm. 'Natalie,' he says, and his voice is soft — too soft, like he's trying to soothe a cornered animal. 'It's over. You don't have to do this anymore.'

'Do this?' I snap, my breath coming in short, sharp bursts. 'You don't get to come here and act like you understand me. Like you know anything about me.'

'I know more than you think. You're my wife. How am I not going to know everything about you?' His voice is steady, but his eyes — there's something in them I can't quite place. Pity? Sorrow? 'I know what happened to Cat. You were caught on one of the cameras. I haven't shared that information with anyone yet.'

A wave of nausea hits me hard. My fingers tighten on the edge of the car door. 'You don't know anything,' I hiss, though the tremor in my voice betrays me.

'I know you called the helpline. I know that's how you met her,' he says, taking another step closer. 'She was trying to help you, wasn't she? But you couldn't let her. Because then you'd have to tell her the truth.'

'Stop!' The word bursts out of me, loud and ragged, but he doesn't stop.

'She cared about you, Natalie, didn't she?' he says, his voice cracking slightly. 'And you killed her. Did she work it out? Was that what happened?'

The world tilts, the wind roaring around me, blowing icy rain in little tornados. His words shatter the thin walls I've built around myself. Cat's face flashes in my mind — her wide, terrified eyes, the sickening crack as her head hit the car door. *I didn't mean to*, I tell myself, like I always do. But the truth has claws, and it's tearing through me. She was too smart. Too quick reading *between the lines*.

'You don't know what you're talking about,' I manage, my voice barely a whisper now.

'Don't I?' He's closer now, just a few steps away. 'I see it, Natalie. This is how you are, but you just don't see it. The way you twist things. The way you turn it all around until you're the victim. But you're not. Not this time. I'm to blame. I should have done something about it sooner. I'm sorry. I failed you and now I'm as much to blame for Cat's death as you are.'

'No,' I whisper, shaking my head. 'You made me this way. You did this to me.'

His face crumples, and for a moment, he looks as broken as I feel. 'I never wanted to hurt you,' he says softly. 'I only ever wanted to love you. But you—' He stops, swallowing hard. 'You need professional help, Natalie. Real help. I can't cover for you anymore. I've come to take you home. You know you need help. Your temper is out of control.'

That word again. *Help*. It scrapes against my raw nerves, taunting me. 'I don't need anything from you!' I shout, my voice rising with desperation. The wind tears at my words ripping them from my mouth, carrying them away. 'You're the police. You can't let this go.'

But Royce doesn't move. He doesn't fight me. He just stands there, letting the silence settle between us. And in that silence, the weight of everything I've done crushes me.

I see Cat's lifeless body on the floor, the blood pooling beneath her. I see Royce flinching, stepping back when I raised my fist so many times, the bruises he tried to hide. The excuses to his family. I see the fear in his eyes, the same fear that's in mine now. How he couldn't defend himself. Because that would mean hitting a woman. And he'd never do that.

My knees buckle, and I sink to the ground, the cold seeping through my clothes, biting at my skin. I know he's right. My ankle suddenly begins to throb. I'm shaking, my breath hitching in uneven gasps. I know I'll need hospitalisation. I know I have a problem. I'm scared.

'I'm so tired,' I whisper, barely able to hear my own voice over the gusts of wind. Tired of defending myself when I know I'm in the wrong.

Royce kneels in front of me, his movements slow and deliberate. He doesn't touch me, not yet, but his presence feels steady, like an anchor in the chaos. 'I know,' he says gently. 'But it's over now. Let me help you.'

I want to lash out, to scream, to shove him away. But I can't. The fight is gone. The rage, the fear, the lies — they've hollowed me out, and there's nothing left. I came here to end it all. On my own. To release him from me. I haven't been fair to him.

In the distance, I hear the ruckus of student voices cutting through the storm. It's all over. He'll have to bring me in. If I'd done what he wanted earlier, Cat would be alive. As it is, she's dead because of me.

I don't resist when Royce helps me to my feet, his grip firm but careful. I don't look back at the guest house, at the broken pieces of my life scattered behind me. Because there's nowhere left to run.

Nowhere left to hide.

And for the first time, I feel the weight of it all settle fully on my shoulders. The truth. The guilt. The end. I need his strength. I lean into him letting him take my weight. Like he's always done.

EPILOGUE

William

I suppose I always felt there was a piece missing from the puzzle of your death. I kneel by your grave, unwrapping the flowers with care. I cut the string and trim the stems, fitting them neatly into the little brass flower holder. You used to talk about wanting to make a difference, about doing something meaningful that helped others. Back then, I didn't really understand what you meant. I remember feeling cornered whenever you tried to explain it to me, like you were speaking a language I refused to learn. I never gave you the time you deserved. I thought you were just talking, just dreaming aloud, not that it was something you truly wanted for yourself.

Looking back now, I see how much distance had grown between us, especially after all the failed IVF attempts. Without realising it, we let that heartbreak wedge itself between us. Or maybe I should say *I* let it. I resented you for not being able to get pregnant, as if it were your fault. And then, when we found out about my low sperm count, I turned that resentment inward. I became bitter, defensive, a proper prat, if I'm honest. I let my pride get in the way, and I hurt you because of it.

I suppose you felt invisible for a long time, and I get that now. I know I made you feel that way. Looking back, it's painfully clear. That's when you met Jake. I imagine there was something dazzling about him, wasn't there? The way he didn't know your history, your pain. He saw you as sexy, desirable — as *you*, not just someone trying to have a baby.

Jake told me you were sad the night you met him. It was after one of our rows. Do you remember? Of course you do. How could you not. We'd finally got pregnant, and you carried longer than ever that time. I was so hopeful. But you — well, you didn't want to hope. You said it would jinx it. I didn't understand. But you lost it. I wanted to take you out to that restaurant you loved, Double Chances, to take your mind off it. I told you to get dressed up, that it was going to be okay.

And then I took that call. God, Cat, I keep thinking, if I hadn't taken it, maybe you'd still be alive. People say everything happens for a reason, but does it? Really? Or is life just a series of 'Sliding Doors' moments? If I hadn't taken the call. If I hadn't had to leave. If, if, if.

But we'll never know, will we?

Jake told me you stayed at our table for ages that night before moving to the bar. I'll never know what was running through your mind because you never told me. You said you left not long after, and you did, but not alone.

I didn't see how lonely you were. I didn't see the growing chasm between us. I wish I could undo it all, but the cracks had formed long before that night. I became complacent, and you grew more distant with each passing day. Did you sleep with him before you started the physiotherapy sessions? Or did that happen later? Did you try and stay faithful, but the loneliness and the tug of desire was too strong? Was that it? He never told me what happened that first night. He might have taken you home. I think he was trying to hurt me by keeping it vague. Letting me think what I wanted.

Looking back now, it's so clear. The endless events, the drinks parties, the dinners with my friends, the client meetings. I dragged you along, oblivious to the torment I was putting you through, so wrapped up in myself that I never truly saw you.

Lucy told me she saw it. She said she tried to talk to me, but I wouldn't listen. I was arrogant, dismissive, angry that she'd dare to interfere. What could she possibly know about my marriage? The very idea of her giving me advice was infuriating at the time.

But by then, you'd already switched off. That's what you told Jake. He said when the affair began, you couldn't stop thinking about each other, couldn't keep away. Even then, I felt something shift between us, but I ignored it. Maybe I didn't want to see it. Maybe I couldn't bear to admit what was happening.

* * *

Cat

I was obsessed with Jake. He was new, exciting and unburdened by the weight of everything we'd been carrying. All I wanted was freedom. The kind of freedom where sex wasn't tied to hope or heartbreak, where I didn't have to wonder if this time it would lead to a pregnancy. It felt liberating. Jake encouraged me to do what I wanted, to live for myself. That's when I signed up for the helpline. I wanted so badly to tell you, William. I really did. But I was scared. Scared you'd put me down or dismiss it. So, I kept it to myself, just like I kept Jake. And if I'm honest, I enjoyed the secrecy of it all. The thrill of living a life you didn't know about.

I think, in some twisted way, I wanted to hurt you. Jake was everything you weren't — free-spirited, bold, someone who faced life without overthinking it. You were always so serious, so measured, even about the smallest things. You'd check restaurant reviews before we went anywhere, while Jake chose places simply because he'd passed by and liked the look of them. That spontaneity, that recklessness — it's what I loved about him.

I'm sorry I caused you so much pain, William. I loved you, but I couldn't stop seeing Jake. That night you left me at the restaurant, I think I lingered at the bar on purpose, hoping for something to happen. I don't even know what I was hoping for. And then he was there, sitting beside me, asking if I was all right, offering to help. I guess I must've looked sad or lost. That's how it started. But I swear I didn't know at the time where it was headed. I had a stiff neck. He told me he was a physiotherapist and gave me his card. He got me a taxi. Two days later I called for an appointment. It was platonic at first, but it changed. I think I wanted it to change.

I didn't know I could feel the way I felt with Jake. That rush of lust and abandon — it was addictive. I still remember that night at the restaurant. The rain after weeks of dry weather, the smell of petrichor in the air. I wasn't trying to hurt you, William. I just felt rash like I needed to do something dangerous. I needed it for myself, though. I needed to feel something different. I want you to understand that. I never planned to have an affair. But once it started, I couldn't stop. The more I had, the more I wanted.

And then, one day, I found out I was pregnant. When I told Jake, I was confused and terrified. I admitted I didn't know who the father was. He said he didn't care. He told me he loved me and would stand by me no matter what. Jake had even found the helpline for me. He encouraged me to go for it. But I'm ashamed to admit the reason he did was because, in some ridiculous, desperate moment, I told him you'd hurt me. I told him you'd abused me. It wasn't true. I don't even know why I said it. Maybe I didn't want him to see me as just a bored, lonely wife looking for an escape. Maybe I wanted him to feel like my saviour.

Jake made plans for us. He made plans for everything. He wanted us to be together. It was moving too fast for me. He wanted me to leave you. He wanted to tell you about us. And I — I said I would. I thought I wanted that too. But as time went on, he grew impatient, even agitated, because I kept putting it off. I wasn't ready. I told him he was being ridiculous, that I couldn't just walk away from my life so easily. And deep down, I hesitated because I thought the baby might be yours.

But before you came home the night before, Jason showed up. He said he needed to talk. We went for a walk in the park. It was dark, so I brought the torch you'd given me. He was furious with me, accusing me of interfering in his life. He said I had no right to judge him.

Then Jill rang me the morning I disappeared. She begged me to meet her, said she was scared. I wasn't supposed to. It was against the rules. But I'd already bent the rules for her before. She needed me, and I wanted to help. But Jason turned up too. I went with him to the park before Jill arrived, but he was being weird, and I felt unsafe and said I had an appointment. I took the side roads and entered the house through the side street he doesn't know about.

* * *

Natalie

I remember the first time I met Cat. Even then, convincing her to meet wasn't easy. She told me it was against the rules, and I could tell she lived by those rules. It wasn't just a policy to her — it was who she was. That's when I realised, I had to lie. Because if she knew the truth, she wouldn't help.

So, I made you the villain, Royce. I said you were abusive, cruel. A wife-beater. And Cat believed me. She validated my every word.

It shouldn't have been so easy, but it was. I still had the marks on my wrists from that fight. The fight where I wanted so badly for you to break. Do you remember that day? You were calm, as you always were, even as I screamed and threw everything I could at you, desperate to provoke you. But you never retaliated. You never gave me the satisfaction of breaking you.

Looking back, I think you always knew what I was capable of. You were so careful not to leave marks, as though you understood, even then, that I might use them against you. But that day, I pushed too far.

I remember standing by the ironing board, the iron hot and within reach. The thought struck like lightning: *grab it, end this*. And when I reached for it, you reacted. For the first time, you grabbed my wrists, squeezing until I dropped the iron. It clattered to the floor, shattering the corner of the granite countertop on the way down.

And then it was my turn to break.

I collapsed to the floor, sobbing uncontrollably. I wasn't prepared for the rush of shame, the overwhelming weight of what I'd become. I looked up at you and saw something I hadn't expected — fear. But not fear of me. Fear *for* me.

You knelt down beside me, your face soft with concern, and pulled me into your arms. And I let you. I buried my face in the curve of your neck, breathing in your scent, woodsy and warm, like safety.

How could you still be so kind to me? So gentle?

I'd so wanted to go to Cornwall and see the family, but I knew you didn't trust me around the kids. I couldn't go knowing you'd be worried that something might happen. I know in my heart that's why you never wanted children. You're too sensitive and gentle to ever say it to my face.

I hated you for it, Royce. For being everything I wasn't. For loving me even when I didn't deserve it. And I hated myself even more for needing you, for clinging to you despite all the pain I caused. I wanted to be good for you, but deep down, I was terrified you'd leave. That one day you'd finally look at me and see what I really was.

But you didn't leave.

You stayed, even when I gave you every reason to go. When I lashed out, when I screamed, when I threw your love back in your face — you stayed. You never stopped trying to reach me, even when I made it impossible.

And that's why I broke down that night. Because your love showed me what I couldn't bear to see: myself.

I cried for hours, and when I couldn't cry anymore, I called the helpline. That's when I met Cat.

She was so kind, Royce. Her voice was steady, calm and non-judgemental. She made me feel safe in a way I hadn't felt in years. I told her everything — well, almost everything. I didn't tell her about you. About how you weren't the monster I'd made you out to be. About how you were the one who loved me even when I couldn't love myself.

I told her lies because I thought the truth would scare her away. And she believed me.

When we finally met in person, I thought I could start afresh. No more lies. I told her the truth about everything — about the fights, about my temper, about how I wasn't running to save myself but to save *you*.

But the moment I told her, something changed. Her kindness hardened. She looked at me differently, like I was a stranger. A threat. She saw the ugliness inside me.

She told me I was deceitful. That I was dangerous. That I needed to stop calling her. She was there to help the abused not the abusers.

We were standing in this desolate, forgotten place — a graveyard of rusted cars and broken things. It felt fitting, somehow.

I reached out to her, desperate to explain, to apologise, but she stepped back, her eyes wide with fear. I begged her to understand, but she shoved me away.

And then, I lost control.

I pushed her back, harder than I meant to. She stumbled, tripping on something, and hit the edge of a car. Her head struck at an odd angle, and blood began to pool beneath her.

I froze, Royce. I couldn't move. I couldn't breathe. I watched as her eyes fluttered, as her body went still.

She was gone.

I wanted to scream, to beg her to wake up, but I knew it was too late. And all I could think was that no one would believe me. Not you. Not the police. Not anyone.

So, I ran. But before I left, I couldn't leave her on the ground, so I put her inside the car.

I ran from Cat, from you, from the life we'd built and the wreckage I'd made of it. And as I ran, all I could think about was the look on your face the last time you held me. How your love made me feel safe. How it made me want to be better.

And how, no matter how far I run, I'll never be able to escape what I've done.

* * *

Royce

What captivated me most about you was your face. So radiant, so breathtakingly beautiful. There was a kind of innocence, a purity in your expression that completely stole my heart the moment we met. I was lost in you from the very beginning.

I remember that weekend in St Andrews, our first time away together. We were supposed to go abroad, but I had a case starting, and we sneaked away for a long weekend instead. Looking back now, some might say I should have walked away after that trip. God knows, part of me knew it even then.

Do you remember what you said to me after it happened? 'I'm sorry, I don't know what came over me. I think I had too much to drink and got carried away.' I wanted to believe you. I *needed* to believe you, but deep down, I didn't. Even when I had to pull you off me, yanking you by your ponytail as you screamed in pain, I felt guilty. I thought I'd hurt you. And when I squeezed your arm to comfort you, to let you know I was still there for you, you looked so shattered, so remorseful. 'I feel like the worst person in the world,' you said. 'It won't happen again. I'm so sorry, Royce.'

I told myself I could fix it, fix *you*. But the truth was bothering me, even then. Something about it all felt wrong, and yet I stayed. I stayed because I loved you, because I couldn't imagine walking away.

Years passed, and the outbursts became less frequent, just flashes, usually when you'd had too much to drink. I convinced myself we could live with it. I couldn't stand the way you tore yourself apart afterwards, the way you begged for forgiveness. I tried to get you help, but you shut me down every time. 'I can stop on my own,' you'd say. And for a while, you did. Until the next time.

Eventually, I stopped trying to fix it. I stopped fighting. I buried it, convincing myself this was our normal. But when you began twisting things, when you turned the blame on me, making it seem like *I* was the one hurting *you*, something broke in me. The way you cried, the way you played the victim, it was so believable, so terrifying. And when you threatened to go to my boss, to tell them I was the abuser if I ever left you, I knew I was trapped. I should have left years ago. I knew that. But by then, it felt too late. I told myself this was my fault — that I had let it get to this point.

And yet, I didn't want to leave you. I wanted to help you. God, Natalie, all I ever wanted was to save you.

Then I found the paperwork you'd hidden, tucked away beneath the carpet, beneath the pile of books as if burying it there could somehow keep the truth from coming to light. My heart sank as I read it, the words blurring together under the weight of what they meant. You were planning to leave me. Part of me felt an unexpected relief, a fleeting, shameful sense of freedom that whispered, *maybe it could finally be over*. But that relief was swallowed almost instantly by a crushing sorrow. The idea of losing you, of you no longer being in my life, hit me like a blow to the chest. I wasn't ready to let go, not of you, not of the dreams we'd once shared, not of the hope I still clung to, no matter how fragile. And then I found the note. Your suicide note. The words on the page ripped through me like a storm, leaving devastation in their wake. The thought that you'd not only planned to leave me but to leave *everything* — to leave this world — was unbearable. The relief I'd felt moments before twisted into guilt, regret, and a grief so heavy it was almost suffocating.

I had no choice but to find you. I couldn't involve my colleagues in the police. I was terrified of what you might say to them if they got to you first.

And now, we're here. You've killed someone. Cat is gone. Manslaughter. That's the word for it, isn't it? I have to call it in. I have to tell the truth. I have to face her husband and explain what happened.

But I can't. Holding you in my arms, I can't do it. I can't lose you, Natalie. Not like this. Not after everything. God help me, I can't let you go.

THE END

THE JOFFE BOOKS STORY

We began in 2014 when Jasper agreed to publish his mum's much-rejected romance novel and it became a bestseller.

Since then we've grown into the largest independent publisher in the UK. We're extremely proud to publish some of the very best writers in the world, including Joy Ellis, Faith Martin, Caro Ramsay, Helen Forrester, Simon Brett and Robert Goddard. Everyone at Joffe Books loves reading and we never forget that it all begins with the magic of an author telling a story.

We are proud to publish talented first-time authors, as well as established writers whose books we love introducing to a new generation of readers.

We won Trade Publisher of the Year at the Independent Publishing Awards in 2023 and Best Publisher Award in 2024 at the People's Book Prize. We have been shortlisted for Independent Publisher of the Year at the British Book Awards for the last five years, and were shortlisted for the Diversity and Inclusivity Award at the 2022 Independent Publishing Awards. In 2023 we were shortlisted for Publisher of the Year at the RNA Industry Awards, and in 2024 we were shortlisted at the CWA Daggers for the Best Crime and Mystery Publisher.

We built this company with your help, and we love to hear from you, so please email us about absolutely anything bookish at feedback@joffebooks.com.

If you want to receive free books every Friday and hear about all our new releases, join our mailing list here: www.joffebooks.com/freebooks.

And when you tell your friends about us, just remember: it's pronounced Joffe as in coffee or toffee!